Sarah Mallory grew up in the West Country, England, telling stories. She moved to Yorkshire with her young family, but after nearly thirty years of living in a farmhouse on the Pennines she has now moved to live by the sea in Scotland. Sarah is an award-winning novelist, with more than twenty books published by Mills & Boon Historical. She loves to hear from readers, and you can reach her via her website at: sarahmallory.com.

Also by Sarah Mallory

A Kiss to Stop a Wedding
The Earl's Marriage Dilemma
Wed in Haste to the Duke
Snowbound with the Brooding Lord
The Night She Met the Duke
The Duke's Family for Christmas
Cinderella and the Scarred Viscount

Lairds of Ardvarrick miniseries

Forbidden to the Highland Laird
Rescued by Her Highland Soldier
The Laird's Runaway Wife

Discover more at millsandboon.co.uk.

RESCUED BY THE RAKISH LORD

Sarah Mallory

MILLS & BOON

All rights reserved including the right of reproduction in whole or in part in any form. This edition is published by arrangement with Harlequin Enterprises ULC.

This is a work of fiction. Names, characters, places, locations and incidents are purely fictional and bear no relationship to any real life individuals, living or dead, or to any actual places, business establishments, locations, events or incidents. Any resemblance is entirely coincidental.

Without limiting the exclusive rights of any author, contributor or the publisher of this publication, any unauthorised use of this publication to train generative artificial intelligence (AI) technologies is expressly prohibited. HarperCollins also exercise their rights under Article 4(3) of the Digital Single Market Directive 2019/790 and expressly reserve this publication from the text and data mining exception.

® and TM are trademarks owned and used by the trademark owner and/or its licensee. Trademarks marked with ® are registered with the United Kingdom Patent Office and/or the Office for Harmonisation in the Internal Market and in other countries.

First published in Great Britain 2026
by Mills & Boon, an imprint of HarperCollins*Publishers* Ltd,
1 London Bridge Street, London, SE1 9GF

www.harpercollins.co.uk

HarperCollins*Publishers*, Macken House, 39/40 Mayor Street Upper, Dublin 1, D01 C9W8, Ireland

Rescued by the Rakish Lord © 2026 Sarah Mallory

ISBN: 978-0-263-41877-4

04/26

Printed and Bound in the UK using 100% Renewable Electricity at CPI Group (UK) Ltd, Croydon, CR0 4YY

Lesley Cookman

Rest easy now, Lesley. We miss you,
but we still have great memories, and your books.

Chapter One

'Quick, quick, the mail's a-coming!'

Tom the pot-boy's urgent cry sent the already busy kitchen into a frenzy. Passengers on the cross-country mail would be given only as much time as it took to change the horses and collect the mail before they were off again. Cook was already issuing orders as she sliced more beef, fresh coffee pots were filled, potatoes piled high in dishes and meat pies pulled out of the oven.

Selina retreated to a corner of the inner hall, out of the way, but where she could observe both the kitchen and the public rooms. She was always impressed by the speed and efficiency with which food was delivered to the customers, but she needed to be ready to maintain the peace between those busy preparing the food and the harassed servants running back and forth to the coffee room and private parlours.

When the initial rush was over, she helped carry

the empty pots and plates through to the scullery for the maids to clean, despite Cook's protests.

'Tedn't your place to do such menial work, Miss Wynter,' objected that tyrant of the kitchen. 'You bein' a lady an' all. What your father would say I don't know!'

'Then we won't tell him, Mrs Trew.' Selina replied cheerfully. 'There is no one else available today and, since I am responsible for you being short-handed, it is only right that I should be here to help.'

Cook scoffed at that. 'Don't see you could do much else, other than turn off the landlord, his missus and that slatternly daughter of theirs. Turning the White Horse into a bawdy house, they was!'

Selina agreed, but it had left the posting inn severely lacking in serving men and maids. Some help had been found in the village, but a sudden crisis this evening meant she was obliged to bring James and Alice, two of her own servants from Reigney Abbey, to fill the gap while she helped in the kitchens and soothed ruffled feathers whenever Mrs Trew's temper got the better of her.

Once the mail had departed, the activity in the inn slowed and Cook ordered Selina out of the kitchens. However, Alice and James were still working in the coffee room and Selina, who hated to be idle, took up a broom and began to sweep up the leaves that had blown into the garden passage.

She had just finished collecting up the leaves when

sounds of an altercation could be heard and she went back inside to investigate. James and Alice were in the inner hall, trying unsuccessfully to usher a couple of drunken travellers out of the building. Selina hesitated, the inebriates were not local gentlemen, but she was still loath to become involved.

Not that anyone would recognise her: even Papa would not know her now, she thought, with her cheeks flushed from the kitchens and tendrils of hair escaping untidily from beneath her beribboned mob cap.

The two men were growing more vociferous and evading all attempts to move them out to the small yard, which was used only by the inn servants. James and Alice were trying their best, but service at Reigney Abbey had not taught them how to deal with obstreperous guests.

The men had reached the belligerent stage of intoxication and when they began threatening James, Selina took up her broom and intervened. Telling Alice to open the outer door, she briskly ordered the two men to leave. Her appearance had the desired effect: the servants immediately grew in confidence while the two drunken men were cowed by her air of authority, not to mention the besom she waved menacingly in their direction.

'I'll not tell 'ee again,' she declared, adopting a strong country accent, 'Be off with 'ee, now.'

The men hastily backed away out of the door and into the lamp-lit yard. The first man stumbled and his companion tripped over him, bringing them both crashing down onto the cobbles. Selina stood in the doorway, fists on her hips, mimicking her old nurse in one of her rages as she watched the men scramble unsteadily to their feet.

She stepped out of the door, brandishing the broom.

'Get off my property now, or I'll give 'ee such a beating!'

One of the revellers, an ox of a man, glanced around. There was no one else in sight, although sounds from the busy stable-yard could be heard through the adjoining passage. He turned back to Selina, a triumphant look on his bullish features.

'Ha, you think you can thrash me?' he snarled, bunching his fists and advancing upon Selina. 'Damned impudent wench!'

She gripped her broom more tightly, determined not to back away, and was preparing for battle when a deep, amused voice sounded from the shadows.

'*She* might not be able to thrash you, my friend, but I certainly can!'

The drunken reveller halted and Selina dared to take her eyes off him to glance at the figure strolling out of the adjoining passage. In the flickering light of the yard lamps, she thought the newcomer looked far more dangerous than her assailant. He was a tall man, his broad shoulders made even bigger by a caped greatcoat, which hung open to expose a small sword hanging at his side. He was dressed completely in black, any white linen hidden beneath the dark muffler tucked into his riding jacket. His whole bearing exuded power, from the black tricorne worn at a jaunty angle to the shiny black top boots.

The erstwhile reveller continued to stare at the stranger, who addressed him cheerfully.

'Yes, my fine fellow. You would be wise to consider your next move very carefully. I'd suggest you leave now and save yourself a deal of trouble.'

'I see what it is,' spat the ox-like man, helping his fellow traveller to his feet, 'You intend to have the wench for yourself!'

'My intentions need not concern you,' drawled the stranger, walking over to stand between Selina and the drunken pair. He rested one hand on the hilt of his small sword. 'My actions should, however, because if you tarry here much longer, I shall lose patience.'

The second man was on his feet now and tugging at his companion's arm.

'Come away, Nathan,' he hissed. 'Let's find our horses and leave this place.'

For a few moments the ox-like man hesitated, glowering. Then, keeping away from Selina's broom and making sure he did not come within sword's reach of the dark stranger, he shambled off with his companion.

Selina watched the men disappear into the shadows

of the passage, on their way back to the stable-yard. She glanced at the stranger.

'Thank you for your intervention, sir.'

'It was no trouble. I had stopped here to dine, then the arrival of the mail coach meant my departure was even more delayed. I was whiling away the time by exploring a little when I heard voices.'

'And helped me to send those two drunkards on their way,' she remarked. 'I only hope they do not fall off their horses!'

'A night in a ditch won't do them much harm.' He turned towards her. 'Well, mistress, do you think my efforts worthy of a reward?'

He had pushed his hat back so that the lamplight fell on his face. A handsome countenance, thought Selina. If one liked lean cheeks and dark eyes set beneath straight black brows. He grinned then, and she was unable to resist smiling back.

'I shall order a tankard of ale to be put aside for you in the taproom.'

'What, is that all, Dolly?' He moved closer. 'I had heard there might be something more on offer...'

He reached out, but Selina quickly stepped back, raising her broom to hold him off.

'I am not Dolly,' she retorted. 'And whatever you have heard, sir, it is not the case at the White Horse!'

Laughing, he put up his hands. 'Outmanoeuvred, by Gad. Well done, madam!'

Selina laughed back at him, strangely not a whit

afraid, her spirits still bubbling with energy following the recent contretemps. There was no denying she was enjoying herself.

'I have been avoiding unwanted attentions since I was a child,' she told him, cheerfully. 'When gentlemen would invite me to sit on their knee in exchange for a *bonbon*!'

'Ah well. Pity. It seems I was misinformed about this place.'

She should retire now, and let the man return to the main yard, but something made her want to delay.

'Possibly not,' she said. 'Dolly was the landlord's daughter, and of the same dubious character as her parents. I was obliged to turn off the whole family two weeks ago.'

'You are the new landlady, then?'

He was regarding her with interest, a tiny smile playing about his mouth, and it was at that point Selina realised she should not be bandying words with this man, however handsome he might be. In fact, being handsome made him all the more dangerous!

She glanced towards the door, where the servants were watching her anxiously.

'James, pray come and escort this gentleman to the taproom, and set him up with a tankard—no, make that a *blackjack*—of ale.'

He laughed at that. 'Hell, madam, do you wish to make me too cast away to travel on to London? A tankard will do, thank you.'

The footman hurried up. 'If you will come this way, sir. The taproom is off the main yard.'

'Very well, lead on.' He flashed a final grin at Selina. *'Au revoir*, fair maid, until the next time.'

'Goodbye,' she corrected him, trying not to laugh. 'There will not *be* a next time. Now you had best follow James, before I revoke my hospitality.'

'Gad, madam, I vow you are a managing female.'

'One has to be, in my position. Now be off with you, sir!'

Not noticeably dashed, he swept off his hat and made her a flourishing bow before following James away into the darkness.

Selina stood for a moment, her spirits fizzing like champagne. Only when she was sure he would not reappear did she close her eyes and breathe out a long sigh. What on earth was she doing? That could have gone so horribly wrong, and not just the danger posed by two drunkards. It was a miracle she had escaped discovery.

Her avenging angel might not have guessed her identity but she knew his. She had seen his tall, imposing figure two weeks ago at the assembly ball. Where he had been pointed out to her as the notorious rake, Devil Blackbourne.

Chapter Two

Selina remembered that evening at the Torrisford Assembly only too well. She danced the first dance with Sir Alfred Kenton, the squire, and then with two more of her father's elderly friends. However, when Mr Keith brought the Honourable Clifford Fremington to her as a prospective partner, she had refused, point-blank, to stand up with him.

He was the son of their closest neighbour, but his repeated marriage proposals, including one earlier that evening before the dancing had even commenced, had become tiresome. Not all the charm of the master of ceremonies, the scowls of Lord and Lady Fremington, nor the threat of censure from some of the haughtier patrons could persuade her to change her mind. Even when it was pointed out to her that having refused Mr Fremington, she could not stand up with anyone else for the rest of the evening, she stood firm.

It was at that very moment that half a dozen gentlemen had walked in and the atmosphere in the room changed immediately. Word spread like wildfire that Viscount Graddon was here with his guests—all single gentlemen—who were staying at Graddon Hall for several weeks' hunting.

Selina had felt the sudden sting of frustration. For once, there would be sufficient partners for every lady who wished to dance. It irked her, but she was philosophical. What was done was done. She took a seat next to Papa amongst the more elderly residents of the neighbourhood and watched as the gentlemen were presented to every one of her female friends. No one would think to look for a dance partner here, on these back benches.

One figure in particular had attracted her attention. A tall, dark stranger, immaculately dressed in a very plain black evening coat and breeches; a severe contrast to his snowy linen and white satin waistcoat. Even his hair was black, gleaming like a raven's wing and tied back from a lean face that was undoubtedly handsome with dark straight brows, clean-shaven cheeks and a strong jaw.

Selina might have considered him attractive, but she saw him raise his quizzing glass and survey his company with a look of slightly bored amusement. His dark eyes swept around the room, but as Selina and her father were sitting a little in the shadows, she had escaped his notice.

It had not been not long before she learned that the gentleman in question was Lord Deveril Blackbourne, a man of such dubious reputation that he was called Devil Blackbourne, even by his friends. Despite this notoriety, there was no shortage of partners for him. He danced with all the most handsome and vivacious ladies, and although Selina told herself she was grateful not to have attracted the attention of such a rake, she had to admit it was a little galling to sit out, unnoticed.

But thank goodness, she thought now, in the light of what had just occurred!

That had been a fortnight ago, and since then Selina had heard more than she ever wished to hear about the gentlemen at Graddon Hall from her friends and neighbours. Husbands and fathers who met them during the hunt were urged by their wives or daughters to invite the Viscount and his guests to dinner, and several families even arranged little parties for their guests, including the occasional, impromptu dance.

Selina had been too busy with the troubles at the White Horse to accept any of these invitations, and since Papa was content to stay at home of an evening with his books and his port, she had so far avoided all contact with Lord Graddon's hunting party.

Until tonight, when Lord Deveril had walked out of the shadows and appointed himself her champion.

'Well, it was fortuitous that he is leaving Torrisford,' she muttered, making her way back into the inn. 'If we should meet again, he would be sure to recognise me, and then I should be in the suds!'

***

Upon reaching the taproom, Lord Deveril accepted his tankard of ale and retired to a quiet corner to think. The footman who had escorted him back through the busy stable-yard had been damnably close-lipped about his mistress and Deveril was intrigued.

He smiled now as he recalled his first sight of her, confronting those two rogues. She had been standing in the doorway, every curve of her womanly figure defined against the light from the hall behind her. And she had the daintiest ankles he had seen for a long while.

She might not be the delectable Dolly his friends at Graddon Hall had spoken of, but he was impressed by the way she had advanced upon the two fellows, brandishing her broomstick with such vigour it was not surprising they fell back before her.

And she had resisted his advances with good humour and not a hint of fear. But who was she? She had definitely told those two drunken sots to leave *her* property, and she had mentioned turning off Dolly and the landlord.

Clearly, she was a woman accustomed to being obeyed, so why had that serving man, James, not confirmed that she was the owner of this establishment? Unless she was perhaps the owner's mistress. That idea found no favour with Deveril. She did not seem to him to be mistress material, and he had some experience in the matter.

He finished his ale and made his way outside, where fresh horses were finally being put to his post-chaise. A few discreet enquiries of the ostlers and an aged stable hand proved equally fruitless. No one was willing to talk about the Junoesque serving maid, and that struck him as damned odd.

'There is some mystery here, and I should like to get to the bottom of it,' he muttered. 'Perhaps I will stay in Devonshire, after all.'

That would not cause any problem, beyond perhaps a teasing from his fellow guests. Richard, Lord Graddon, was a close friend and Deveril had accepted the invitation to join him at Graddon Hall to alleviate his growing restlessness. But Deveril was not enamoured of hunting, the main form of entertainment on offer at the Hall. He relished the hard riding of the chase, but he did not enjoy the kill, which was why he had elected to return early to London.

Now, however, there was the prospect of a different kind of sport to divert him. He wanted to know more about the bold wench who could see off two drunkards with nothing more than a broom, and who could also turn aside his advances so adroitly.

He strolled across to his waiting coach and addressed the postilions.

'Change of plan. We are going back to Graddon Hall!'

It was late when Selina returned to the Abbey. She sent James and Alice off to their beds and was about to creep up the stairs when her father's valet appeared in the hall. One look at his face and she guessed what he was about to say.

'What is it, Pensford, is Papa not asleep?'

'No, miss. He has been asking for you.'

'Oh dear, does he know where I have been?'

'I'm afraid so, miss. Leighton let it slip at dinner, and the master insisted upon staying up until you returned. You will find him in the drawing room.'

'Thank you, Pensford. Give me five minutes to tidy myself and I will go to him.'

The valet nodded. 'I've built up the drawing room fire, miss, and I will have a glass of wine sent in for you.'

Selina hurried off to her room, where she quickly shed her cloak and bonnet and removed the bib and apron she wore over her gown. Then she let down her petticoats, which she had raised by the simple expedient of turning them over at the waist, and loosened the strings of her skirts to lower them to a more seemly level.

She had already discarded her mob cap by the time her maid came in and she put up a hand to forestall her long-suffering maid's rebuke.

'Now, Nancy, pray do not ring a peal over me!'

'As if I would dare,' retorted Nancy, mendaciously. 'You knows I don't approve of you goin' to that inn, but it don't mean I won't help when you comes back. You should've called me. The least I can do is help to make you presentable so you don't worry your poor papa into an early grave. Now then, you'd best let me tidy your hair before you goes to see him.'

Selina gave her maid a kiss on the cheek.

'You are a *darling*!' she said, sitting down at her dressing table.

It took only a few minutes to tidy her dark curls and after a last, critical look at the mirror, Selina rose to her feet.

'Thank you, Nancy, that is much better.' She gave her skirts a final shake. 'This polonaise gown might not be my finest attire, but Papa will think it perfectly respectable. Don't wait up for me!'

She found her father in the drawing room, dozing beside the fire. There was a glass of port on a table at his elbow, an open book on his lap and an array of lighted candles about him. As she entered the room he stirred.

'Is that you, Selina?'

'Yes, Papa.' She closed the door gently and moved forward into the light.

'You have been to the White Horse.'

It was a statement, not a question, and Selina did not even consider prevaricating.

'I have, sir. They were very busy tonight and I took James and Alice to wait on tables. Then I stayed to ensure Mrs Trew did not fly up in the boughs again. She is such a good cook and manages the kitchens very well, but she can be short tempered when things get busy, and we cannot afford to lose any more servants.'

She broke off as a footman came in with a glass of wine for her. She took it and smiled at her father.

'Now, let us drink our wine together and then we may both retire.'

But her father was not listening. He said plaintively, 'You should not go there, Selina. A common inn! It is not seemly for a young lady to be visiting such places.'

'Nay, sir, it is a very respectable posting house.' She squeezed his arm. 'Pray, do not be anxious, Papa. I never enter the public rooms, no one sees me.'

Well, no one who knows me.

She went on, 'It should be the last time I need to play peacekeeper there. The new landlord and his family arrive tomorrow and I have great hopes that he will do very well.'

Her father shook his head. 'But if it is not the White Horse, it will be something else. Poachers in the Home Wood, perhaps, or dealing with villagers' complaints.' He sighed. 'Reigney is too much for your young shoulders, Selina.'

'Now, that I will not allow,' she interrupted him, with mock severity. 'You know how much I enjoy running the estate. I like to be active and doing something.' She laughed and added, thinking of tonight's encounter with Lord Deveril, 'I have been told that I have a very *managing* disposition.'

But her father was too agitated to be amused.

'Yes, yes, but this trouble at the inn has been very worrying. You should let Ashworth deal with it. He is land steward, after all.'

'And he has plenty of other things to occupy him. Besides, I am far better at keeping the peace. This was only a little hitch, Father, and from tomorrow I hope that I shall not be required to go there again for some while. But you must see that we needed to look after the mail coach passengers, as well as the horses. The mail provides a very lucrative trade and we cannot afford to lose it.'

She put her wine beside his on the table and sat down on the little footstool at his feet.

'Dearest Papa,' she said, taking his hands, 'you must not fret so. I love Reigney, and I *like* the challenges it offers, whether it be making a success of the White Horse or discussing new breeds and crops with the tenant farmers. I cannot bear to be idle!'

'But you are so young, my darling girl. It is not right that you should have these cares on your shoulders. You should be enjoying yourself more, going out with friends to parties of pleasure.'

'You know quite well I would find a constant round of visits and parties very dull. You and I see quite enough of Society.'

He fidgeted in his chair. 'If only I was not so dependent upon you! Since your mother's sad demise, I find myself sadly pulled down. She was such a strong lady, always putting duty before self. Oh, Selina, I miss her so much, and try as I might, I cannot do half as much as I should. Sometimes I think it will be a blessing for everyone when I quit this earth and join her.'

'Hush now, Papa. You are only saying that because you are overtired, and I am a beast to have caused you such worry tonight.' She picked up his wine glass and handed it to him. 'Come along, Papa, let us drink together, and then I will take you up to your room. Pensford will have warmed the sheets for you by now and you will see, once you have had some sleep, how much better everything will look in the morning.'

They sat together in silence for a while, but Selina could see that her father was ill at ease.

She said gently, 'We rub along very well here, do we not, Papa? You have your books to amuse you and old friends with whom you correspond, and I am very happy looking after Reigney. I believe it is an ideal arrangement.'

He frowned. 'But no one is looking after *you*. You need a husband, Selina. We should find you one.'

'What, give control of my life to someone else?' She laughed. 'No indeed! I am quite capable of running Reigney and I have no wish for any man in my life, Papa. Other than yourself.'

She had a sudden image of the black-clad figure striding out of the shadows at the White Horse. Not that she had needed his help, of course, and she had heard enough about men like Lord Deveril Blackbourne to know they were not the sort to make a woman happy. At least, not as a husband.

'It is not right,' her father said again. 'You should be out in the world, meeting suitable gentlemen, making new friends and acquaintances.'

'But I do, dear Papa! We go to the assemblies, do we not?'

'Once a month. That is not enough,' he told her. 'If only my sister were still alive to invite you for another Season in town.'

Selina grimaced, remembering the short time she had spent in London with her aunt.

'I so disliked being stared at and, and *weighed up* by everyone I met there. I really did not enjoy being assessed at every turn. My clothes, looks, family and fortune discussed as if I was merely a bundle of goods to be valued and sold to the highest bidder. And nothing to do but decide what to wear for the next party!' She shuddered. 'No thank you, sir. I prefer to remain here in Torrisford. I have friends enough here and have no wish to go anywhere else.'

It was not strictly true. Selina would have liked to travel, to see more of the world. But she had long ago resigned herself to the fact that she could not leave Papa and he, in his turn, did not wish to leave Reigney.

'I suppose we must make do with the assemblies in Torrisford,' he said, giving her a faint, rueful smile.

'Yes indeed,' agreed Selina, keen to encourage this line of thought. 'And you find them most enjoyable, do you not? Seeing all our neighbours, talking to our friends. You see, we are not exactly hermits.' She rose from her little footstool. 'Now, sir, you should go to bed and stop worrying. Mr Gurney is coming to play chess with you tomorrow, and you will need a clear head for that, won't you?'

She accompanied him up the stairs, knowing that by the morning he would be once more immersed in his books and content to potter around his library while he waited for the vicar to arrive. Then, with harmony restored, she would be able to spend the day writing letters, paying bills and catching up on the accounts.

Chapter Three

The light was still shining from the dining room windows at Graddon Hall when Deveril returned. He found the Viscount and those of his guests who had not already sought their beds gathered around the supper table, which was littered with plates, glasses and decanters.

'Damme if it ain't Blackbourne!' exclaimed Lord Ancrum, regarding him with a bleary eye. 'Thought you'd left for town!'

'I changed my mind.'

Another of the guests laughed. 'Hah, if that ain't just like you, Dev.' He splashed wine from one of the decanters into his glass and raised it in a mocking salute. 'Never known a fellow like it for setting off on a whim!'

'Quite.' Deveril grinned and walked across to the sideboard, where he helped himself to some of the meat pie, 'That's it precisely, Henry. An hour alone in the post-chaise and I was already regretting my decision.'

That caused some laughter from those around the table, and a few ribald comments on his capricious behaviour, but he did not respond. He filled his plate with pickles and cheeses and carried it back to the table, where he sat down beside his host.

Lord Graddon poured a fresh glass of wine and pushed it towards him.

'Perhaps now you will tell us the real reason for your return.'

'But I explained it, Richard,' said Deveril, with a wave of one hand. 'I realised town would be devilish dull without you all.'

'Fustian!' cried Lord Ancrum, sitting opposite. 'Don't believe that for a moment. London could never be dull for you, not with the lovely Lady Fylde waiting for you.'

Sir Henry sniggered and glanced around the table. 'I'd wager it was her letter that came two days ago. Wrote to hurry your return, eh?'

'No mistaking it was from a woman,' declared Charles Penkridge, his lips twisted in distaste. 'It positively reeked of scent.'

Deveril sipped at his wine but said nothing. They were quite correct; Amanda had written with an ultimatum; come back to town immediately or she would find herself another lover.

The beautiful young widow had returned to London

in the spring with the sole purpose of finding a paramour and it was not long before they were engaged in a passionate *affaire*. However, it had not taken Deveril long to discover that the lady's beauty did not extend beyond her outward appearance and he had soon tired of her selfish, grasping nature.

The final straw had been her demand that he buy her a high perch phaeton. His refusal resulted in a tantrum, which was when he had decided to accept Richard's invitation to join him in Devon.

Lady Fylde's letter had given Deveril a reason to leave Graddon Hall, but he had not been returning to London for Amanda's sake. He was tired of the incessant talk of hunting. He had no objection to bagging a brace of pheasant or grouse for the pot, or even shooting a deer, if the venison was to grace the table, but he disliked killing any poor creature for sport. He rarely visited Graddon Hall during the hunting season, but this time the invitation had coincided with Amanda's sulks and he had thought it prudent to remove himself from town.

A few weeks with his hunting friends had proved more than enough, but now he had the mystery of the woman at the White Horse to occupy him and he was happy to stay in Devon a little longer. As for Amanda… He drained his glass. The high perch phaeton would be his parting gift to her. He would write to Roberts tomorrow, and tell him to arrange it.

'Well, man?' demanded his friend. 'Lady Fylde wrote to hasten your return, didn't she?'

'On the contrary,' drawled Deveril, 'she gave me my *congé*.'

Exclamations of surprise greeted his announcement, and Deveril was obliged to endure his friends' good-natured mockery for several minutes until they lost interest in teasing him. The chiming of the clock drew attention to the lateness of the hour. Lord Ancrum yawned and declared he was for his bed, and soon the others followed, leaving only Deveril and his host at the table.

Lord Graddon fetched the decanter of brandy from the sideboard and carried it and two glasses across to the table.

'Perhaps now you will tell me the truth, Dev,' he said, charging the glasses and pushing one towards his friend. 'I don't for one moment think Lady Fylde has broken with you.'

'You think I am too irresistible?' murmured Deveril, raising an eyebrow.

'I think you are too rich.'

'Richard, Richard, that is brutal. Are you saying the lovely Amanda only wants me for my fortune?'

'You are a handsome dog and charming, too, confound you, so perhaps that has something to do with it. But 'tis common knowledge Fylde left her with only a modest income.'

'It's my belief she bled him dry before he died.'

'Is that why you are not going back to fight for her?'

'I have never yet felt obliged to, er, fight for a lady.'

'You mean you have never cared enough for any woman to put yourself out for her.'

'Precisely, Richard.'

'By heaven you are a cool one!'

Deveril heard the note of censure in his friend's voice and his lips twisted into a self-deprecating smile. 'I have often been told I have no heart.'

The Viscount looked up at him from under frowning brows. 'Fustian. You have been good enough to me when I have needed it.'

'But you are a friend, Richard. You would do the same for me, would you not?'

'Of course. Anything in my power.'

'And there you have it. I have never met a woman who would do that.' Deveril raised his glass twisting it this way and that as he studied the amber contents. 'Oh, they are very willing to *give*, but it always comes at a price.'

He saw that Richard was regarding him with a frown and raised his brows. 'Are you feeling sorry for the lovely Amanda? I assure you she is more than capable of securing herself another lover, and one who is prepared to indulge her every whim.'

'It is not Lady Fylde I feel sorry for, it is you, my friend. You are a restless soul, never staying long with any woman or in one place.' The Viscount drained his glass. 'Oh well. I am glad to see you back here. I know you are not a great one for hunting, and I only hope you won't be bored, my friend.'

'No, I don't think I shall be,' said Deveril, thinking of the woman at the White Horse. 'I am sure I shall find something to occupy me.'

Deveril was eager to make enquiries about the woman he had met at the posting inn. However, Lord Graddon and his party had been invited by Lord Tawton, the Viscount's cousin, to try a few days' hunting on Dartmoor. Having returned so precipitately to Graddon Hall, Deveril decided he owed it to his host and fellow guests to accompany them to Lord Tawton's estate in South Devonshire the next day.

The distances involved kept the whole party away several days and it was a week later before they rode back to Graddon Hall. It was not the best of journeys. The rain started soon after they set off and persisted all day, so that when Lord Ancrum spotted a small inn nestled in a valley at Salcoombe, some miles from Torrisford, they all agreed they should call a halt. The local ale and a good fire proved very much to their liking, and they decided to dine there. The grooms having been dispatched to take their horses back to the stables and return to collect the revellers at midnight, the party settled down to dry their sodden coats and enjoy themselves.

They had finished a very good dinner and were gathered around the fire when the landlord came in.

'Beggin' your pardon, sirs, but Lord Fremington and his son have arrived and was askin' if they might warm themselves by the fire, there bein' only the one private parlour, here, see.'

Lord Graddon glanced at his friends then said cheerfully, 'Aye, why not? The more the merrier.'

The landlord retreated and a few moments later two men entered the room. Deveril remembered seeing them at the Torrisford Assembly. An old Devon family, he had been informed, biggest landowners in the area, and they swaggered into the parlour, assured of their welcome.

Lord Fremington was of stocky build with a bagwig over his greying hair while his son wore his own sandy locks, badly powdered. There was no mistaking that the two men were related. The Honourable Clifford was a little taller than his father, but of the same heavy build and they both had rather pale, protruding eyes. But where Lord Fremington was smiling broadly, his son's mouth had a distinctly petulant look.

'Much obliged to you, my lord,' declared Fremington, shrugging off his damp greatcoat and shaking it out. 'We have been visiting friends. They begged us to stay the night, but we decided to ride home, ain't that right, my boy?'

'You decided, Father,' muttered the younger Fremington, although his father did not appear to hear him, for he continued with barely a pause.

'Didn't think it would rain quite so hard, though,'

he remarked. 'That's why we stopped here, to sit it out for a while. It seems you had the same idea, eh, my lord? Nothing better than a good fire and a glass of wine or home brewed, what? Ha ha, I hope you don't mind us joining you, but no one wants to be sitting in the taproom with the scaff and raff, eh?'

'No, of course not,' exclaimed Sir Henry, waving his wine glass at the newcomers. 'No need for that. Move up, Penkridge, and you, Ancrum, we can easily make room for two more!'

After a few moments' shuffling everyone was seated, more or less comfortably, and the landlord was sent off to fetch more refreshments.

'Well, this is very pleasant,' declared Lord Fremington. 'A warm fire and good company, we could not ask for more eh, Clifford?'

His son muttered something, but Fremington did not wait for a reply and turned immediately to the Viscount.

'Have ye been far, my lord? I didn't think there was any hunting on the moors today.'

'We have been south for a few days, hunting with Lord Tawton.'

'Tawton, eh?' Lord Fremington slapped his thigh in delight. 'I know him well. A very good sort of man. He has some of the finest hounds in the county, so I am sure you have had good sport! But I hope you've had better weather than we have enjoyed in Torrisford. Rain's been relentless these past few days. I shall be surprised if it don't wash away some of the roads.'

'It's a constant problem, ain't it?' remarked Sir Henry. 'Keeping the roads in good repair. Don't you find that, Lord Fremington?'

It was a promising subject. Deveril sat back while the others shared their stories of perilous journeys over poor roads. He had no wish to join in. He was content to drink his wine and listen, lost in his own thoughts. Until he heard Charles Penkridge mention the White Horse.

'Jesmond and I changed horses there on our way to join Lord Graddon some weeks back.' He paused, grinning. 'They made us very welcome, didn't they, Henry? Especially that pretty daughter of the landlord…'

'Never mind that now, Charles,' said Ancrum impatiently. 'We heard enough of the dainty Dolly at the time. Damme, I never saw a man so moonstruck over a yellow-haired chit!'

So, thought Deveril, the woman he had seen was definitely *not* the landlord's daughter. He had only seen her by torchlight, but she had been dark-haired, as well as being far too curvaceous to be described as dainty.

'Aye, and then she goes off with her father, never to be heard of again.' Penkridge went on, shaking his head sorrowfully, until a snarl from Lord Ancrum brought him back to the matter in hand. 'But, yes, it was a very good road. We made damned good time to Graddon Hall, ain't that so, Henry?'

Sir Henry was nodding in his chair and looked up, bleary-eyed. When he did not answer, the conversation veered off on quite another subject, but Deveril saw an opportunity. He turned to Clifford Fremington, who was sitting nearby.

'I came that way too and made excellent time,' he said. 'The White Horse appears to be a very busy place. Is it part of your estates?'

'What?' Clifford Fremington's head jerked up. 'Oh. Oh no. That land, west of Torrisford, belongs to Reigney Abbey.'

'Church land?' asked Deveril.

'Are you talking about Reigney?' Lord Fremington broke off his own conversation with Charles Penkridge to call across to Deveril. 'The Abbey is at present owned by my neighbour, William Wynter.'

'At present?' Deveril looked at him, his brows raised.

Lord Fremington shrugged. 'Wynter is an old man and he has no son to carry on.'

'But there is a daughter, isn't there?' put in the Viscount. 'She was at the last assembly.'

Deveril was on the alert now, although he maintained his look of only faint interest in the conversation.

'Was she, by Gad,' exclaimed Penkridge, 'I don't recall seeing her.'

'That's because she was not dancing. She was sitting at the side of the room with her father.'

'An heiress and not dancing?' Charles Penkridge shook his head. 'Whatever is wrong with her?'

Deveril did not miss Clifford Fremington's scowl, nor the hasty way his father jumped in with an answer.

'Nothing at all, she merely chose not to dance that night.' He paused. 'I think perhaps I should tell you, sirs, that the lady is, er… Well, there has been an understanding between our two families for some time. Our lands march together, you see, and the children have known each other forever. What could be more natural than a union between our two families?'

'Aye,' said Clifford Fremington, his chin jutting pugnaciously. 'Miss Wynter and I are as good as engaged.'

'Ah, I see,' said Penkridge, satisfied. 'That explains everything.'

It explained nothing, thought Deveril, noting the way Lord Fremington frowned at his son.

Deveril's first thought, upon hearing that Mr William Wynter had a daughter, was that she must be the woman he had met at the White Horse. However, it was impossible to imagine that vivacious, Junoesque creature sitting idly by while others danced. Or being betrothed to the stolid young man now sitting beside him. Confound it, she would run rings around him!

'You are to be congratulated, Mr Fremington,' he

said, raising his glass in a salute. 'I look forward to meeting the lady.'

'Ha ha, be careful there, Fremington,' cried Lord Ancrum, who was by now in boisterous spirits. 'Blackbourne will steal this Miss Wynter from under your nose if you don't look out. For some reason the ladies can't seem to resist him. Ain't that so, Charles?'

'You are right,' affirmed Penkridge. 'He's broken more hearts than I care to remember. Damme he only has to smile at a chit and she's smitten!'

Clifford Fremington was looking thunderous and Deveril tried to frown down his companions. He said dampingly, 'You exaggerate, Charles. For heaven's sake can we not talk of something more interesting?' He looked towards the Viscount. 'Or play at cards. What say you, Richard, a friendly game of brag, perhaps?'

The suggestion was taken up with enthusiasm by everyone except Sir Henry Jesmond, who could not be roused from his slumber.

As the gentlemen returned to the table, Deveril moved closer to the Viscount.

'Richard, I suggest we set the stakes beforehand,' he said, sliding a quick glance towards Clifford Fremington, who was looking anxious.

His friend did not disappoint him. With the faintest of nods, he declared. 'No high stakes tonight, gentlemen. We will agree the limits in advance.'

Lord Fremington puffed out his chest. 'Pho, not on

my account, sirs. I've played my share at Boodle's. I shall stand buff.'

'I am sure you would, my lord,' replied Richard smoothly. 'But on a night like this, when we have been travelling all day and our carriages will be arriving in a couple of hours, I'd rather not play deep.'

'Good plan,' declared Lord Ancrum, taking the new packs of cards from the landlord. 'Just a few games to see us to midnight, what? For small stakes. We ain't out to ruin anyone this evening!'

'Aye, that's much safer when one is playing against Blackbourne,' chuckled Penkridge. 'He'll take any bet, however outlandish!'

Deveril shook his head. 'Not true, Charles. I like at least a chance of winning.'

'Ha, your life has been one long list of outrageous bets, to say nothing of the mistresses, scandals and duels! Like the time you wagered Arthur Jardine the new Lady Somersal would be in your bed within a month?' He laughed heartily and dug an elbow into his neighbour, who just happened to be Clifford Fremington. 'She'd married Somersal a year earlier but when they came back to town, she made it quite clear she was ready for a liaison. And by heaven, Jardine was hot for her! Boasted he would make her his mistress, but one dance and a few compliments from Blackbourne and she would not look at anyone else. Practically fell into his arms!'

'And has fallen into plenty of other men's arms

since then,' snapped the Viscount in repressive accents. 'I think that says more about the lady than Blackbourne.'

Deveril frowned. 'Let be, Richard. It is a very old story and reflects ill upon all those involved.'

But Charles Penkridge had not finished.

'It was the *on dit* of the Season, I recall. Blackbourne here ended up being called out by the husband *and* the would-be lover!'

Deveril raised a hand. 'I would rather forget the matter, gentlemen. It was not well done of me, although Jardine was being a bore.'

'He behaved outrageously,' retorted Richard. 'He suggested the wager and pressed you so much, you had little choice but to accept.'

Lord Ancrum rapped on the table. 'Enough chatter now, or there will be no time for a game! So, gentlemen. Brag, yes? For penny points!'

They settled down to play, although in far more relaxed fashion than would be tolerated at any London club, and Deveril was able to join in while at the same time thinking back to the events at the White Horse. Surely the mysterious woman could not be Miss Wynter. No respectable young lady would be abroad, pretending to be a serving wench. On the other hand, she had been very self-assured, and at times her broad accent had slipped a little.

There was only one thing for it. He must call at Reigney Abbey and see this Miss Wynter for himself.

* * *

Selina awoke to an exceptionally fine morning. Too fine to waste it indoors. When she learned that her father was taking breakfast in his room, she decided she would ride to the White Horse and visit the new landlord and his family. They had been in residence for a week now, and she was eager to know how they were settling in.

This visit was far less eventful than her previous one. This time she was not masquerading as a servant, nor becoming embroiled in an altercation and bandying words with a notorious rake, and she came away feeling much more optimistic for the future. Not only was the new landlord proving himself to be a sensible and hardworking man, Mrs Trew was quick to voice her approval of him and his wife, who was a friendly, outgoing woman with experience of running a busy inn.

No, thought Selina as she rode back to the Abbey, she was unlikely to be called upon to intervene quite so drastically in matters there again.

The short February day was nearing its end when Selina reached Reigney and she was surprised to see the squire's carriage standing in the stable-yard. She hurried to the house where the butler informed her that Lady Kenton was waiting for her in the drawing room.

'My dear ma'am, is something amiss?' she asked. 'Is it Helena, perhaps, or the squire? It must be serious to bring you here at this time of day.'

'No, no, everyone is very well, thank you. Leighton told me your father was taking a nap and I would not have him disturbed. In fact...well, it is you I wish to see, Selina.' Her ladyship rose and held out her hand. She went on, with only a tiny hint of censure, 'Forgive me if I do not kiss you, my dear, but you have, er...'

She tapped her own cheek and Selina laughed. 'Is my face spattered with mud? I beg your pardon. I should not have come here in all my dirt, but I was afraid your news might be urgent! Do you have time to wait while I go and change?'

Lady Kenton gave her a motherly smile. 'Yes, Selina, my news will keep a few more minutes.'

'Good, then I shall ask Leighton to bring in wine and cake while you wait for me!'

It was not much above a quarter of an hour later that Selina returned to the drawing room, her muddy riding habit replaced by a day dress of butter yellow and with her thick dark curls tamed and confined with a matching ribbon.

'There, is that better?' she said, coming in and helping herself to a glass of wine and one of the fancy cakes before taking a seat opposite her friend.

Lady Kenton nodded approvingly. 'Much better, my dear. I worry that you think me a trifle critical, but I was your mother's dearest friend...'

She hesitated and Selina filled in the gap by saying

cheerfully, 'You are afraid I am becoming a hoyden. I quite understand and do not hold it against you.'

'No, no, my love!' Lady Kenton was quick to disclaim. 'However, your circumstances, looking after your father, spending all your time taking care of the farms and estate business—it has made you a trifle more...*independent* than is usual for a gently bred young lady. Your dear mama would not like you to be considered anything less than ladylike.'

Selina accepted the censure with a nod. Lady Kenton meant well, but like the rest of the neighbourhood, she did not approve of Selina's living at Reigney without a chaperone. It did no good for Selina to say that Papa was chaperone enough, because everyone would argue that he did not accompany her when she was riding around the countryside or dealing directly with local traders and farmers.

She could only be thankful that none of them knew of her visits to the White Horse.

'I am a sad trial to you, am I not, ma'am?' she said ruefully. 'However, I am five-and-twenty and I have been running Papa's affairs since Mama died. I could not do that if I was not allowed a little more freedom than a chit from the schoolroom.'

'No, of course, and everyone agrees you have been remarkably successful,' replied Lady Kenton. 'However, it is important that you do not allow your independence to carry you too far. Which brings me to the reason for my coming here today.'

'Oh?'

Selina adopted a look of mild interest, but inside her heart was sinking. Somehow word had got out about her activities at the posting inn!

'Yes, my dear. It is a rather delicate matter. It concerns Lord Graddon's guest, the one with the roguish epithet Devil Blackbourne.'

'Oh no!'

'*Yes!*' Lady Kenton declared, nodding. 'You will recall we all thought he had quit Graddon Hall.'

'Did we?' Selina replied cautiously.

'Well, perhaps you had not heard it, my love, because you have not been into Torrisford this past week, but it was commonly understood that he had left and returned to London. There was much talk of it—the young ladies being disappointed, while their mothers were uniformly relieved to see the back of such a rake!'

'But he has returned?'

Lady Kenton nodded. 'Apparently, he went only as far as the first change, then turned about and came back the very same night! Not that anyone knew of it. You see, Lord Graddon took his party off to South Devonshire for a few days and they did not return until the early hours of this morning. A groom from Graddon Hall went into Torrisford to collect the post, where he met Mrs Babbage, from the haberdashers, who winkled everything out of him. And as you know, she is as good as any town crier.'

'And now, I suppose, it is all over the town and all the poor mamas are once again anxious for their chicks. But is this all, ma'am?' she asked, not yet relieved of her worries. 'I cannot think it warrants you coming here especially to tell me.'

'You are quite correct, if it was only the rake's return I would have left it until we met, or you heard it from one of your other friends. As it is, Sir Alfred heard a most extraordinary report today and as soon as I learned of it, I came to warn you.'

Selina was now thoroughly alarmed. Was news of her masquerading as a serving maid all over Torrisford now? She waited anxiously while Lady Kenton tapped her fan against her palm, clearly struggling to find the right words to express herself.

'Oh, my dear Selina,' she exclaimed at last, 'the rogue has made you the subject of the most outrageous wager!'

Chapter Four

'A wager?' Selina felt the colour draining from her cheeks. 'I d-don't understand.'

'No of course not, you have never even met the man.' Selina thought it best not to correct Lady Kenton, who went on, 'That is why I had to come and see you as soon as I could. You will recall I pointed him out to you at the last assembly, and I suppose he must have seen you there. And now, having made this wager he will soon be seeking you out!'

'But I do not understand,' Selina repeated, bemused. 'How did you learn of it? I hope you will explain everything to me.'

Her ladyship sighed. 'I can see I must.'

Selina folded her hands and waited anxiously for the older lady to begin.

'Sir Alfred went to Torrisford early this morning and returned, deeply troubled. As squire, you know that people are always telling him things, but he rarely disturbs me with them. However, this worried him so much that he disclosed it to me, and suggested I should drop you a hint.'

'Quite right, if it concerns me.' Selina sat up very straight. 'Pray do go on, ma'am. The word with no bark on it, if you please!'

'Very well.' Lady Kenton drew in a breath and said, slowly, 'It would appear Lord Deveril has wagered five hundred guineas that he will be the first man to...' She hesitated, then squared her shoulders and went on, 'You are no longer a child, Selina, so I will tell you straight what Sir Alfred said to me: Devil Blackbourne is determined to be the first to seduce you.'

'What!'

'Yes! Sir Alfred had it from Lord Fremington, who was present when it was all agreed.'

'Five hundred guineas.' Selina put a hand to her cheek. 'How, how abominable!'

'Well, the squire told me his lordship said Blackbourne had *laid a monkey on it*, which I *think* means five hundred guineas.'

Despite being young and unmarried, Selina's contact with her father's tenants and market traders had made her far more worldly wise than most ladies of her acquaintance and she said, 'I believe it can also mean five hundred pounds, ma'am. Not that that makes it any less odious.'

'Indeed not! I was so angry when I heard of it.'

'But how did it come about, and how does Lord Fremington know of it?' asked Selina, suspiciously.

Lady Kenton clasped her hands in her lap and sat forward.

'It seems he and Clifford took shelter from the rain yesterday at The Ram—you will know it, a small inn at Salcoombe?'

'Yes, yes, although I have never been inside.'

'No, I should think not. But to continue: they found Lord Graddon and his party were there, doing the same thing. The Fremingtons joined them in the parlour and they all sat down to play cards. Lord Fremington says that was when the wager was struck. One of the Graddon Hall party explained how Lord Deveril had made a similar wager concerning a lady in London, and challenged him to do the same in Torrisford and...' Lady Kenton drew a deep breath. 'And your name was mentioned.'

'Oh, that is *scandalous*,' exclaimed Selina, jumping up. 'How dare they talk about me in that way!'

'Yes, it was quite despicable. Lord Fremington says he tried to put a stop to it, of course, but drink had been taken by then, which made everyone a little free in their behaviour. Lord Deveril more than most, apparently. He said he would wager a monkey with each of them that he would win you!'

'Goodness,' exclaimed Selina. 'How many were there in Lord Graddon's party, six, seven? Can the man be that rich, or does he expect to repair his fortunes with this wager?'

Lady Kenton frowned at her. 'Pray do not make light of it, Selina.'

'No, of course not,' said Selina, contrite. 'Pray continue.'

'Well, once the wager had been agreed, of course, there was nothing Lord Fremington could do. He told Sir Alfred that Clifford was most incensed at Blackbourne's behaviour, and he had great trouble stopping him from calling out his lordship.'

'I should have thought better of Clifford if he had done so!'

'Selina, my dear, you cannot mean that.'

'No, of course not.' She threw Lady Kenton an apologetic look. 'I beg your pardon. I know full well that would set even more tongues wagging.'

'Yes, that was Lord Fremington's worry, and why he came looking for Sir Alfred first thing this morning. He wanted him, as squire, to go to Graddon Hall and put a stop to such nonsense.'

'*Could* he do so?'

'That is the problem, Selina. If Sir Alfred mentions the wager to the Viscount, he is bound to know it came from the Fremingtons.'

'And that would be considered quite unacceptable behaviour by a gentleman, I suppose,' said Selina, bitterly.

'Quite. And imagine how difficult it would be for Lord Fremington to meet the Graddon Hall party in Society, once it was known.'

'Yes, I can see it would make things a trifle awkward. But it would be just as difficult for Sir Alfred, would it not?'

'Yes, it would. I am so glad you understand that, Selina.' Lady Kenton threw her a grateful look. 'Alfred really does not like to be on bad terms with his neighbours. In the end he decided the best thing would be for him—or rather me!—to mention it to you, my love. To put you on your guard.'

'Yes. Thank you.'

'We will of course do our best to help. I am always ready to chaperone you, for example.'

'My dear ma'am, I have done without one for years and see no need to be chaperoned everywhere now!' retorted Selina. 'No, you have warned me, and I shall make sure I give Lord Deveril no chance to importune me. I cannot think he would actually force his attentions upon me, would he?'

'No, no, I am sure he would not. These London rakes, you know, they are mostly all bluff and bluster. Besides, I understand the Viscount's party were all drinking freely and they might all have forgotten about the wager by now. But we cannot be sure, so at the very least, Selina, you must take a servant with you when you go out.'

'When I leave the estate, perhaps, but it cannot be necessary here at Reigney, where everyone knows me!'

Lady Kenton gave her a grave look. 'Of all Lord

Graddon's guests, Blackbourne is the most notorious. There was some tragedy in his youth, I believe.'

'Oh?' Selina could not help being curious.

'Yes. He was engaged to a young lady, but she died before they could marry. It is said he took it very hard, always wears dark colours now and has sworn never to take a wife. Not that it has prevented him taking comfort from any number of women, if the rumours are to be believed.' Lady Kenton's gaze flickered towards Selina and she added darkly, 'Mistresses.'

'Perhaps his heart was truly broken,' said Selina, thinking how unhappy her own father had been since his wife's death.

'Perhaps, although it is no excuse for his wild behaviour. It is said he leaves a trail of broken hearts and broken heads wherever he goes! However it may be, none of this has diminished his attraction to the fairer sex.' She pursed her lips. 'It would seem he only has to smile at a young lady for her to fall in love with him.'

Having experienced that smile for herself, Selina could understand it. Not that she was in any danger of losing her heart to such a rake.

'There is no doubt he is exceedingly charming,' Lady Kenton went on. 'I thought so myself, and by the end of the assembly all the young ladies were talking about him!'

'Not all of them, ma'am.'

'No, my love, you spent most of the evening sitting with your papa, did you not? You avoided the rake's eye, and you cannot know how relieved I was about that! But if he has decided to pursue you, it can only be a matter of time before your paths cross. You must be vigilant, my love. One cannot afford to take any chances with a rake.'

'No. Of course not.' Selina responded automatically, her mind racing. She was sure Lord Deveril had not recognised her at the inn, and her own servants and those at the White Horse were all too loyal to give away her secret. Her dress that night, and her actions, must have convinced him she was nothing but a servant. His return to Graddon Hall must be totally unrelated.

Yet even if this was nothing more than a coincidence, if he should seek her out, Selina knew he could not fail to recognise her. Why, she had bandied words with him for several minutes!

'How long are they expected to remain in Devonshire?' she asked, as casually as she could.

'Oh, a few more weeks yet. I believe the Viscount will not remain at the Hall beyond Lady Day.'

Another month, then. She could live with that. The hunting party never ventured this side of Torrisford, and she would be able to find things to keep her occupied on the estate. She would excuse herself from any engagements where Lord Deveril was likely to be present, and keep herself hidden away until he had left Devonshire. No one would think it unusual. She often spent weeks at a time without leaving Reigney.

'I can see you are shaken by this news,' remarked Lady Kenton, looking at her with some concern.

'I am, ma'am,' she replied with perfect truth. 'I shall keep to the house and estate until the hunting party has gone.'

But that did not satisfy her ladyship.

'Pho, there is no need to bury yourself here at Reigney,' she said. 'You spend far too much time on your own as it is, and do not tell me you have your father for company, because I know it is not true. I have a great fondness for Mr Wynter but he has always been in poor health and something of a recluse. I would not be surprised to learn you see him for little more than an hour each day, if that!

'No,' Lady Kenton went on, 'if you ride out then pray do not do so unaccompanied, but as for keeping to the house, that is not necessary. I shall be quite happy to accompany you to any parties you wish to attend. Most of them are given by our friends and neighbours, so it is most likely I shall be attending anyway.'

'I will not trouble you to do that, Lady Kenton. Believe me, I shall survive quite happily without parties of pleasure.'

Lady Kenton leaned forward. 'My love, I had no intention of you living like a hermit for the rest of the winter! No, no, that will not do at all. Even if I am not available, you have any number of friends here who can act as chaperone.'

Selina realised it was useless to argue any further

now. She would find excuses to remain at Reigney, and perhaps invent a slight malaise to keep her at home for a couple of weeks, by which time the Graddon Hall party might well have left Devonshire. Not that she would tell Lady Kenton that, of course.

'Well, having given you the hint, I must go,' said her ladyship, rising. 'Sir Alfred will fret if I am late for dinner. Give my regards to your papa, my dear Selina, and remember, do not leave the house without an escort!'

And with this, Lady Kenton sailed out, leaving Selina to sink down on the chair and put one hand over her eyes.

How could she have been so foolish! She had always been so careful to keep out of the way at the inn. She had always dressed soberly and stayed in the background. She had never given anyone reason to look at her twice.

Until a week ago.

Having driven the two drunkards out into the yard she should have left the servants to see them off the premises. How she wished now that she had not allowed her temper, and the temptation to prove herself, get the better of her.

However, it was too late to worry about what could not be changed. She must think of the future, but even the scandalous news that Lady Kenton had told her did not overly concern Selina. 'Forewarned is forearmed', was a favourite saying of Papa's and there was not the slightest possibility of Lord Deveril worming his way into her affections now she knew of that wicked wager. She would go on as always, looking after her father and the estate, and she would deal with this Devil Blackbourne if—or when—their paths crossed.

It had always been Selina's intention to ride out the following morning if the weather was fine. She wanted to call upon her father's tenant farmers and then to visit the Home Farm, where she wanted to see for herself the recoating of the barn's thatched roof.

The day dawned cloudy but dry and she saw no reason to change her plans. After all, she would be riding on her own land, where everyone knew her. She ordered Orion to be saddled and went up to change into the mannish jacket and buckskins that she kept for such occasions. Some twenty minutes later, she was galloping away from the Abbey on her rangy black hunter.

She returned to the Abbey several hours later, tired and muddy, to discover that Lord Deveril had called earlier in the day.

'I informed him there was no one at home to receive him, as you instructed,' the butler explained. 'The master had retired to his bed to rest so that was perfectly correct. The gentleman left his card.'

'Thank you, Leighton, you may give it to me.'

She took the card and studied it for a moment. So, it seemed his lordship was intent on pursuing her.

Putting the card in her pocket she went upstairs to change for dinner. It was futile to hope his lordship would not call again, but at least she had delayed the confrontation a little longer.

Chapter Five

Selina stayed well within the boundaries of the Reigney estate when she did go out, but for the most part she remained at the Abbey. Her father was suffering from a slight chill and this provided her with the perfect excuse to instruct Leighton that she was not at home to any visitors except Lady Kenton, should she call. It also allowed her to decline the flurry of invitations that arrived, one to ride out with friends and several more offering a number of entertainments that ranged from informal dinners and card parties to an impromptu dance. She was quite happy to refuse them all, knowing perfectly well that these sudden activities had all been devised for the sole benefit of entertaining the gentlemen from Graddon Hall.

It was a full week since Lady Kenton's visit and Selina had spent much of it with Ashworth, her father's steward, riding over the estate and agreeing upon a plan of works for the coming months. It was not yet March, and under the cloudy skies the landscape looked grey and lifeless, but Selina was still glad to be out of doors.

This morning, the sun was shining and Selina decided to reward herself for all her hard work with a ride to Reigney Ridge. Lord Deveril had not called at the Abbey again, neither did Lady Kenton seek her out to tell her that her exploits at the White Horse were now being discussed throughout the county. Selina should have been reassured by this, but she could not be easy. She was no innocent schoolroom miss—she had read any number of novels and heard enough gossip from her married friends to know that unscrupulous rakes would go to extraordinary lengths to ruin respectable ladies.

She thought it inevitable she and Lord Deveril would meet at some point and he would be sure to recognise her now. When that happened, she had no doubt he would try to use that information against her and she was surprised how much that hurt.

She had thought him a rogue, but an honourable one. It was very silly, fanciful, even, but when he had smiled at her, she had felt a connection, as if she had met a kindred spirit, and the idea that he was now planning to seduce her, as he had most likely seduced any number of women before, was humiliating, and painful as a wasp sting.

'If he means to intimidate me into agreeing to his horrid plans then he will soon discover he has the wrong sow by the ear,' she muttered, pushing the final pins into her hair with unwarranted force. 'I do not consider my actions sufficiently scandalous to warrant my agreeing to anything I do not wish to do!'

She was about to ask Nancy to put out her breeches and riding jacket but then thought better of it. Today she must wear her plum-coloured riding habit. The hunting party was still in residence at Graddon Hall, and it would be foolish to risk being caught at a disadvantage.

As soon as she was dressed, she joined her father for breakfast, but it was nearly noon before she could leave the house. First she had to settle Papa in his library with his books and a good fire, then there was her daily meeting with the housekeeper, followed by a short discussion with Mr Ashworth, her father's steward, before she could set off to ride up to Reigney Ridge.

It was a glorious day, cold and crisp, and after the overcast skies of the past week the sun was a welcome reminder of the coming spring. The valleys and farms were soon left behind and she made her way up onto the hills. There was a good track across this stretch of the moor and Selina gave Orion his head, revelling in the hunter's speed and power as he flew over the ground.

She slowed as they approached the ridge, where the ground fell sharply away into a wooded valley. Bringing Orion to a stand, she took in a deep, refreshing breath and gazed out across the landscape. In the distance she could just make out the horses and riders of the Torrisford Hunt. She could not see the hounds, but occasionally the faint sound of their baying floated through the still air as the hunters streamed down from the open moors to the valley below. No doubt Viscount Graddon and his friends were with them, thought Selina, watching the tiny figures disappear into the trees on the lower slopes of the valley. She shivered a little and turned away, hoping that whatever they were chasing today managed to escape.

A movement further along the ridge caught her eye. She put a hand up to shield her eyes from the sun and saw a lone rider approaching. As the horseman drew nearer, she recognised the upright figure as Lord Deveril, dressed all in black and mounted on a handsome grey horse.

Selina felt a sudden kick of apprehension. If she galloped off now, she knew she could avoid him. However fast the grey might be, Orion was on home ground which would give her the advantage. But she hated the idea of running away: she would have to deal with the man at some point, so why not now, without the eyes of Torrisford Society upon her?

Decision made, she waited for Lord Deveril to come up, her anxiety mixed with an equal amount of relief that the moment had finally arrived.

When he was within hailing distance he raised one hand in greeting.

'Miss Wynter, we meet again!' His dark eyes were

full of laughter. 'You are a deuced elusive lady. I have been riding around here for days, hoping to see you.'

'Do I know you, sir?' She treated him to a haughty stare. There was still a possibility he might not recognise her.

He grinned. 'Not formally, no, but I wanted to find you, to thank you for that tankard of ale.'

Only for a moment did Selina consider disclaiming any knowledge. It would be futile, so instead she gave him a look intended to depress pretension.

'Well now you have thanked me, so you may go on your way. Or rather, you should return the way you came. Perhaps you are unaware that you are trespassing.'

'No, am I? This way leads to Reigney Abbey, does it not?'

She turned Orion, saying pointedly, 'Goodbye, Lord Deveril.'

'If you are going back to the Abbey then pray allow me to accompany you.'

He rode up alongside her, so close she could reach out and touch the buckskins covering his muscled thigh, if she so wished. Even more alarming, he could reach *her*.

'I do not wish you to accompany me.' She edged Orion away, widening the distance between them.

'Then I shall follow you. To call upon Mr Wynter, you understand. I should like to make his acquaintance.'

Deciding that any further remonstrance would be childish, Selina pressed her lips together and set off at a canter. She was not surprised to find Lord Deveril kept pace, but when the grey began to edge in front, she could not resist the challenge.

She gave Orion his head and the black surged forward. Immediately Lord Deveril responded and soon both horses were galloping neck and neck across the hill. The wind tugged at Selina's hat, pulling curls free from their pins, and a laugh of pure joy bubbled up. She must look like a hoyden, but for the moment she did not care.

They were approaching the lower slopes of the hill where the track descended more steeply. They both slackened their pace but the grey stumbled, pitching the rider over the horse's head. Selina hauled on the reins and Orion came to a plunging halt.

'Deveril!'

She slipped to the ground and ran across to where he was lying, motionless. He was on his back, eyes closed, and she dropped to her knees beside him. Gently she smoothed the black hair away from his brow, anxiously scanning his body for signs of injury.

'My lord, are you hurt?'

'Forgive me while I catch my breath,' muttered Deveril, keeping his eyes shut while he assessed the situation. 'I do not *think* I have broken anything.'

'Thank heaven for that. Can you get up?'

He opened his eyes to find Selina gazing down anxiously into his face.

'Now why should I want to move, when you are looking at me like that?'

The ready laughter sprang to her eyes and she sat back, shaking her head. 'You are irrepressible, my lord! Tell me, truthfully, how do you feel?'

'I *feel* I want to kiss you.'

'Well, you cannot!' she said, blushing and laughing at the same time.

He grinned. 'Can I not?'

'No! We must ascertain that you have taken no injury.'

He sat up slowly. 'I may have a few bruises, I think, but nothing more serious.'

'I am very glad about that.' She jumped up and held her hand out to him. 'Let us see if you can stand.

'Well?' she asked, when she had helped him to his feet. 'Is there any damage?'

'Only to my pride.'

'That will soon be mended!' She was standing before him, her face alive with merriment, and Deveril's breath hitched. The fall had winded him, but not like this! It seemed the most natural thing in the world to pull her into his arms and, when she did not resist, he lowered his head and kissed her.

She leaned against him, her palms resting on his chest, her mouth soft and sweet against his. He deepened the kiss and she responded, her tongue flickering tentatively for a moment and then she was pushing him away.

Immediately he released her and she stepped back, her cheeks flushed. Without a word, she began to shake out the voluminous skirts of her riding habit. Deveril watched her for a moment, then he scooped up his hat.

'Should I apologise?' he asked her. Selina kept her eyes lowered, giving the skirts a more vigorous shake while she tried to make sense of her feelings. He had kissed her! She should be furious with him, but how could she let him take all the blame, when she had kissed him back so outrageously?

She could not recall the last time she had felt so… so *alive*. The gallop, Deveril's sudden fall and the knowledge that he was unhurt had left her buzzing with nervous energy. And then that kiss! It had set her body tingling from her head to her toes. Even now she could feel the blood pumping through her veins. She knew she could have stopped him from kissing her, if she had tried. If she had wanted to do so. It would be wrong, churlish, to dissemble.

'It was not entirely your fault, my lord.'

'Wasn't it?'

'No. I was curious.'

'I see.' He did not appear to be shocked by her admission. 'Did I live up to your expectations?'

She looked up. He was smiling, his eyes full of mischief, and Selina was obliged to smother the laugh bubbling up inside. This was dangerous ground and she knew very well that Lord Deveril was experienced at flirtation. Yet for the life of her she could not bring herself to snub him.

She looked around. 'At least we did not frighten the horses.'

He laughed. 'Thank goodness for that! I must check that Colonel has taken no hurt.'

She followed him across to where the horses were standing together, heads down and quietly cropping the turf. Gathering up Orion's reins she thought how fortunate it was he had not galloped back to the Abbey. Imagine the uproar if the big hunter had arrived home riderless. Papa would have been beside himself with worry.

She watched Deveril as he inspected the gelding, gently running his fingers over the horse. If she had not broken off that kiss his hands might now be caressing her, just as gently. She looked away, the very idea of it making her feel faint.

'Well, there seems to be no damage,' he said at last. 'I suggest we continue our ride. Shall I help you to mount?'

'*Can* you do so?' She regarded him with some amusement. 'I am no lightweight.'

He grinned. 'But I cannot resist the challenge!'

He walked over and linked his hands, ready for her to step up, then he threw her expertly into the saddle.

Selina hooked her leg over the pommel and made

herself secure, then she spent a few moments decorously arranging her skirts and trying to work out why she was not blushing furiously. Lord Deveril had kissed her, and now she had given him an excellent view of her ankles. Another excellent view, she corrected herself, remembering how she had tucked up her skirts when she was at the White Horse.

Good heavens, they had still not been introduced, but she was acting more freely with him than any other man of her acquaintance! What had happened to her resolution to have nothing more to do with Devil Blackbourne?

Deveril kept one hand on the bridle while Selina made herself comfortable in the saddle. The lady intrigued him. He was more used to helpless females who would cling to him, fluttering their eyelashes, wanting his protection. This woman was different. If there had been a convenient log, he knew she would have preferred to use that as a mounting block rather than accept his help.

She gathered up the reins, saying, 'Thank you, I can manage now.'

Thus dismissed, he walked over to Colonel and scrambled into the saddle, wincing a little. Despite his hope to the contrary, he guessed he had suffered some bruising to his body. Which was possibly an advantage at present, for the pain was diverting his thoughts from more lustful imaginings.

They set off again in silence, but it was companionable enough. There was no awkwardness between them and when, after a while, she glanced across at him, he risked saying what was on his mind.

'I admit, when I first saw you on that horse, I had my doubts about your ability to handle him. But not now. You are an excellent rider, Miss Wynter.'

'Thank you. I confess I do not often have an opportunity to race Orion, as we did today. It was a little irresponsible, but I enjoyed it very much.' She nodded towards his own mount. 'I am relieved neither you nor your horse suffered injury from that stumble.'

'So too am I.'

'But I should not have given into the temptation.'

He grinned. 'Oh, I don't think there is any harm in that, occasionally.'

Selina quickly looked away, alarm bells clamouring in her head. She could blame the excitement of the gallop for why she had allowed him to kiss her. It could also explain why she had acted so freely with him, but the exhilaration had faded now, giving way to the inevitable slump in her spirits.

She leaned forward and smoothed her hand over Orion's neck while she tried to gather her thoughts. What was she doing even *talking* with this man, when he had had the audacity to bandy her name amongst his friends, to make her the object of a wager. Did she not understand? He intended to seduce her!

Not that he would succeed. She would never allow him to succeed.

No? When he has already stolen a kiss. And made you laugh, when you should have slapped his face and left him.

She glanced across at her companion. He looked quite at home in the saddle, riding with an easy grace and seemingly indifferent to her silence. In fact, she thought crossly, he was completely at his ease, while her nerves were stretched taut. If he was trying to discompose her, she had to admit he was succeeding all too well! She felt quite, quite *hunted*.

Which brought a question to her mind: 'Why are you not riding to hounds today, my lord?'

'Hunting with dogs has never appealed to me.' She looked at him, surprised, and he went on, 'Although that does not mean I do not enjoy the chase.'

The glint in his dark eyes brought the heat rushing to Selina's cheeks and she scolded herself for such weakness. The blush revealed only too clearly that she understood his meaning. She saw the gleam deepen to real amusement and was alarmed at how much she wanted to smile back. So much for her ability to keep him at a distance!

Several responses came to her mind, each one teasing, flirtatious and certainly not the sort of thing a respectable young lady should say to any gentleman, least of all a rake.

Then say nothing, Selina. That way lies danger!

Sensitive to her mood, Orion jibbed and she was glad to give her attention to calming him. If only she could calm herself so easily. But what unnerved her most was the fact that, despite the impropriety of this exchange, she was enjoying herself. Just as she had that night at the inn.

Heavens! She needed to be free of this man's presence, and quickly.

They had reached a fork in the road and she stopped, glancing up at the sun, which was already low in the sky.

'We keep early hours at the Abbey. My father will be resting now before dinner and will not see you. Or anyone. You would do well to follow the other road, back to Graddon Hall.'

'Or I could accompany you to the Abbey and you could invite me to step inside, for some refreshment.'

Selina chose to take offence at his audacity. She said coldly, 'I think not.'

'I believe I might be a little overset. From the fall, you understand.'

She was not in the least fooled by the innocent note in his voice. After a slight pause he went on.

'Ah. I see what it is. You are anxious for my safety, if I am obliged to ride back later in the dark.'

'I am not in the least anxious—' She stopped, pressing her lips together. He was teasing her and she was angry with herself for rising to the bait.

'There is a moon tonight, you know,' he remarked.

'Sufficient for me to find my way to Graddon Hall. Or even for a moonlight stroll, if you cared to accompany me.'

She almost gasped at his audacity. The man had no shame, how could he even suggest such a thing?

She said sternly, 'Lord Deveril, I have no intention of flirting with you!'

'Well, that is a pity.'

'For you, perhaps. But I am sure you will soon find some other poor female who will welcome your advances.'

He sighed. 'Yes. Sadly there are far too many of 'em.'

Selina now discovered Lord Deveril Blackbourne could shock her and make her want to laugh at the same time.

'That, that is an outrageous thing to say!'

'But it is true. I met any number of them at the last assembly.'

'I know, I saw—'

Again, Selina was obliged to break off, but the damage was done: he laughed. What was it about the odious man that made her forget propriety and talk to him so freely? He was a rake, a libertine. It should be no surprise that his manner was disarming. How else would he make his conquests?

'So you *were* there,' he said. 'Why did I not see you?'

'I kept well out of your way, that is why!' She gave

him a haughty look. 'Your reputation precedes you, Lord Deveril.'

'If my reputation is so very bad, why are you here now, talking with me?'

'I should not be,' she admitted.

Her friends and acquaintances in Torrisford would be scandalised if they knew she was riding alone with any man, even one far more respectable than Lord Deveril Blackbourne. Thank heavens she had decided to wear her riding habit rather than the buckskins!

Then there was her behaviour at the White Horse three weeks ago. That had been quite scandalous. No *respectable* female would enter into a brawl with two drunken men. Nor would she engage in friendly banter with a complete stranger. She scolded herself for doing so, especially now, when she remembered what Lady Kenton had told her about that wager.

'I am very glad you are talking to me,' he remarked. 'I welcome the chance to become better acquainted.'

He was smiling and again Selina felt that strong tug of attraction, but she looked away. This was all part of his plan. It was why he had kissed her.

The memory of that kiss flooded back, sending burning darts arrowing their way through her body and heating her blood. He had planned it all! Well, perhaps not the tumble from his horse, but even that he had shamelessly turned to his advantage. He was preparing the way for her seduction.

And, even knowing what he was about, she had

not given him a set-down. Stupid, gullible fool that she was!

'Ha! So now we come to it,' she exclaimed, allowing indignation to feed her anger. 'Let me tell you, my lord, that I have no intention of submitting to your outrageous demands.'

'I beg your pardon? I have made no demands.'

Deveril's surprise caused his hands to tighten on the reins and Colonel shied. What was she talking about? She gave an angry laugh.

'You have mistaken your quarry this time, my lord! You may tell the whole of Torrisford that I was serving at the inn for all I care. I am not ashamed of doing so. It was necessary for someone to help while we were without an innkeeper.' She gave a hiss of disgust. 'How you can be so base as to even *consider* holding such a threat over me, I really do not know!'

'Holding a threat over—' Deveril had been listening in bewilderment and disbelief to Selina's rantings, but this was too much.

'Just what the devil are you implying?' he demanded. 'I have no intention of telling anyone what happened at the White Horse!'

'Do you deny you told your friends that you intend to, to *seduce* me?'

'Yes, I do deny it!' He hadn't even been sure she was the woman he had met there, until he had seen her today. 'How the devil can you think I would behave so scandalously?'

'Why should I think otherwise? You are a rake. A libertine. It is what you do!'

She was sitting tall and straight in the saddle, those sapphire eyes flashing angrily, and Deveril suddenly felt as if he had been punched, and the breath knocked out of him.

There was no denying that she was a beauty. He had thought so when he had seen her dressed as a servant, but now her generous curves looked even better, amplified by the mannish cut of her riding coat. And in the cold light of day there was no mistaking her warm, creamy skin or the luxuriant dark curls that had escaped from her hat and now hung in a riotous tangle about her shoulders. 'Fore Gad, she looked magnificent!

Now, though, it was an icy magnificence. There was no hint of the friendly smile that had lit up the inn yard.

He shook his head. 'Believe me, ma'am, I have no such intention.'

He watched her, noting how she pressed her lips together as she struggled to keep her temper. And failed.

'Ha!' She gave a scornful laugh. 'You are only saying that now because you have discovered I am not a bird for your plucking!'

Her disdain struck him like a slap and a surge of anger welled up.

'Confound it woman, will you *listen* to me?'

Intent upon the argument, she had neglected to keep

the distance between them. Deveril leaned over and grasped Orion's reins, effectively preventing her from riding off.

He said wrathfully, 'Do you really believe I would try to coerce you? Hell and damnation, woman, how can you think I would ever resort to such tactics?'

'Who knows what you would do to a defenceless woman!'

'Defenceless!' Deveril gave a crack of laughter. 'If that don't beat the Dutch! You are the most formidable female I have ever encountered.'

Disturbed by their harsh voices, the grey sidled and suddenly there was no distance at all between them. His leg rubbed against hers, separated by nothing more than a couple of layers of cloth and buckskin, and a bolt of pure lust shot through Deveril.

He stared at her lips, no longer tight and angry, but parted slightly as she stared angrily at him. His breath caught in his chest. He imagined dragging her from the saddle and onto his lap. Kissing that luscious mouth that looked so damned inviting—

'Don't you dare kiss me again!'

Selina's furious exclamation brought him to his senses.

He released his hold on her reins, just in time to catch her wrist as she lifted her riding crop. They were close, their faces only inches apart, eyes locked. The horses were both standing perfectly still, as if recognising the danger of the moment.

Deveril said deliberately, 'I won't be responsible for the consequences if you set about me with that whip.'

He waited until he saw the fire fade from her eyes before he let her go.

'That's better,' he growled as she lowered her arm. 'I had no intention of kissing you.'

It was a lie and they both knew it, but she merely narrowed her eyes at him. Then she nodded and he went on.

'I came looking for you because I was intrigued, but I pray you will acquit me of anything more sinister.'

By heaven how could he say that, when just moments ago he had wanted to ravish her!

His conscience smote him and he added, gruffly, 'I beg your pardon. I did not mean to distress you.'

'Distress me? I am not *distressed*, I am furious! I have never been more angry in my life!'

Having gained her freedom, he expected her to ride off, but although she was still in a rage, she seemed strangely disinclined to move away.

'I am sorry if I misunderstood your intentions,' she said at last, as if the words were forced out of her.

Deveril nodded. He did not deserve an apology, even one so grudgingly uttered, and it did nothing to improve his temper. He was angry with Selina for thinking badly of him, and even more so with himself, for wanting to behave like the worst sort of scoundrel.

Without another word he touched his hat and rode off towards Graddon Hall. By heaven, the woman was a veritable shrew. He set off at a canter, wondering why the devil he had wasted so much time and effort seeking her out.

Selina kept Orion at a stand and watched Lord Deveril ride away. She hated herself for apologising to that insufferable man. He had grabbed her reins; she had been perfectly entitled to defend herself from attack.

She was also convinced that he intended to kiss her a second time, even though he had denied it. She had seen it in the way his eyes darkened, the way everything had suddenly grown so still. What shook her to the core was that she had wanted him to kiss her again! She had yearned for it with every ounce of her being. Even now, just the thought of it turned her insides to water and sent a little shiver of apprehension down her spine. She had never felt like this about any man before, so out of control. She was not sure she liked it.

Orion sidled nervously as Selina's hands tightened on the reins.

'Well, you have surely killed off his interest in you now,' she said aloud, her eyes following his retreating figure.

He was undoubtedly a fine horseman. Some—no, many, she conceded fairly—might consider him handsome, but he was no gentleman. He was boorish and uncouth, she decided, as she made her way back to the Abbey. No better than Clifford Fremington. Let the other ladies of Torrisford simper and fawn over Devil Blackbourne, for her part she hoped she never saw the man ever again!

Chapter Six

A change in the weather gave Selina's thoughts quite another turn. It became colder and wetter, a combination that always aggravated her father's arthritis and for the next few days she did not leave the Abbey. Apart from Mr Gurney's regular weekly visit she was his sole companion, keeping him company and distracting him from his discomfort with chess, or card games.

After a week, however, the symptoms had eased sufficiently for him to talk of attending the forthcoming Torrisford Assembly. Selina had been quite sure that he would not be well enough to go, and resigned herself to staying at home. She should have been delighted, therefore, when her father announced on the eve of the assembly that he was quite well enough to attend. Instead, she felt a swirl of anxiety in the pit of her stomach at the thought of meeting Lord Deveril.

Their last meeting was never far from her mind. She felt giddy just remembering his kiss. It filled her with excitement, but there was also apprehension at the unfamiliar feelings he aroused. In some indefinable way she knew that he threatened her safe, comfortable existence. It would be far better if she did not see him again.

On the day of the assembly, she made one final effort: she suggested her father should go to the assembly without her.

'I am really not in the humour for dancing tonight, Papa. I should much prefer to remain here by the fire, reading my book.'

'What you need is more society, my love, not less. You will feel better for the outing.'

'I do not think so, Papa. Not tonight. But that need not prevent you enjoying yourself. You might travel with the squire and his wife. Sir Alfred and Lady Kenton are always happy to call for you. Truly, you do not need me to come.'

'But I do, my child. I love to see you dancing and enjoying yourself.' He took her hand. 'My dear Selina, you are five-and-twenty, how are you ever to find a husband if you hide yourself away?'

She gave him a look of fond exasperation. 'I have told you, Papa, I do not *want* a husband. I want nothing more than to spend my days looking after you and Reigney and, and becoming an eccentric old spinster!'

But her father was having none of it.

'You say that now, my love, and I confess it adds greatly to my comfort to have you with me, but it is not right for you spend all your time looking after me and Reigney Abbey. You should be out in the world, enjoying yourself. And you should attend not only for my sake, but for our friends. Let it be your duty to give them the pleasure of your company!' He squeezed her fingers before releasing them, saying, 'I will hear no more about your staying at home tonight. I should very much like to have your company at the assembly. And you must put on your new satin robe. It would please me immensely to see you wearing it: I am reminded of your mama, you see. Old rose was always her favourite colour.'

Selina quashed any further objections. Papa was in good spirits this morning, and she hadn't the heart to suggest she was not well. The last time she had used that excuse, her father had become too anxious to leave her alone, and that had made her feel extremely guilty. She knew how much he enjoyed the assemblies and that must be her comfort.

Even if Lord Deveril was present, after their last bruising encounter she thought it unlikely he would approach her.

The George at Torrisford was ablaze with light when Selina and her father arrived for the assembly. Music could already be heard coming from the upper windows as they stepped down from the carriage and Selina was aware of an added excitement in the air when they joined the patrons making their way slowly up the stairs to the assembly rooms.

The matron in front of them broke off her conversation with her daughters to look back and greet them.

'My girls are expecting great things, tonight, Mr Wynter, they have been in high spirits all day.' The two young ladies on the step above giggled at this, while their mother nodded indulgently before continuing. 'I have heard that Lord Graddon will again be bringing his party. It is always more enjoyable, is it not, when there are more than enough partners for everyone.'

Mr Wynter chuckled. 'Well, well, that is good news, Mrs Hexham. It means all the young ladies will be able to dance.'

'Surely, Papa, you do not expect me to spend all my time on the dance floor,' Selina protested, laughing. 'I would much rather sit with you, at least for some of the evening.'

'Then you will be doing me a great disservice,' he scolded her gently. 'It gives me the greatest pleasure to watch you dance.'

'And who knows, Miss Selina, you might catch yourself one of these fine London beaux,' said Mrs Hexham, with a fat chuckle. 'I tell you straight, Mr Wynter, my girls are quite desperate for your pretty daughter to land herself a husband and leave the field clear for the rest of 'em!'

This frank speech did not find favour with Selina,

who blushed and could only manage a small smile in response.

Thankfully she was not expected to reply, for they had reached the landing and Mrs Hexham and her girls sailed off quickly towards the ballroom.

Mr Wynter squeezed Selina's arm.

'Not as delicately put as I should like,' he murmured, 'but I think she meant it as a compliment.'

'The Misses Hexham are welcome to all those *fine London beaux*,' she replied. 'I would much rather they all stayed away!'

Then, having relieved her feelings on the matter, Selina pinned on a smile and accompanied her father into the ballroom.

They made their way through the crowd to where Sir Alfred and Lady Kenton were sitting on the benches at one side of the room, along with their daughter, Mrs Helena Frith, and her husband.

'Mr Wynter! Come and join us sir,' cried Sir Alfred, jumping to his feet. 'We have saved you a seat, as always!'

'No sign of the Graddon Hall party yet,' murmured Lady Kenton, when Selina sat down beside her.

'I expect they will be fashionably late, Mama,' remarked Mrs Frith.

Selina gave her a quick, sideways glance. 'Perhaps they will not come at all.'

Alas, her hopes were not realised. She was going down the dance with the squire when a sudden commotion at the door announced the arrival of Viscount Graddon and his party. Her gaze was immediately drawn to Devil Blackbourne, his tall, upright figure in a plain black frock coat was unmistakable amongst the bright colours and patterned coats of his companions.

He had his back to her and she felt free to study him. He wore his hair unpowdered, the glossy black locks just long enough to curl over the edge of his velvet collar. As if aware of her scrutiny he turned suddenly and looked straight at her. Even across the room Selina could feel the power of his glance. It hit her like an arrow and she was all at once breathless, her heart thudding against her ribs. She turned her head away, determined not to give him the satisfaction of knowing just how much he unnerved her.

Shaken, Selina missed a step and was thankful for Sir Alfred's steadying hand as she recovered her place in the dance. She concentrated hard on the final movements, giving all her attention to her partner, but even when she had regained her outward calm, her mind was racing wildly with conjecture.

She had expected Lord Deveril to snub her tonight. They had parted on bad terms and he would want to punish her. He would laugh and flirt with the other young ladies, determined to pique her interest, to show her what she was missing. It was a game she had often observed being played between ladies and gentlemen and Selina wanted no part of it. She was quite prepared to appear equally indifferent, but the expression in Lord Deveril's eyes had confounded her. It was hot, angry, and it had burned her like a branding iron. Good heavens, had she made that deep an impression upon him?

'My dear Miss Wynter, are you quite well?' Sir Alfred asked as he raised her from her final curtsy. 'You are trembling—is it possible you have caught a chill?'

'What? Oh, no, no, sir. I am quite well, but you will have noticed I missed my step in the dance. I am quite mortified!'

He laughed. 'Don't be—if we all knew the contra dances as well as you, the assembly would be a great deal more entertaining! Now, are you engaged for the next—but of course you are. Here comes your partner now!'

Selina immediately thought it must be Lord Deveril, waiting to pounce, but when she looked around, she saw the Honourable Clifford Fremington approaching. Of course, how foolish of her. Sir Alfred knew of that scandalous wager; he would never have relinquished her so cheerfully to Devil Blackbourne as he did now to Clifford Fremington. With a bow the squire withdrew and Clifford held out his hand.

'Well, Selina, will you dance with me, or do you intend to snub me again as you did at the last assembly?' he demanded.

Her reply was equally blunt: 'Perhaps I will dance with you, if you promise not to propose to me again.'

'You made your feelings very clear the last time!' he muttered. 'It doesn't mean I shall give up, though.'

Selina hesitated. She had known Clifford for many years and despite his boorish ways, she felt a little sorry for him. He was an only child, like herself, but whereas she now had the running of Papa's estates to occupy her, Clifford had nothing to do but amuse himself. His parents made their son a generous allowance and indulged him shamefully, but he was allowed no say in the management of the lands that would one day be his.

Clifford's parents were standing nearby, his mother fidgeting nervously while his lordship's eyes were fixed upon his son, and Selina thought it very likely that he had ordered Clifford to dance with her. Lord Fremington wanted them to marry, because when Papa died, she would inherit Reigney, or rather, it would go to her husband, and that would make the Fremingtons the biggest landowners in the area.

Selina knew it would be far kinder to refuse to dance with Clifford than allow Lord Fremington to believe they would ever marry, but at that moment she spotted Lord Deveril talking with Mrs Julia Allen. The dashing young widow was hanging onto his arm, smiling like a cat who had just stolen a whole jug of cream, and something hot and angry flared within Selina. She grabbed Clifford's hand and walked with him onto the dance floor.

'Changed your mind, have you?' he drawled, so smug that any sympathy for him vanished.

'I was feeling sorry for you,' she said coldly. 'I decided to grant you one dance, but mind this, Clifford, I will not stand up with you for the second.'

He glared at her, but his ill humour had no effect upon Selina because she did not notice. Devil Blackbourne had joined their set, with the beautiful Mrs Allen as his partner.

Hell and damnation!

Deveril hid his vexation behind a smile as he waited for the dance to begin. He would have preferred to join any of the other sets rather than to be in such close proximity to Miss Selina Wynter. Her angry glance in his direction as he took his place told him she felt exactly the same.

Yet despite the antipathy between them, he could not keep his eyes from following her as she skipped and twirled with Clifford Fremington. Her Junoesque figure was displayed to advantage in a deep pink satin gown, which shimmered and sparkled with every movement. With difficulty Deveril dragged his thoughts and his eyes back to his own partner. Why on earth was he thinking about ice maiden Selina Wynter when Mrs Allen was giving him every encouragement to flirt with her?

Being in the same set, it was impossible to avoid Selina completely. When the movement of the dance brought them together, Deveril clasped her hand, trying to ignore the sudden awareness when he felt the delicate bones beneath her glove. They were both smiling, as was polite, but she remained cool, aloof, her blue eyes looking through him. It was a relief to return to his own partner and enjoy her warm smiles.

The dance could not end soon enough for Deveril, but even as the final notes were being played, he noticed that Selina was saying something to her partner which made the fellow scowl and walk off as soon as he had made his bow.

What a vixen, he thought, saluting his own partner. He did not particularly like Clifford Fremington but she should not humiliate him with such a public dismissal. The woman had no manners; that famed beauty of hers went no deeper than a pretty face. It was a wonder she could find anyone to stand up with her!

Deveril's eyes followed her as she walked off the dance floor and he tried hard to find fault. She looked agitated, her usually smiling countenance shadowed with a frown and she was clasping and unclasping her hands. His sympathies dramatically reversed; Fremington had upset her, damn his eyes!

A word from his partner reminded Deveril of his duty and he turned his attention back to Julia Allen, smiling and responding to her flirtatious chatter with his usual easy charm, although he had lost all enthusiasm for the dance. He was wondering how much longer it was going to take to make up the sets and begin when the master of ceremonies and his wife came hurrying towards them.

'Ah, Mrs Allen, you have torn your gown,' cried Mr Keith, in flustered accents. 'Look, look, a flounce is come loose.'

Deveril glanced down to see a strip of lace trailing from the back of his partner's skirt.

'Alas, ma'am, you cannot dance like that,' Mr Keith continued. 'You might trip and injure yourself.'

The widow inspected the damage and gave a little tut of annoyance. 'You are right. I shall have to go and pin it up.'

Mrs Keith put a hand on her arm. 'Come along, my dear. I always bring needles and thread for just such an eventuality.'

'Yes, thank you.' Julia Allen gazed up at Deveril, her large eyes soulful. 'How tiresome. I shall have to forgo our second dance.'

He bowed. 'There will be other opportunities to stand up together, ma'am.'

'Oh dear, oh dear,' muttered Mr Keith, as they watched the ladies walk away. 'Such a shame, my lord, to have spoiled your dance.'

'Yes, isn't it.' Deveril responded mechanically.

'We must find you another partner,' continued the MC, looking around. 'Ah, Miss Wynter is free! If you will allow me, sir...?'

The man was smiling up at him and Deveril knew it

would be the height of ill manners to refuse. Whatever his thoughts on the lady—and by heaven they were confused!—he did not wish to embarrass her in public.

With an inward shrug he turned and followed Mr Keith.

Chapter Seven

Helena Frith put out a hand to stop Selina as she hurried off the dance floor.

'What is this, my dear, are you not dancing the next?'

'Not with Clifford Fremington, no!' Selina did not trouble to hide her irritation when replying to her lifelong friend.

'I take it he asked you to marry him again?' Helena shook her head. 'How tiresome for you.'

'No, I had warned him not to do so when I agreed to stand up with him, but he was so, so smug and arrogant that I was tempted to box his ears.'

'Yes, and I believe you would do so, even here!'

Selina's annoyance melted at her friend's accurate reading of her character.

'As a last resort, perhaps,' she confessed with a rueful smile. 'I made it plain to Clifford I would only dance the first with him, but I was obliged to remind him of it, and quite bluntly, before he would go away.'

She sighed. 'One can't help feeling a little sorry for him, because it is his father who is so eager for the match.'

'Well, thank goodness Clifford is more afraid of you than his papa!'

They both laughed at that, then Helena's glance shifted.

'But I do not think you will have to sit out this dance after all, my dear,' she murmured, looking past Selina. 'Mr Keith has found you another partner.'

'Really?' Selina, caught unawares, looked around, still smiling, to find Lord Deveril at her shoulder.

'Miss Wynter, I pray you will take pity on his lordship,' exclaimed Mr Keith, with an entreating smile. 'An unfortunate occurrence has robbed him of his partner.'

She barely heard him. She was so surprised that she could only stare at the tall, handsome figure before her. Her mind was beset by irrelevant details, such as the fact that Lord Deveril's dark coat and matching breeches were not black, as she had originally thought, but a very dark green. The frock coat fitted perfectly across shoulders that were broad and straight. A white silk waistcoat covered the flat plane of his stomach and the dark breeches clung smoothly to his muscular thighs, while snow-white clocked stockings and soft black dancing pumps completed the ensemble. The thought flickered into her head, quite irrationally, that he was the embodiment of a dream.

Selina felt her mouth go dry and found herself wishing that she had another broom in her hands for protection.

Do not be so foolish, Selina. What harm can he do you here?

She dragged her eyes upwards, but could not quite bring herself to look into his face. She fixed her eyes on the ribbon of his quizzing glass, which he had tucked inside his waistcoat, then fixed her gaze on the emerald pin nestled into the snowy folds of his cravat. She should refuse. She wanted to do so, but in the back of her mind was the memory of that night at the White Horse. He was already angry with her, if he chose, he could ruin her with a word.

Well, this is a pretty fix, thought Deveril. The lady was as reluctant to dance as he was, but they were trapped by etiquette. He could not slight her by walking away, although the lady looked as if she might well refuse *him*. A wry smile tugged at his mouth. That would be a new and salutary experience, but he would survive.

He put out his hand.

'Miss Wynter, though we have not been *formally* introduced, I would be honoured if you would dance the next with me.'

Selina swallowed and forced herself to meet his eyes. Tiny devils frolicked in their black depths.

It is only the reflection of the candlelight. Stop being such a ninny!

She was all too aware that Helena was watching them with a lively interest. To hesitate too long or blush now would be sure to draw attention.

Politely she inclined her head and he took her hand, pulling her fingers onto his arm and escorting her back onto the dance floor.

She said, 'I thought you were dancing this with Mrs Allen.'

'The lady had a slight accident with her gown and went off to mend it.'

She glanced at him, her brow creased with suspicion, but his voice and his countenance were perfectly innocent. Not that she thought him innocent. Not for a moment! The musicians struck up the familiar tune and she turned her mind to the steps she needed to perform. Not for the world would she let anyone see how much this man discomposed her.

Selina had to admit she had rarely danced with such an accomplished partner. He moved with such grace and assurance it was impossible not to enjoy oneself. It was, after all, merely a country dance and in full view of all her friends. Nothing improper.

And yet, it felt like so much more. When he took her hand, Selina's skin burned and a delicious tingle ran through her. She was obliged to remind herself that Lord Deveril was nothing more than a charming rake. If everything she had heard about him was true, he had had many mistresses and broken dozens of hearts. Surely, knowing all that would ensure she did not risk losing her own? She was, after all, five-and-twenty, not a giddy schoolgirl. Even though that was exactly how she felt when she was dancing with him!

All too soon the final bars of music were played, everyone came to a stand and Selina curtsied to her partner. There was no denying she felt elated, joyous, which made her disappointment all the greater when Lord Deveril made no attempt to secure a second dance.

Silently she allowed him to escort her across the room to the benches, where her father was sitting with the Kentons. Papa had not yet met Deveril Blackbourne and Selina was steeling herself to perform the introduction when Sir Alfred jumped up and she was relieved of her duty. While the gentlemen conversed together, Selina sank down on the bench beside Lady Kenton and strove to regain her composure. She would not have stood up with Lord Deveril if Mr Keith had not made it impossible to refuse, so why on earth did she feel so disappointed that he had only danced once with her?

After a few minutes his lordship wandered off and Lady Kenton turned to Selina.

'So, my dear, you have finally met the notorious Deveril Blackbourne. And you have danced with him, too. It was inevitable I suppose, since that disgraceful wager is not common knowledge. It would be impossible for you to rebuff the man without giving rise to all sorts of gossip and conjecture.'

'Yes.' Selina nodded. 'However, I am grateful that you told me what he was about.'

Her ladyship hesitated, but could not resist asking, 'And what do you think of him?'

'We only stood up together for one country dance.' Selina tried not to sound peevish. 'One can hardly form an opinion upon that.'

'Lord Deveril has an abundance of charm,' remarked her ladyship, a little wistfully.

'If he is only a fraction as rakish as his reputation, then one would expect him to be attractive.'

'True, Selina, but alas, very few young ladies understand that. I confess, I am relieved he is not making you the object of his attentions. I expect he has realised you are too sensible to be taken in by his wiles and has decided to call off the bet.'

'Yes, very likely.'

Selina knew she should be relieved but, inexplicably, she felt incensed. If he was such an accomplished flirt then he would surely know how to make amends for their earlier contretemps. But if he thought one dance was sufficient to put him back in favour, he must be insufferably arrogant.

'Whatever the reason,' Lady Kenton went on, patting her hand, 'I am very glad you are not in raptures over the man. Unlike most of the ladies here, and not only the young, unmarried ones!'

Selina followed her glance towards the dancers and saw that Lord Deveril was now standing up with Mrs Keith, who was looking flushed and not a little pleased with herself.

'I believe you are being too hard upon Blackbourne,' put in Sir Alfred, overhearing their conversation. 'I think now that we may well have misunderstood the situation.' He leaned down and said more quietly, 'I have never thought Fremington's understanding more than moderate. It is more than likely he got the wrong end of the stick and there is no wager. I have certainly heard nothing about it from anyone else, which is unusual.

'No, no. The more I see of Lord Deveril the more I like him. He is an excellent rider, and very good company, not at all high in the instep. I think him a capital fellow.'

'That is because you have no young daughters to protect,' retorted his fond spouse. 'I am very glad that Helena, like Selina, appears immune to the man's charms.'

'Precisely.' Sir Alfred beamed. 'Which is why I have invited Lord Graddon's party to come to our little soirée on Friday!' He turned to Selina. 'I have already spoken to your father, my dear, and he is very keen to join us. I hope you will come, too, else the ladies will be sadly outnumbered!'

Still beaming, he wandered off, leaving his wife

looking dismayed. She turned an apologetic eye upon Selina.

'There is no withdrawing it now, my dear, but I do wish Sir Alfred had discussed this with me before he issued the invitation.' She gave a little huff. 'If you would rather not come then I will understand. We can send our own carriage for Mr Wynter, and see him safely home again. It will be no trouble,'

'You are very kind, but if my father is well enough to come then I shall certainly be there,' Selina replied. 'Papa would find it very odd if I were to miss one of your parties, ma'am, and he might even decide to stay home himself. No, an evening of music and conversation in the company of friends will be very beneficial to him. He spends far too much time alone with his books.'

And if Lord Deveril was there, it would make not the slightest difference, she decided, watching him go down the dance with Mrs Keith. She had his measure now. She had met many such men in her one, short London Season. Frippery fellows, all of them, outwardly charming but in essence selfish and shallow. She was unlikely to be taken in by such a man.

'Well, my love, are you pleased now that you came to the assembly?' asked Mr Wynter, when he and Selina were in the carriage and on their way home.

'Yes, I very much enjoyed seeing all our friends.'

'And you had partners for almost every dance,' he

went on, a warm note of satisfaction in his voice. 'Lord Graddon's party added a very welcome number of gentlemen tonight.'

Selina could not deny it. She had danced with the Viscount and a few others from his party, although Lord Deveril had not approached her again. She had seen him dancing with several of the young ladies, but his final partner was Mrs Allen, the vivacious widow he had danced with earlier. She was known to be a notorious flirt and they appeared to be very taken with one another. If that was so, Selina was glad: it would save any other young woman from having her heart broken.

'My own dancing days are over,' her father was saying. 'But I do enjoy watching you skipping around the dance floor.'

'And now we have the Kentons' soirée to look forward to,' said Selina, aware of the wistful note in his voice and anxious to cheer him. 'You will enjoy that.'

'Yes, of course.'

His tone was mournful, and Selina hoped it was merely tiredness and not the onset of another bout of illness.

Deveril excused himself from joining Lord Graddon and the others for the hunt the following morning. He made a leisurely breakfast and then ordered his horse and set off in the opposite direction, his hat firmly on his head and his greatcoat collar turned up to ward off the icy late-February winds. He was going to call upon Mr Wynter and his daughter.

He had not intended to dance with Selina at last night's assembly. After what had occurred on Reigney Ridge, Deveril suspected he was the last person she would want as a partner, but the master of ceremonies had rather forced his hand.

Once the dance was over, they had gone their separate ways, but for the rest of the evening he had noticed that Selina's eyes never sought him out, nor did she display anything but indifference when chance placed them in the same set. It was a novel experience for Deveril. For once it had been his turn to be painfully aware of her proximity, to feel his eyes following her when she went down the line with her partner. And when he had gone to bed last night it was Selina Wynter's blue eyes that disturbed his slumbers. He dreamed she had coolly assessed him and found him wanting.

He had awoken this morning conscious of a feeling of dissatisfaction. The coldly correct lady he had partnered on the dance floor was nothing like the fascinating creature he had met at the White Horse. He had missed her rich, throaty laugh, the mischievous gleam that sparkled in her eyes. It had become a matter of importance for him to know which one was the real Selina Wynter.

The most direct route from Graddon Hall took him through Torrisford and then the same distance again on the other side before he had his first glimpse of Reigney Abbey. It was a sprawling stone building with hints of its monastic origins to be seen in the stone mullions and arched doorways. A small garden surrounded the house while woodland covered the rising ground behind it, and on the way there he had ridden past a number of well-maintained farms and cottages as well as fields surrounded by neat hedges. If what he had heard was correct, and Selina Wynter was indeed in charge of everything, then she was a good manager.

He was admitted to the house by a harassed-looking footman, who invited him to sit down beside the hall fire before hurrying away, presumably to speak with his master. Left alone to kick his heels, Deveril could hear raised voices coming from a passage at the far end of the hall. Intrigued, he wandered closer and recognised Selina's voice.

'You have said quite enough, my lord. Please leave now.'

A male voice responded, loud and angry: 'Don't think you can play fast and loose with my son, madam! You would do well to accept his offer.'

'Never. I have made that abundantly plain on more than one occasion! I have no intention of marrying anyone, least of all Clifford.'

Ah. So that irate voice must be Lord Fremington's. Deveril listened as the man became even more incensed.

'It would secure your future and your father's. 'Fore

Gad, madam, be sensible! How much longer do you think you can carry on here? Running an estate like Reigney is man's work.'

'*Good day* to you, sir.'

'By Gad, if I had the taming of you—'

'Leighton, his lordship is leaving.' Selina cut across Fremington, her tone ice-cold and imperious. 'Please show him out now.'

Deveril heard someone, presumably the butler, bidding his lordship to come with him. Hasty footsteps sounded on the wooden floor and Deveril retreated to the fireplace just before Fremington stalked into view. His scowling red face was mottled with anger and when he saw Deveril he halted, causing the butler to stop abruptly behind him.

'Ha, Blackbourne. You lose no time in getting to the chase!' His loud, angry words echoed around the hall. He glanced back the way he had come and added, 'No woman is safe from you, ain't that so, *Devil* Blackbourne?'

The butler coughed and Fremington said testily, 'Yes, yes, Leighton, I am going!'

Deveril watched the two men disappear into the screens passage, his thoughts racing. Selina's icy tones cut short his reflections.

'What do you want here, my lord?'

He looked up to find she had entered the hall and was staring at him, a haughty tilt to her head. He made her an elegant bow.

'After an assembly, it is usual to pay a morning call,' he said mildly. 'Or does that etiquette not apply in Devonshire?'

'We are not at home to visitors today.'

'Ah.' He smiled, not at all discouraged by her cold tone. 'The young servant who let me in asked me to wait. I came to pay my respects to Mr Wynter.'

'That is not possible. After last night's exertions my father keeps to his room today.'

Deveril waited. She might yet thaw and offer him refreshment. He guessed she was struggling between common courtesy and a strong desire to throw him out.

'I will tell him you called. Good day.' She turned her head to address the butler, who was standing in the entrance. 'Leighton, Lord Deveril is leaving now.'

Head high, and with an angry swish of her skirts, she turned and walked off, leaving Deveril with nothing to do but shrug and follow the butler to the door.

'Well, that was interesting,' he muttered as he trotted away along the drive a few moments later. 'I'd say Fremington deliberately raised his voice just now, to make sure his words reached the lady. Why on earth would he wish to discredit me with her?'

The answer was obvious: He wanted the lady to marry his son.

Deveril shrugged. Clifford Fremington was welcome to the lady, he had no real interest in her. She danced very well, but her smiles meant nothing and as for the blushes he had seen on her cheek last night, that had merely been the heat of the room.

He turned his collar up and pulled his hat a little lower over his eyes against the icy wind that was blowing. It was not often he was wrong about a female, but this time he was clearly far off the mark. As he reached a bend in the drive he looked back at the Abbey, the solid oak door firmly shut against the weather and intruders.

'Enough of this nonsense,' he muttered, kicking his horse into a canter. 'Miss Selina Wynter is as cold today as her name suggests, and I have done with her.'

Chapter Eight

Selina stormed off to her bedchamber, running up the stairs and slamming the door with such force that it shuddered in its frame. The action relieved the violence of her feelings, but the fact that she could feel such anger alarmed her. She stood for a moment, fists clenched and breathing deeply until she regained some control over her emotions.

Lord Fremington's visit had been unexpected and unwelcome. She had very nearly lost her temper with the man and when Leighton escorted him away, she had remained by the open door, wanting to be sure he had actually left the house before she relaxed her guard.

It was when she heard his lordship speaking to another caller, one equally unwelcome, that her smouldering anger ignited. She hesitated, but only for an instant. She was too much on edge, too incensed, to wait meekly for Leighton to bring her a calling card, only to send him back again to deny her. Picking up her skirts she marched off to the hall, where she found Lord Deveril standing before the blazing fire, just as large and twice as handsome as she remembered.

Blast his eyes!

Her temper now cooling, she walked over to the window. It looked out over the gardens to the fields and woods that surrounded them. Everything she could see from here was Papa's land. Her inheritance. She had no intention of losing control of Reigney by marrying Clifford Fremington. Neither would she risk losing her reputation to a notorious rake like Devil Blackbourne, who clearly thought that one dance and a few smiles were enough to turn her head.

Shaking out her skirts she made her way downstairs to the study, where she tried to lose herself working on the accounts, but it was difficult to concentrate. Lord Fremington's words kept returning to haunt her.

Running an estate like Reigney is man's work.

She put down her pen and stared at the neat columns of figures. How would she go on here, when Papa died?

She knew as much about Reigney as the land steward, but her neighbours still did not take her seriously. If she went to market without Ashworth she had to work twice as hard to sell livestock or corn. Traders would haggle far more with her than with a man, and her plans to build a water mill in the Shep Valley had to be presented by her father before the bank would consider advancing the money. Even now, with the loan repaid and the mill making good returns, she knew any request from her for another loan would most likely be rejected.

With a sigh she gave up on the ledgers and ordered Orion to be saddled. She needed to be active; she would take Orion for a gallop on the moors and then go on to Shep Mill, stopping off at one or two of the farms on the way.

Today she was more impatient than ever of convention and she ran upstairs to change into the mannish riding jacket and buckskins that she kept for just such days as this, when she wanted to ride hard and fast. She would not be leaving her father's lands and would stay well clear of any public highways. The world might look askance at her behaviour, but Papa's tenants had long ago grown accustomed to Miss Selina's wild ways and regarded her with a lenient eye.

She decided to call on the miller and talk with the tenant farmers, inspect the recent improvements and discuss future plans with them. It would help to reassure her, as it always did, that she was as capable as any man.

Deveril rode briskly away from Reigney Abbey and as soon as he was on open ground he gave Colonel his head and enjoyed a gallop. The hard riding did something to ease his restless spirit, but it did not erase it completely. On reaching Graddon Hall and finding that the others had not returned from the hunt, he decided to spend the remaining daylight hours exploring Exmoor. The Viscount kept several sure-footed, sturdier horses in the stables specifically for riding on the moors, where the going could be boggy and uneven and, rather than risk overtiring Colonel, he ordered one these spare mounts to be saddled.

It was not long before Deveril set off for the hills, accompanied by one of the stable hands. He knew Richard would insist he take a groom, saying frankly that he didn't want any of his guests getting lost or disappearing into a bog. He spent an enjoyable few hours, diverted by the freedom of the moors and the short spring day was fading when he breasted one last hill, knowing it was nearly time to turn back. He drew rein and looked about him, drawing in deep breaths of the crisp clear air as he took in the view all the way to the coast in the west.

Turning, he realised the landscape was equally splendid in every direction and in the distance, he spotted another rider enjoying a fine gallop across a stretch of high, open ground.

'Where is that?' he asked the groom. 'Would it be Fremington land?'

The stable lad shook his head. 'Nay, that's Reigney Ridge, my lord. Part of old Mr Wynter's estates.'

Reigney Ridge. That was where he had met Selina. Where they had first kissed, then quarrelled.

'An' that'll be Miss Wynter, exercising that black hunter of hers,' said the lad.

'No, surely that's a man,' said Deveril, staring hard at the figure.

'Nay, it's Miss Selina all right.' The stable lad grinned. 'Often sees her, we do, riding on that there 'ill.'

Deveril nodded. He remembered the way they had raced across the turf. He had thought then the horse was much too strong for a woman. In the event it had been Colonel who had stumbled and thrown him. The irony of it was not lost on him and a laugh bubbled up inside, but it was soon doused when he remembered her temper, the contempt in which she held him.

He shrugged and turned away, determined not to spend another moment thinking about the woman.

Dusk was falling by the time Selina rode back to the Abbey. She was tired and very muddy but in a much better frame of mind. And she was even more cheered when she went into the house to learn that her father would be joining her for dinner.

'This is a great pleasure, Papa,' she greeted him when she went into the drawing room at the appointed hour. 'I did not expect to see you until the morning.'

'I feel very well, my love,' he said, taking her hand as she bent to kiss his cheek. 'My tiredness is quite driven away by a letter I have received. You will remember my old friend Horace Chewton? He has written to say he is visiting his sister in Cornwall and wishes to call here before he returns to Oxford.'

'Oh, that is very good news, sir!' cried Selina. 'When may we expect him?'

A visit from such an old friend would cheer her father immensely and give him some much-needed companionship, if only for a few days.

'Monday!' Her father sat back, his eyes shining. He waved the letter. 'Listen, Selina. He says, "I have arranged the whole and by the time this missive reaches you I shall already be on my way from Falmouth. I shall arrive in Torrisford shortly after noon on Monday next, but if that is at all inconvenient for you, my dear friend, only leave word at the Half Moon in Exeter, where I am putting up Saturday and Sunday night, and I can easily rearrange my plans".'

Selina laughed. 'Well, he has certainly made his preparations!'

'Horace was always a very practical fellow. I have already written a note to say how happy we will be to have him stay. I hope you do not object, my love?'

'Not at all, it will be a pleasure to have Mr Chewton here, for as long as he wishes.'

'Thank you, Selina,' he said, rising and offering her his arm. 'Chewton has always been such a good friend, and his presence will bring some much-needed cheer to the Abbey. Now, shall we go into dinner?'

There was no doubt that Mr Chewton's letter worked like a charm upon Mr Wynter. His lethargy quite disappeared and he was in very high spirits at the Kentons' soirée the following night, eager to tell his friends of the forthcoming visit. After accompanying her father on an initial circuit of the room, Selina guided him to a chair. It was out of the draughts and from there he might watch and listen in comfort to Helena, who was entertaining everyone with an accomplished performance on the harp.

The guests chattered and laughed while footmen glided around the room, moving silently between the groups with trays of wine and negus and lemonade. Helena's music provided an elegant accompaniment, the soft strains of the harp filling any lull in the conversation.

Standing beside her father, Selina watched Lady Fremington approach. The two families might be neighbours, but they had never been close friends and Selina was surprised that the lady was singling them out. After talking of unexceptional subjects for a few moments, Lady Fremington issued an invitation to Selina to come and stay at Fremington Court.

'It, it must be a little lonely for you at the Abbey, Miss Wynter,' she said, with a nervous smile, 'without a mother to bear you company.'

'Oh, do you think so?' Mr Wynter shifted uncomfortably in his chair. 'I had not considered. That is, *are* you lonely, Selina?'

'No, no, Papa. Not at all.'

Selina put a hand on his shoulder. She felt sorry for the small, colourless woman, whom she suspected was bullied and browbeaten by her husband and her son, and she declined the invitation as gently as she could.

'Papa and I rub along very well, you know. And do not forget I have the work of the estate to occupy me.'

'But you would be doing me such a service, my dear,' said her ladyship, a little desperately. 'With no daughters of my own, I should very much like to have you stay, even for a few days. Oh, please, Miss Wynter, do say you will come.'

But Selina was adamant. She knew the invitation was nothing more than a ruse to throw her into Clifford's company.

'Well, my dear, have you asked her?' Lord Fremington came up, smiling with false bonhomie. 'My lady always feels a trifle low in these dull February days, Miss Wynter. Then she hit upon the excellent idea of having you stay. Quite set her heart on it, she has!'

This jovial speech left Selina unmoved. In fact, it roused her indignation. If Lord Fremington had forgotten their quarrel the previous day, she had not. But she had some sympathy for his poor wife, which made her bite back her harsh retort and reply with a smile.

'I am of course honoured by my lady's invitation. However, I am afraid it is not possible for me to leave Reigney at present, even if I wished to do so. You see, we are expecting a visitor soon. An old friend of my father's.'

'What is this?' said the squire, who was passing at that moment. 'A visitor you say?'

'Why yes, Sir Alfred,' she replied. 'Mr Horace Chewton. You may remember him. It was some time ago, but I believe you met when he last came to stay.'

'Aye, I do remember him, very well. An excellent fellow and a very entertaining dinner guest, as I recall. Never at a loss for a good story, eh, Wynter?'

'Very true, sir, very true. We have enjoyed many battles on the chessboard, and backgammon, too. I must say I am looking forward to seeing him, his visits always cheer me up.'

'Is Chewton travelling post?' enquired Lady Kenton, who had followed her husband over to the little group.

'No, the mail.'

'Ha, I wish him luck with that!' exclaimed Lord Fremington, 'I never travel anywhere without my own cattle these days!'

'Sadly, we are not all so fortunate,' replied Mr Wynter in a tone of gentle reproof. He turned back to Lady Kenton. 'Chewton is travelling from Cornwall, you see, and breaking his journey at Exeter, where he plans to attend a Sunday service at the cathedral. It is some years since I was in Exeter but I am eager to know what he thinks of the medieval vaulted ceiling, and of course the misericords, which are considered very fine.'

'Oh Lord!' muttered Lord Fremington, rolling his eyes and taking another glass of wine from a passing servant while the squire and his guest discussed stone elevations and flying buttresses.

'Horace Chewton shares Papa's interest in architecture,' Selina murmured to Lady Kenton, her eyes twinkling.

'Well, well,' exclaimed Sir Alfred, 'you must bring your guest to dine with us one evening, Wynter. We should be delighted to renew our acquaintance with Mr Chewton, would we not my dear?'

'We should indeed,' his wife agreed. 'It must be, what, three years since his last visit?'

'Nay, 'tis four.' Mr Wynter sighed. 'How time flies.'

'I suppose you will have to collect your visitor from Torrisford,' put in Lord Fremington.

'We will. Or rather, Selina will meet him from the coach and bring him back to the Abbey. I shall reserve my energies for the evening,' he added, chuckling. 'I think dinner that night could be quite protracted.'

'Yes, I expect it to be a very late night, Papa,' Selina agreed. 'I intend to retire and leave you and your guest to enjoy yourselves!'

Sir Alfred gave a crack of laughter. 'Aye after four years, they will have much to catch up on, eh, Wynter?'

A movement at the door caught his eye.

'Ah, and here is Lord Graddon and his party come in.' He held out his arm to his wife, saying, 'If you will excuse us, ladies, gentlemen!'

As they moved off an elderly gentleman came up to

speak with Mr Wynter and Selina took the opportunity to slip away. She had spotted Lord Deveril's imposing figure amongst the Viscount's party and now made sure she kept her eyes well away from him. She would give him no encouragement to approach her.

Deveril saw Selina the moment he walked in and noted how she turned away after one brief glance in his direction. Which was just as well, since he would not be seeking her out tonight.

Yet, despite his good intentions he could not prevent his eyes from straying in her direction. Confound it, he defied any man not to be drawn to the striking picture she presented. She was wearing a *robe à l'Anglaise* of emerald satin with a cream-coloured underskirt and trimmed at the neck and sleeves with cream lace. Her luxurious dark hair was unpowdered and one glossy ringlet hung down on her shoulder, accentuating her slender neck and the smooth whiteness of her skin.

She was standing beside her father's chair, laughing with their hosts, while Lord Fremington and his wife hovered awkwardly on the edge of their group.

As well he might, thought Deveril, after the argument he had overheard yesterday. Not that he could blame Selina for refusing to marry the Honourable Clifford Fremington. He was a very dull dog. Deveril looked about him and spotted the fellow at the centre of a group of young bucks, holding forth about something. He judged Fremington to be around thirty, his own age, but the young men around him appeared much younger and they clearly admired their neighbour. It was no surprise that the fellow was puffed up in his own importance.

In Deveril's experience it was only very young ladies who were attracted by that bluff and bluster. More assured females like Miss Selina Wynter would want something more.

Bah, what are you doing even thinking of that woman?

A servant was passing with a tray of glasses and Deveril took one as he followed Lord Graddon and the rest of the party further into the room. It was claret, and not a bad one at that. He took a few more sips and then, schooling his face into a smile, he joined his friends in making themselves agreeable to the other guests.

He succeeded very well for the next couple of hours. The calming sounds of the harp were replaced by those of the pianoforte played by a very young lady who stumbled through the first few bars but improved considerably when she realised how few people were actually paying attention to her. He admired her courage, remembering his own early forays into polite society.

The last ten years had changed him from a shy, awkward boy into a polished and fashionable gentleman. It always amused him that in town he was regarded as an asset to any aspiring hostess. He had a large number of friends, and a name for fair dealing at the gaming table. He was also renowned as a dangerous rake. He was justly proud of the first reputation, but the second was as unwarranted as it was undesired.

He never promised more than a flirtation with any woman who threw out lures, but somehow it had become the fashion for those ladies to declare themselves heartbroken. Some of them even sank into a very public decline worthy of that great tragedienne, Mrs Siddons herself.

This evening, however, he was at pains to be the perfect guest. He was civil to everyone, chatted as easily with the young, single ladies as with their mothers and was careful not to snub any young gentleman who struck up a conversation.

'With the result,' murmured Lord Graddon, when they found themselves momentarily alone at one side of the room, 'that everyone is in transports over you. They think you are the epitome of a Polite Gentleman!'

Deveril grinned. 'And so I am, Richard, so I am.'

'Ancrum and Penkridge will be demanding blood by the end of the night. They are most put out that you have stolen a march with all the prettiest ladies here!'

'I cannot help it if I cast the rest of you in the shade.' He patted his friend on the shoulder. 'They have nothing to fear. I am merely being polite. I make sure they do not think I mean anything more.'

'I wish to heaven you did mean something,' exclaimed Richard, suddenly serious.

Deveril frowned, aware of the familiar black cloud descending on his spirits. The Viscount put a hand on his arm.

'Dev, it's been nine years since Belinda Roding died. Isn't it time you looked to the future, to giving your heart to some other lady?'

'My heart, Richard?' he said lightly. 'You know I have no heart. I buried it with my fiancée.'

'I don't believe that! Damn it all, Deveril, you are not yet one-and-thirty, a young man still! I would be failing as your friend if I did not want to see you happy.'

'I am perfectly happy. I have my friends and sufficient fortune to do as I please. As for women, I do not wish to sound conceited, but there are plenty willing to share my bed, so why should I take a wife?'

The Viscount shook his head. 'Perhaps marriage is not the answer, but in the years since Belinda's death you have changed, become more…distant, somehow. More restless. Oh, the others don't see it, but they don't know you as I do.'

Deveril was shaken by Richard's perception. Belinda Roding had been his first, his only love. After a lonely childhood, reared by servants while his parents were little more than strangers, he had looked forward to a life of happiness and companionship with Belinda and he had never recovered from her untimely death.

After a full year's mourning he had returned to Society, hiding the pain of his loss beneath a cheerful exterior but determined never to risk his heart again.

Even now he could not bear to have the wound touched, even by his best friend. He summoned a smile and answered Richard in a lazy drawl to disguise his true emotions.

'Your concern is touching, Richard, but unnecessary. I go on very well as I am, you see, a confirmed bachelor.'

With that he turned and strolled away to join a lively group discussing the recent death of Charles Edward Stuart, the infamous Bonnie Prince Charlie.

Chapter Nine

Selina was enjoying the soirée far more than she had anticipated. Her father was in good spirits and happily conversing with his friends, Lord and Lady Fremington had not repeated their invitation for her to come and stay and she had exchanged no more than a dozen words with their son all evening. Even Lord Deveril kept his distance. She mingled with her friends and neighbours and was even persuaded, towards the end of the evening, to take a turn at the pianoforte.

Like all the young ladies of her acquaintance, music was one of Selina's accomplishments. She enjoyed playing, but knew herself to be a competent, rather than a brilliant pianist. She was therefore happy to perform at the end of the evening, when almost everyone was engaged in cards or conversation and paying scant attention to the music.

She sorted through the sheets of music beside the pianoforte and began with pieces that she knew Papa would enjoy before moving onto a Mozart sonata that was a particular favourite of her own. She was so engrossed in her playing that she had finished the first movement before she realised someone had come up and was watching her. She looked up, fingers lingering on the last chord.

'I beg your pardon, please go on,' said Deveril quickly.

She looked so startled to find him there that he thought for a moment she would jump up and run away. He leaned forward to turn the page, saying, 'There are two more movements yet.'

She took a breath, composing herself before she continued to play. Deveril studied her, noting the moment she began to relax and lose herself in the music again. She had removed her gloves and, in the candlelight, he could see faint cuts and scratches on her hands. Evidence that she did not 'sit on a cushion and sew a fine seam,' as the nursery rhyme went.

He watched her fingers flying over the keys and remembered those same bare hands gripping the broom when she confronted the drunkards at the White Horse. What a strange creature she was. All the breeding and accomplishments of a lady, but the temper and spirit of a tavern wench.

He felt again that tug of interest, but he quickly squashed it. This was Richard's doing, blast him, reminding him of his dead fiancée and wanting him to find another woman to love. That certainly would not be Selina Wynter. She bore no comparison with Belinda, who had been a gentle soul, softly spoken and sweet-natured. She had died so young, before they had had a chance to do more than share a few chaste kisses.

His eyes were drawn to Selina's lips. He remembered how they had felt beneath his when he kissed her. Soft, warm, the slight hesitation before she responded, albeit briefly. He felt his pulse quicken at the memory. It had hardly been a kiss at all but it had ignited a fire that still smouldered within. It meant nothing, no more than attraction for a pretty woman. A damned nuisance, but it would pass, given time. It always did. Better to think of the cold way she had received him at Reigney Abbey. How she had looked at him as if he was not fit to clean her boots and dismissed him forthwith.

Deveril turned and walked away. Of all the females he had met, Selina Wynter was the very last woman who would ever capture his heart.

The final notes of the sonata died away and was greeted with warm applause.

'Brava, Miss Wynter,' cried the squire, clapping loudly. 'You will delight us with another piece, will you not?'

Selina's smile was perfunctory. Lord Deveril had walked off before she had finished the second movement and he was now the centre of a lively group standing by one of the windows, paying no heed at all to the music. He must consider her performance very mediocre after the London salons.

She said, 'Thank you, Sir Alfred, but the other ladies...'

'Everyone else has taken a turn,' he assured her. 'I pray you will play for us again, my dear. Having had such a fine instrument transported here from London, Lady Kenton and I enjoy nothing better than listening to it being played, and so proficiently, too!'

Lord Ancrum leapt up from his chair. 'If you need someone to turn the music, Miss Wynter, I am at your service.'

'No, no, let me do it,' cried Charles Penkridge, another of Viscount Graddon's party. 'Ancrum here can barely read a note!'

Their cheerful enthusiasm was infectious. Selina laughed and put up her hands. 'Thank you, both, but I do not require music for this next piece.' She glanced over at Helena. 'And afterwards, perhaps Mrs Frith will join me in a duet?'

She rattled off from memory a sonata by Mr Arne, then performed with Helena a piece for harp and pianoforte, which was very well received, but that was enough. Her father was nodding in his chair.

'It grows late,' she said, moving over to join him. 'I think it time we took our leave.'

'Of course, my dear,' said Lady Kenton. 'I shall send for your carriage immediately.' She took her young friend's hands, saying earnestly, 'But you have enjoyed yourself, have you not?'

'Very much, ma'am.'

'Then you should do it more often. You are too young to hide yourself away, Selina. You need to go into society more and enjoy yourself.'

'I do enjoy myself, ma'am,' she replied, laughing. 'As for society, we have Mr Chewton arriving on Monday, which will be entertaining.'

Lady Kenton did not look as if she thought the addition of a second elderly gentleman at the Abbey would provide much amusement for her young friend, but she did not say so.

'Then let us hope the weather holds,' was her only comment. 'It has been so much colder today.'

'One must expect that in February,' Selina replied. 'We are well stocked with provisions. I just hope any snow does not come until Mr Chewton is safely arrived at the Abbey!'

Setting off for Torrisford on Monday morning to collect Horace Chewton, Selina remembered her conversation with Lady Kenton. The sky was the colour of lead and an icy wind was blowing. Despite the warm brick at her feet, she shivered and pulled her cloak a little closer around her walking dress as the carriage negotiated the narrow lanes.

By the time they arrived at the George it was snowing steadily, but she was encouraged by the landlord's assurances that it would not yet have caused problems on the Exeter Road.

'You are in good time, though,' he went on. 'The mail ain't due in for a while yet. Perhaps you'd like to sit in the private parlour and I will have something fetched up for you. Coffee, or tea?'

'Nothing yet, thank you,' Selina replied. 'I have a few purchases to make from Mrs Babbage, but I will step in for a cup of coffee when I return.'

With that she set off along the high street to the haberdashers.

She soon completed her shopping and came out with a neatly tied package containing a length of linen and coloured silk thread, which she planned to make into handkerchiefs for Papa. It was snowing quite heavily now and she pulled her hood up to cover her hair and her frivolous blue bonnet before setting off for the posting inn.

She was halfway back to the White Horse when she heard her name and found Clifford Fremington hurrying up behind her.

'Miss Wynter—Selina! Thank the Lord I have found you.'

She looked at him in surprise. 'Clifford, whatever is the matter?'

'Mama!' he uttered. 'She has been taken ill.'

'Oh, I am so sorry to hear that, I hope it is not serious?'

'Yes, yes, it is serious!' He shifted nervously from

one foot to the other, his eyes darting here and there as he struggled with his words. 'It's...that is, the doctor says there is no hope.'

'Oh, my goodness!'

'I know. But she keeps calling for you, Selina.'

'Me? But why should she do that?'

He waved a hand and said impatiently, 'I don't know, ma'am, but I pray you will come with me now and talk with her.'

'I am sorry, that is not possible, I am in Torrisford to collect Mr Chewton. Once I have delivered him to Reigney I will drive over—'

'That could be too late,' he interrupted her. 'Every moment is precious! Please, Selina, my carriage is waiting for us, you see, a few yards back there. Come with me now.'

Thick snowflakes were settling on his hat and shoulders. She had never seen him so agitated. She nodded.

'Very well. Only let me take this to the White Horse and instruct my driver, then I will come with you.'

'No, no,' he cried wildly. 'That will not do at all! You must come *now*. This minute! We have not a moment to lose!'

'I have never seen you like this, Clifford!' She put a hand on his arm, trying to calm him. 'Surely if your mother is so very ill you should be at her bedside.'

'I am fulfilling her dying wish, and if it is you she

wishes to see then I must bring you to her! Please, Selina, she was calling for you so pitifully.'

He was wringing his hands and could not keep still, moving constantly and clearly labouring under great distress. He turned and beckoned to his driver.

'It will be best if we go immediately,' he told her. 'My man can take your package to the White Horse and give it your servants. He will explain that you have been called away on an errand of mercy. Will that do?'

'Yes, I suppose so,' she said as he took the parcel from her hands. 'But he must tell them you have taken me to Fremington Court and that I shall be returning to the Abbey this evening. In fact, if I am not back by five o'clock then my father must send the carriage for me.'

'You may direct him yourself,' said Mr Fremington, as the coach came to a halt beside them.

A groom clambered down, his hat pulled low over his brow and the muffler covering his nose and mouth against the cold, and Selina duly repeated her message while hunting in her reticule for her purse.

'And here is sixpence for your trouble,' she told the man. 'And please be sure to relay my message just as I have told you, is that clear?'

The man nodded and touched his hat.

'Aye, ma'am, that I will. Just as soon as I've seen you off,' he said, holding open the carriage door.

Clifford uttered a sigh of relief.

'Thank you, Miss Wynter. Come along now, not a moment to lose!'

He took her arm and helped her into the carriage then quickly jumped in behind her after a quick word with the groom. Even as the door was slammed shut the chaise lurched forward, sending Selina sprawling onto the seat.

'Good heavens,' she said, settling herself in the corner. 'Your driver is very impatient.'

'Aye, he has orders to spring 'em,' said Clifford, collapsing down beside her.

'However ill your mother is, it will not help if we break an axle en route,' said Selina tartly.

To her surprise, her companion laughed at that.

'Oh, she ain't ill at all,' he told her, his voice smug. 'That was just a ruse to get you into the coach. I am abducting you.'

Chapter Ten

'So, you are not coming with us this morning, Blackbourne,' remarked Charles Penkridge, when Deveril joined his friends in the hall.

'No, but I have stirred myself sufficiently to rise at this ungodly hour and see you off.'

It was not yet dawn and the hall glowed with light from the many lamps, as well as the fire blazing in the hearth.

'You will be missing the last hunt of the season,' Sir Henry warned as a servant helped him into his greatcoat. 'As well as the opportunity to ride with the North Devon Staghounds.'

'Leave him be, Jesmond,' muttered Lord Ancrum. 'You know he's squeamish about the kill.'

Deveril knew this was an attempt to shame him into accompanying them, but he was not to be moved. He merely shrugged. 'I have never enjoyed seeing any animal hunted down merely for sport.'

'There is every possibility the creature will outrun us.'

'True, Ancrum, but there is also the very real possibility that it won't.'

Penkridge gave a snort of laughter. 'Blackbourne prefers to spend his days prowling about the house, brooding over the loss of his mistress, the fair Amanda.'

Deveril did not reply, but the accusation was very wide of the mark. In truth he had hardly thought of Amanda Fylde since coming to Graddon Hall.

'You must of course do what you think best, Dev,' said the Viscount, heading for the door. 'But I do hope you will find something to occupy you, while we are gone.'

'Or someone! I am sure that pretty widow, Mrs Allen, would be delighted to keep him company.'

Deveril ignored Sir Henry Jesmond's sly comment and responded to the Viscount.

'You have a well-stocked library here, Richard, so I shall not be bored. And I shall probably go for a ride this morning. Colonel will be fretting when he sees all the other horses going off and will need some exercise.'

'Well don't leave it too long,' Charles Penkridge warned him. 'My man heard from the kitchen boy that there might be snow here later.'

'I won't. I shall go just as soon as I have broken my fast.'

'If you are going into Torrisford I have a letter to be taken to the post,' said the Viscount. 'I have already franked it, perhaps you would take it for me?'

'With pleasure.'

'I do believe you were right, Charles!' exclaimed Sir Henry. 'He hopes there will be a letter for him from Lady Fylde, saying she has changed her mind and begging that he return to London with all speed!'

Deveril greeted this final sally with nothing more than a grin. 'Enjoy your sport, my friends. I shall not look to see any of you until tomorrow evening, at the earliest.'

'Come along now,' cried Lord Ancrum, shepherding his fellow riders towards the door. 'We must be gone. By the time we are all mounted it will be light enough to see our way.' As the others trooped out the door he turned and waved his crop at Deveril. 'Enjoy yourself, Blackbourne—I just hope you ain't bored to death here on your own!'

With that they were gone, the cheerful chatter replaced by near silence, and Deveril made his way to the dining room, to enjoy a solitary breakfast.

It was beginning to snow as Deveril rode away from Graddon Hall later that morning. He was well wrapped against the weather, but by the time he reached Torrisford, snowflakes were beginning to settle on his hat and his heavy greatcoat.

The town was unusually quiet, which he attributed to the weather. When he turned into the main street, he noticed a travelling chariot pulled up a short way ahead and he recognised Clifford Fremington's stocky figure by the door. Even as he watched, Fremington jumped in, a servant slamming the door shut as the carriage drove off at speed.

The man made no effort to scramble up onto the back of the departing coach but set off along the pavement and as Deveril rode past, he noted that the fellow was carrying a package. The brown paper wrapping was already dotted with snowflakes, and he thought idly that it would soon be sodden if the man was going any distance.

Deveril trotted on to the White Horse, where an ostler ran out to take his horse as he rode into the yard. He tossed the man a coin and dismounted, informing him he would not be long before hurrying towards the inn door. He recognised Mr Wynter's carriage drawn up at one side of the yard and nodded at the driver. Ah yes. He would be waiting for the noon mail and his master's guest.

'Good day to you, my lord.' The landlord greeted him in a friendly fashion, recognising him as one of Lord Graddon's friends and one who was very free with his blunt. 'Can I be getting you something to drink, sir?'

Deveril pulled out the Viscount's letter and waved

it. 'Not today. Just on my way to the receiving office with this.' He hesitated and glanced towards the coffee room. 'Is Miss Wynter inside?'

He cursed himself the moment he had asked the question. The woman was no concern of his.

'Oh no, sir, she ain't. She be gone off to do 'er shopping before the coach comes in from Exeter,' replied the landlord. 'We's expectin' that any minute now.'

Deveril nodded and went into the office to hand over Richard's letter. When he came out again the Exeter mail had arrived and the yard was bustling as the ostlers raced to change the horses.

Two of the stable hands were loading a large trunk into Mr Wynter's carriage while the driver and a tall, thin gentleman with an impressive set of white whiskers sheltered under the carriage arch, deep in conversation with the man Deveril had seen walking along the street.

He heard the driver say, 'What d'ye mean, she's gone off?'

'Just that,' retorted the man, holding out the package. 'She left 'er shopping with me an' she give me a tanner to bring it here for you to take home for 'er.'

Intrigued, Deveril moved closer, listening closely as the man continued.

'Miss Wynter says you're to go on without 'er. Take your visitor to Reigney Abbey an' she'll be back as soon as she can. Now, I've done as she asked and I 'ave to get on. So I shall bid you good day, sirs!'

With that the man tugged his forelock and walked off.

Deveril paused, watching as the old gentleman climbed into the carriage, then he sauntered over to the driver.

'Was that one of Fremington's men?'

'Aye, that would be it.' The driver's brow cleared. 'I knew I'd seen him before somewhere. And that would make sense, wouldn't it? Lady Fremington being sick and asking for Miss Wynter.' He scratched his head. 'Queer start, though, if you ask me. It's not as if the families 'ave ever been that friendly.' He shrugged. 'But, there's no fathoming the ways of Quality—beggin' your pardon sir,' he added hastily.

Deveril merely grinned at that. 'No, no fathoming it at all. But did he not say it was Lady Fremington?'

'Well, no. Just that Miss Wynter'd gone off to see a sick friend. But knowing it was Lord Fremington's man makes it all right. Don't it?'

The driver fixed him with an anxious eye. Deveril hesitated, then he nodded.

'Yes, that's most likely what the fellow meant.'

With that he went off to find his horse, but he could not be easy. There was something odd about the whole business. Surely the man should have made some mention of his master, if he had come from Fremington Court. There had been something odd about the hurried way Clifford Fremington had jumped into the carriage before it had driven off at speed. And not in the direction of his home, either.

Deveril left the White Horse and rode out under the arch. He stopped to look up and down, but there was no sign of the servant who had delivered the package and the message. It was still snowing, but lightly, and it had not yet obscured the few tracks on the road. There were the unmistakable marks of the Exeter mail where it had turned into the White Horse, but there were just two sets of tracks heading out of Torrisford, the wide marks of the farm wagon he could see lumbering away along the high street, but in between those tracks were the much thinner lines made by coach wheels. Mr Wynter's carriage had not yet left the inn yard, so these tracks could only be from the travelling chariot he had seen driving off at such speed a few minutes earlier.

Deveril turned Colonel and set off in the opposite direction to the way he had come. He distinctly remembered seeing the coach drive past the entrance to the White Horse and he looked for signs that it had turned around in the wide high street and headed back towards Fremington Court. There were none. Puzzled, Deveril continued to follow the thin tracks.

Once he had carefully overtaken the farm wagon, the chariot's tracks were perfectly clear and he followed them until they turned off, taking a narrow lane northward. Deveril frowned. He had been to Graddon

Hall several times and was sufficiently familiar with the roads around Torrisford to know that this lane did not turn back on itself or lead in a roundabout manner to Fremington Court, nor even back to Torrisford.

He was pretty sure that it led only up onto Exmoor.

Selina huddled into the corner of the coach and stared out at the snow. It was falling heavily now and beginning to stick to the windows. Soon she would not be able to see out at all.

She was still trying to make sense of Clifford Fremington's announcement that he was abducting her. At first, she had been incredulous. She had scoffed at him, but he merely laughed. Then she tried to open the door and jump out, but when she scrabbled for the handle, he threw her roughly back onto the seat, and told her if she did not behave he would tie her hands.

That had sent her into a rage, but she concealed it, realising that she would have to use cunning, not brute force, to get out of this predicament. So she settled back and asked him, quite calmly, why he was abducting her.

'I am going to keep you with me until you marry me,' he said simply.

She laughed. '*That* will never happen!'

He patted his pocket. 'I have a special licence!'

'What!'

'A special licence.' His arrogant smile made her

want to hit him. 'M'father sent his man of business to London to obtain one. So you see, we can be married as soon as may be, and then I will take you back to Torrisford.'

'I will never consent to it!'

'No? I think you will soon change your mind about that. Once everyone knows we have been living as man and wife, your reputation will be ruined.'

'Not once I tell them the truth, that you abducted me.'

'Do you think anyone will believe you? When it is discovered that we are both missing everyone will think we have eloped!'

She was silent for a moment. 'Your mother is not really ill, then.'

'No, that was a ruse to get you into the carriage,' he replied, looking so pleased with himself Selina longed to hit him.

'And I suppose your man will not pass on my message!'

'No. Your giving him that package was a nuisance, though.' He frowned over that for a moment, then shrugged. 'Not that it matters now.'

'What matters is getting back to Torrisford,' Selina told him. 'I insist you turn around this minute!'

'You are in no position to insist on anything,' he retorted. 'I am not taking you back until you are my wife.' He leaned back in the corner and stretched his legs out, as if making himself comfortable for a long journey. 'The licence is valid for three months. I do not think you want to be away from Reigney for that long, now, do you?'

His words and the leering smile he gave her chilled Selina more surely than the snowy weather. She hunched a shoulder and turned away from him, determined not to let him see her dismay. She would not plead, or cry, but somehow or another she would find a way out of this dilemma.

They travelled on for what seemed like hours, the snow on the glass gradually reducing the light inside to a gloomy twilight. Although she could not see out of the windows, Selina guessed they were climbing steadily, towards the moors.

'Where are you taking me?' she demanded.

'Somewhere I can keep you safe. Where no one will find us.'

'If this snow continues, we will not be able to go much further.'

'Nonsense. It is only a flurry.'

She heard the uncertainty in his voice and, strangely, that gave her courage.

'You know as well as I that these narrow lanes can quickly become thick with snow,' she told him. 'We will be stuck in a drift and die of cold. There are always tales of winter travellers expiring on these moors.'

'Be quiet,' he snapped at her. 'Merton has driven these lanes many times. He knows what to do.'

'I hope so,' she muttered, turning away from him again. 'Or you will have my murder on your hands.'

She heard a growl of exasperation and felt a certain satisfaction at having rattled him. Now she must wait for a chance to escape.

Chapter Eleven

The snow was falling heavier now, fat white flakes that coated horse and rider, but Deveril's main concern was that it was covering the tracks he had been following.

He searched his memory for details of where this road might lead. He could only recall it winding upwards to the moor and when he reached a turning, he decided to see where it went. He had not gone far before it became clear to him that no carriage or wagon could pass along the narrow, rutted track. Frowning, he turned back and continued up the hill.

He was obliged to stop regularly to clear the snow from Colonel's hooves and could only hope that the chaise was making poor time, too. Having discounted the only two tracks leading off this lane, he was confident he would not lose them, but he wondered how much further he would be able to travel.

You should go back, whispered a voice in his head.

You don't even know if Selina Wynter is in that coach. Nor is it any of your business!

But Deveril had seen the servant holding the door for Clifford Fremington to climb into the carriage. That same servant had then given Selina's parcel to her driver. He was convinced now that Selina had already been in the coach and until he was sure, then he couldn't give up.

Due to Selina's insistence that she would be violently ill if she was obliged to travel in a coach with no light, they stopped at intervals to clear the snow from the windows. This task fell to Clifford, the driver maintaining that without a man to hold the horses' heads he would not dare to leave them unattended to do the job himself.

The opening of the door allowed in a blast of cold air, but Selina did not complain. She had assured Clifford that she needed to see out of the front window as well as the side ones, which meant he was obliged to climb out each time. And each time she wrapped herself tightly in her cloak and ignored his mutterings as he wiped the fresh snow from his coat.

After the third stop they set off even more slowly. It was growing dark and the horses were straining to move through the thick snow. They had not gone very far when the carriage finally came to a stand.

'What the devil!' Clifford opened the door and jumped out. Selina stared out of the window into the gathering dusk while he conducted a short, terse conversation with his driver.

'Well?' she said, when at last he climbed back in. 'What is happening?'

'Merton refuses to go much further tonight, damn him,' he told her. 'The snow is so bad now the road is sure to be blocked higher up on the moors, but he says there is a small inn just ahead where we can take shelter.'

'You could order him to turn back. If you take me home now, we can forget this whole ridiculous escapade.'

'He won't do that, either. Says the way it's been snowing the road behind us is sure to be blocked by now.'

'Very well, tell him to stop and I will *walk* back.'

'In this weather?' Clifford huffed out an angry breath. 'We have come at least ten miles. You would not last two hours. No, it must be the inn.'

Ten miles! Selina's spirits sank and she slumped back into the corner as the carriage lurched forward again. It would be impossible for her to walk that far. And she was not yet in such despair that she was willing to risk perishing in the snow!

She pulled her cloak tighter and stared out of the window. The lane had become very narrow by this point and it was impossible to see anything save the falling snow and the black shape of the high bank at the side. Ten miles from home! It was most likely they were in Exmoor Forest. She and her father rarely came this way, but she knew much of it to be a wild and desolate place.

The landlord of a small, remote inn would not have heard of a Mr Wynter, but it was very likely that he knew the Fremingtons. Whether or not that would work in her favour or against she did not know, but it was not the secure house Clifford had planned to keep her, and that had to be an advantage.

Her musings were cut short as the carriage finally came to a halt. She looked out. It was growing dark, but the lying snow made it possible to see that they had stopped in front of a two-storey thatched building, set back a little from the lane. The door opened and a light appeared. Selina could just make out a man standing in the entrance and peering out through the falling snow.

Clifford jumped down. 'Come along. The landlord is waiting.'

Rejecting his outstretched hand, she stepped down unaided into the ankle-deep snow.

'If you say we are married I shall deny it and tell him you have abducted me,' she muttered, expertly flicking her hood up into place before hurrying towards the open door.

The landlord stepped back and Selina found herself in a dimly lit cross-passage with doors leading off each side. She recalled visiting old farmhouses like this. At the far end, a lamp burned on the wall next to an outer door.

'Are you indeed an inn?' she asked doubtfully. 'Do you have rooms?'

'Aye, ma'am, this be the Rising Sun. As for rooms, we 'as some, and if we didn't, we'd find 'ee a bed somewhere. Lord love 'ee, I wouldn't leave a dog out in this weather.'

The man's rough cheerfulness was encouraging and she smiled at him.

'Well, that is something.'

She glanced at Clifford, who had followed her in, and said firmly, 'My friend and I require *two* bed-chambers.'

A young woman in a mob cap and apron was bustling along the passage. She looked very stout, and as she came into the lamplight Selina realised that she was heavily pregnant.

'Two rooms, is it?' said the woman, beaming. 'Well, we can do that, ma'am. Jennock, my dear, you go off an' see to the 'orses, an' I'll take our guests into the parlour.' She opened one of the doors and beckoned Selina to follow her in. 'I'm afraid tedn't very warm, because we wasn't expecting no visitors tonight so we've let the fire die down, but I'll get Mildy to see to that before she makes up the beds.'

She led the way into a large panelled room furnished with a dining table and chairs at one end and two wing-back chairs and a settee at the other, grouped around a fireplace where the remains of the log fire still glowed. The furnishings were old-fashioned and a little worn but in good order, and the size of the room, plus the large bay window that looked out toward the lane, suggested it had once been the home of a prosperous farmer.

Not that Selina was interested in the history of the building at that moment: her main concern was that after the icy weather outside, it felt blessedly warm.

'Thank you,' she said, sinking into one of the armchairs beside the hearth as the landlady went around the room, lighting the lamps. 'You are very kind.'

The woman beamed. 'Aye, well, you make yourselves comfortable and Jennock will fetch you in some wine, or ale, just as soon as he comes in from seeing to the horses. We sent the pot-boy off home when it started to snow and the stable lad's gone off to work with his brother, see, so there's no one else to do it.'

She bobbed an ungainly curtsy to Clifford, who had followed her in, before hurrying away and closing the door behind her.

'Do not think this changes anything,' muttered Clifford, scowling at Selina. 'I am not going to let you go.'

'I cannot see you have any choice. The landlord and his wife seem to be good people, I am sure they will help me if I ask them.' She met his scowl with defiance. 'I shall tell them of your villainous plans if I must.'

'Tell them.' He grinned suddenly, and something

in his assured manner caused her blood to chill. 'The landlord knows my father and he'll be loath to go against him. I think you will find Jennock and his wife will not object to anything I may choose to do here.'

'I shall tell them you abducted me. Sir Alfred is the magistrate, when he hears of this—'

'It will still be your word against mine, and then there's Merton and my footman. They'll both say you agreed to come with me.' His loathsome smile grew. 'And Jennock and his wife, of course. They will not dare to cross a Fremington if they know what's good for them.'

A knock at the door prevented Selina from replying. Which was perhaps as well, she reflected as she watched the young maid deftly coaxing the embers back to life. Losing her temper would not help her now. She needed to stay calm and not inflame the situation.

Deveril shrugged himself deeper into his coat. The cold was beginning to seep into his bones. The snow had eased but it had formed a thick covering on the road and was building up on Colonel's hooves, despite the thick greasing they had been given before he had set out that morning.

Was it only that morning? It felt like a lifetime ago since he left Graddon Hall. The sky had been overcast then and it had only got darker as the heavy snow clouds piled in. For some time he had been riding through a grey twilight which would soon turn to darkness now the sun had set.

Colonel skidded and Deveril reined him in. He dismounted and used his pen knife to gently clear the snow from the gelding's hooves before setting off again, the road dipping sometimes into a valley but generally they were climbing higher and higher, towards the open moors.

'This is madness,' Deveril muttered as the road began to rise again. He should turn back. 'If it isn't already too late.'

He urged Colonel on and when they reached the crest of a hill he stopped and turned to look back the way he had come. Heavy clouds blackened the horizon but the banks were lower here and in the fading light he could see something of the lanes behind him, which wound away like a white ribbon now into the darkness. Then he turned to look at what lay ahead.

Below him, not far ahead and set back a little from the road, was a long, thatched building.

And to one side, next to the low byre, a travelling chariot.

Selina raised no objection when Clifford declared that they should dine early. The landlady had explained everything perfectly: with the weather, and only herself, Jennock and the maid Mildy to do everything, their guests would have to choose which they wanted, the bedchambers prepared or their dinner first.

They had been in the parlour for an hour now and it was finally warm enough for Selina to remove her cloak. She put her wine glass on the mantelshelf while she untied the strings and laid her cloak carefully over the seat that ran the length of the big bay window.

Clifford had been drinking steadily since their host had brought in refreshments, but she had barely touched her wine, knowing she needed to keep her wits about her, especially if the drink made him belligerent.

Not that she was afraid of him. Clifford Fremington was nothing more than a bully and she had never considered him particularly intelligent. He was strong, however, and capable of overpowering her, if she put him in a rage. She must tread carefully.

She remained by the window while she removed her bonnet and unbuttoned her mannish jacket, all the time watching Clifford. He topped up her glass and poured the rest of the wine into his own, drinking it down in one go before he continued pacing the floor.

'Confound it,' he burst out. 'If it wasn't for this damned snow we would be snug in—'

'In where?' she demanded. 'Pray tell me where you planned to take me.'

He waved one hand. 'Oh, nowhere you would know. A snug little hunting lodge. The devil of it is I sent my own people on ahead to prepare the house.' He threw her an angry glance. 'They would have ensured you did not escape. But this place ain't secure. I am not sure I can trust Jennock and his wife to keep you from escaping.'

Her lip curled. 'No, you will have to watch me constantly, won't you?' she said, walking back to the chair beside the fire. 'Even when you are dog-tired and ready to sleep, because as soon as you close your eyes—'

'What.' He caught her wrist as she passed him. 'You'll run away? Or perhaps you plan to bludgeon me with a candlestick.'

He yanked her closer, holding her to his chest so that his wine-soaked breath was in her face. 'I'd best make sure of you now, then.'

He grabbed her hair, holding her head fast while he kissed her roughly. Selina struggled violently and when he raised his head her hand came up and she slapped him, hard.

'How dare you!' she raged, trying to push him away.

'Oh, I dare,' he hissed. 'You have always thought yourself too good for me, haven't you, Mistress High-and-Mighty Wynter, but I'll show you!'

His grip on her hair tightened painfully while his free hand tore the muslin fichu from her neck. Then he slid his arm about her and held her against him with an iron grip.

He tried to kiss her again but she managed to keep turning her head and avoiding his mouth.

'Do you mean to fight me all the way, madam?' He laughed savagely. 'By God, it will be a pleasure to break your spirit.'

His eyes were gleaming wildly and Selina knew he had gone past the point of reason. Her only hope was to scream, but he was crushing her so tightly against him now that she could not draw breath. He forced her backwards. She felt the edge of the sofa behind her knees and they fell, his weight pinning her down against the cushions.

'No. No! Get off me!'

She struggled desperately, trying to push him away, but he was too heavy, crushing her beneath him. Her strength was waning, but then she heard voices in the passage and renewed her efforts. She was desperately trying to find enough breath to scream when the door opened and a deep, amused voice drawled,

'Ah, I beg your pardon. Am I interrupting?'

Distracted, Clifford looked up and Selina took her chance. She pushed him, hard, and he tumbled away from her and onto the floor. Quickly she scrambled to her feet.

Only then did she look up to see who had entered and her lip lifted in a curl of disgust.

'You!'

Chapter Twelve

Deveril was cold and dog-tired, his hat and greatcoat were white with snow, but his reception raised in him a wry, inward smile. Selina had retreated behind the sofa and was glaring at him with loathing. As if *he* had been the one attacking her.

'I thought you would be rather more pleased to see me,' he said. 'Or anyone, for that matter.'

His eyes shifted to Clifford Fremington, who was climbing unsteadily to his feet.

'This is a private parlour, Blackbourne. Get out!'

Deveril was tempted to knock the fellow straight back down again, but Fremington was clearly drunk, and it was beneath him to pick a fight with such a man. He ignored him and strolled over to the hearth. Calmly he took off his hat and brushed the melting snow into the fire, where it hissed and disappeared.

'Did you hear me, sirrah?' Fremington barked at him. 'We would be obliged if you would leave, now.'

Deveril threw his hat down on one of the chairs

beside the fire. 'Regrettably I am unable to do that.' He shrugged off his greatcoat and shook that over the hearth before draping it across the back of the chair to dry. 'The roads, you see. Totally blocked. I was fortunate to get here. And the landlady tells me there is only one parlour in this establishment.'

Fremington's face was already an angry red, but now it darkened to a very unbecoming puce.

'Well...well, take yourself off to the kitchens, then,' he blustered. 'You are very much in the way here!'

'Am I, though?' Deveril's gaze moved to Selina. 'What do you say, Miss Wynter, do you wish me to leave you alone with this fellow?'

'It would be very ill-mannered to turn you away from our fire, my lord,' she said, bending to retrieve her muslin kerchief.

He felt a spurt of annoyance at her cool response. Devil take the woman, could she not show a little gratitude? From her dishevelled appearance it was quite evident what was going on, and what would have happened if he had not come in when he did.

Then he noticed how badly her hands were shaking as she tried to arrange the torn muslin decorously around her neck. His irritation was replaced with concern. She did not trust him any more than Clifford Fremington. And why should she, given his reputation?

There was a light scratching on the door and the landlord looked in.

'Your horse is stabled all snug now, my lord.'

'Thank you, Jennock.' Deveril lifted the empty bottle on the table and studied it. 'Damme if I expected to find wine in such an out of the way place, but if Mr Fremington thinks it drinkable then we'll have another bottle, landlord, if you please.' He glanced at his companions; Fremington was scowling viciously at him, while the lady stood, pale and tense. 'I hope you will both join me in a glass, while we wait for dinner?'

He did not wait for their reply before nodding to the landlord and waving him away.

'There now, it is arranged,' he said, all politeness, as if this was a fashionable London salon. 'Now, I had best move my coat and hat out of the way, and we can all sit comfortably.'

Selina walked slowly towards the fire, fastening her jacket as she went. Retrieving her wine glass from the mantelshelf, she sat down in the empty armchair. She felt very tired and, unusually for her, close to tears. The last person she wanted to find her here was Lord Deveril Blackbourne. She could not deny his arrival had been timely but she thought, with a flash of her usual spirit, that if he expected her to fall upon his breast in gratitude, he very much mistook the matter. Just now she wished all men at Jericho!

The three of them sat around the fire in silence. Lord Deveril had taken possession of the second armchair and Clifford, too slow to act, was obliged to pull up a dining chair. He was looking mutinous. There was no love lost between the two men and Selina wondered if she could use that to her advantage.

When the landlord returned with a fresh bottle and glasses, he announced that the lady's bedchamber was now prepared.

'Mrs Jennock thought that'd be the best one to do first,' he told them cheerfully. 'And Mildy's taken up a jug of hot water for 'ee, ma'am.'

'Excellent, thank you, I shall go up now,' declared Selina, draining her glass. 'Perhaps you could show me the way.'

Clifford jumped up. 'I'll escort you!'

'You will do no such thing,' she snapped. 'That would be most improper. Pray lead on, Master Jennock.'

Then with a last, fulminating glance at Clifford, she followed the landlord out of the room.

Fremington stared at the closed door, his fists clenched as he muttered angry curses.

'If you are afraid she's going to run away, you are very wide of the mark,' Deveril told him. 'The snow is too deep for anyone to get far. And it is snowing again,' he added, glancing towards the window.

'That woman is capable of anything, curse her,' retorted Fremington. 'You saw how she turned on me then. Like a damned wild cat!'

He went over to the table where the landlord had left the wine and filled two fresh glasses. He handed one of them to Deveril before sitting down in the vacated armchair, where he sipped his wine and scowled into the fire.

'Then why pursue her?' asked Deveril, thinking more drink might loosen the man's tongue.

'For the land, of course! Old Wynter won't sell, so I must marry Selina.'

Deveril's lip curled with contempt, but he said, mildly, 'And you think abduction is the way to go about it?'

'It's the *only* way. Damme, she's refused me numerous times!'

'So, you are not as *good as engaged*,' said Deveril, remembering what Fremington had told him on their first meeting. He laughed. 'If I were you, I'd forget the lady and find a more accommodating bride.'

'Blast you, my father won't hear of it! Reigney Abbey lands march with ours to the south and west of Torrisford. He has coveted the estate for years.'

Fremington sat for a while, hands around his glass and staring into the fire. Then suddenly he looked up and glared at Deveril.

'I have heard about you, Devil Blackbourne,' he snarled. 'Don't think for a moment that I shall let you get in my way here. Selina Wynter is mine.'

Deveril raised his brows and regarded the man. He had no personal interest in such a virago as Selina Wynter, but neither would he stand by and allow Fremington to seduce her against her will. And from what he had witnessed earlier, the lady was definitely *not* willing.

He was still deciding how to reply when Selina returned. Both men rose to their feet as she walked in. She had tamed her thick dark curls into some semblance of order and removed her jacket. The torn muslin was now arranged modestly around her neck and shoulders, the ends tucked into the low bodice of her gown.

Deveril acknowledged a grudging admiration for her. Most women of his acquaintance would have been in hysterics after what had occurred today. At the very least they would have ordered their dinner to be sent up to their room.

Aware of his scrutiny, she raised her chin.

'You are wondering, perhaps, why I have not changed out of my travelling clothes, my lord. It appears that while *my abductor* had the forethought to bring a portmanteau for himself, he took no account of my needs for the journey he had planned!'

This forthright speech had Fremington smothering a curse. Deveril cast a derisory look in his direction.

'Now that was a grave error, sir.'

'Doubtless not one you would make, my lord!' snapped Selina.

'Well, no.' The look she gave him told Deveril clearly that she thought him quite capable of such depravity and his lips twitched. 'But then, I have never found it necessary to abduct anyone. Yet.'

Something in her manner changed. He saw her eyes flash, but not in anger. More the way they had at the White Horse, on their first meeting. She was well aware that he was jesting and he had the distinct impression she was trying not to laugh. He felt another stab of admiration.

She was undoubtedly a singular female! In this situation, imprisoned in an out of the way place with two men she did not trust, she should be frightened out of her wits.

Fremington said slyly, 'His lordship is a man of the world, Selina. He understands only too well your predicament. Obliged to spend a night here, without a chaperone.'

'Oh, but I am happy to play the role of duenna,' said Deveril blandly.

'Fustian!' Fremington snorted. 'The knowledge that a notorious rakehell is snowed up with us will only make matters worse!'

'Not at all,' Deveril replied cheerfully. 'During the day we can both play chaperone and ensure the lady is never alone, with either of us. As for the nights, I am sure Mrs Jennock will make up a bed in Miss Wynter's bedchamber for that little maid of hers.'

'For a fee, which I ain't going to pay,' Fremington interjected, looking at Selina.

'And I have only a few pennies left in my purse.' She threw another angry glance at him. 'I was not expecting to need more today!'

'Since you insisted upon having your own room, here, madam, my own purse is spent!'

'Then put it on credit,' she retorted. 'You said the landlord is acquainted with your father—he will know you are good for any sum.'

'I'm damned if I will!'

Deveril could not deny he was enjoying this exchange, but it would not do to allow tempers to become too frayed. He went to the table and poured a glass of wine for Selina.

He said, 'If that is your only concern, madam, allow me to lend you the money for anything you require.'

He heard Fremington's growl, a mixture of rage and frustration, but he was more interested in the lady's reaction. She was biting her lip, looking every bit as annoyed as Fremington by the suggestion. As Deveril had known she would be. The lady would dislike intensely the idea of being in his debt.

He held the glass out to her, saying, 'I shall, of course, keep an exact tally of expenditure. You can reimburse me once you are safely returned to Reigney Abbey.'

Selina took the glass but she stood, still biting her lip. Lord Deveril was regarding her, his eyes full of unholy amusement, enjoying her present discomfiture. She had to concede that she trusted him slightly more than she did Clifford Fremington, but it didn't stop her wanting to throw this wine in his face.

At last, she inclined her head and said with admirable calm, 'Thank you, my lord. I am most obliged to you.'

Clifford muttered a curse and jumped to his feet.

'Confound it, Blackbourne, I expected better of you. I warned you not to get in my way. The woman is mine!'

Selina retreated as he lunged towards her but Deveril was already between them, grabbing Clifford's arm and twisting it up behind his back. The languid manner was quite gone and his voice, when he spoke, was full of quiet menace.

'This woman is a *lady*, Fremington, and don't you forget it.'

Clifford gave a gasp of pain. 'Enough, my lord, enough. Let me go, damn you!'

'Very well.' Deveril released him and stepped back, his fists clenched at his sides. 'But in future you will remember your manners when a lady is present.'

Clifford rubbed his arm and glared at him. 'Damn you, Blackbourne, you'll meet me for this!'

Selina did not miss the look of contempt that flickered across Lord Deveril's face. He looked ruthless, and every bit as dangerous as his reputation. She shivered, thinking how little she knew of Devil Blackbourne.

She put her glass down on the table with a snap.

'Enough of this foolishness, both of you!' she said, before Deveril could respond to the challenge. 'For pity's sake, can we please get through the rest of this evening without causing a scandal? Mrs Jennock will be coming in at any moment to set the table for dinner. 'Tis bad enough that we are stuck here for the night. Do you think I want it known all over the county that I have been the cause of a quarrel between two...' She paused. 'I hesitate to call either one of you a gentleman!'

Her scathing words were met with silence. Had she gone too far? Tension crackled around the room, Selina could feel it, ready to explode into violence at the slightest thing.

Lord Deveril was the first to speak, and he did so quietly.

'You are quite right, ma'am, I beg your pardon.' He looked across at his opponent, who was scowling blackly. 'Come, Fremington. Let us call pax for this evening.'

'Yes, pray do so, Clifford,' Selina urged him. 'If I return unharmed to the Abbey tomorrow, you have my word I shall say nothing of your disgraceful behaviour.'

She glanced at Deveril. 'I hope, my lord, I can rely upon your discretion?'

'You can, madam.'

Satisfied, she turned back to Clifford. 'There. This can all be resolved without a scandal. But you must make it plain to your father that under no circumstances will I marry you. And be warned, sir. I will make this evening's work known to the whole of Torrisford if you importune me in future.'

'You wouldn't dare say anything,' snarled Clifford. 'Your reputation—'

She snapped her fingers. 'I do not give *that* for my reputation! I have done nothing wrong and I will not be cowed by your threats. Let me be clear, Clifford. All I want is to live in peace with my father at Reigney. I have *no intention* of marrying anyone. Do you understand me?'

She was standing with her bunched fists resting on her hips and her eyes sparking fire. Deveril was not surprised that Fremington shrank beneath that fierce stare and a laugh bubbled up in his chest. He was reminded very much of how he had felt when his old nanny gave him a severe scold.

Although Selina Wynter looked nothing like Nanny, he thought now. Selina's cheeks still bore an angry flush and her dark hair curled wildly about her head. And as for her eyes, they were positively aglow in the dim light. She reminded him of Nemesis, the goddess of retribution.

He dragged his eyes away, reminding himself that any man foolish enough to leg shackle themselves to such a woman would have no peace!

'Beggin' your pardon, madam, sirs, I needs to come in and set the table for dinner.'

The landlady's entrance broke the silence. Fremington stalked across to the window, where he stood looking out into the snowy night, and it was Selina who replied to the landlady.

'Yes of course, Mrs Jennock.'

She spoke with a laudable amount of composure but Deveril noted how she clasped and unclasped her hands nervously.

He said, 'Shall we return to the fire, Miss Wynter?'

She looked at him for a moment, as if she had forgotten his presence, then with a slight nod, she picked up her glass and went back to her chair.

Deveril sat down opposite and filled the silence with innocuous remarks while the landlady bustled about, preparing the table. Selina made no reply, her thoughts clearly elsewhere, but when Mrs Jennock went out to fetch another tray, she interrupted his flow of small talk.

'My lord, I hope I can rely upon you not to speak of what has occurred here. That is, to say nothing beyond the fact that we were all obliged to take shelter here for the night. I am well aware that just the fact of the three of us being snowed in together is sufficient to give rise to jesting and merriment amongst men of your...'

She broke off, biting her lip.

'Men of my ilk,' he finished for her, hiding his annoyance behind a silky tone. 'You have a very low regard for me, do you not, Miss Wynter?'

Her eyes flew to his face, but the landlady came back in at that moment and whatever reply she had intended remained unspoken. With an inward shrug Deveril sat back in his chair. Lord, he could not remember when he had ever been more impatient for an evening to be over!

Selina watched the landlady preparing the table and was tempted to say she would take dinner in her room, but after a moment's reflection she decided against it. She, more than anyone, knew how much extra work that would make for Mrs Jennock and the maid. As difficult as it would be, she would sit it out, although she would be counting the minutes until she could make her excuses and retire for the night.

When the meal was eventually served, Clifford consumed his in sulky silence. To his credit, Lord Deveril attempted some polite conversation and Selina joined in. It was a little stilted at first, but gradually she felt the tension easing. It was Clifford's glowering presence that reminded her of the very real dangers of her position: she could not afford to drop her guard at all.

Mrs Jennock proved to be an excellent cook and the dinner was far better than Selina had expected. Clifford grumbled throughout, finding fault with the wines, even though he continued to drink them, and complaining that there were not enough dishes on the table. Comparing the two men, she began to think better of Lord Deveril. He declared himself satisfied with everything set before him and even took the trouble to praise the landlady on the cooking, when she and the maid came in to carry away the last of the dishes.

'Why thank 'ee me lord,' stammered Mrs Jennock, flushing with pleasure. 'We does our best. Now, if you've had enough of the wine, Jennock has a very good cyder that he'd gladly share with you, it having been a 'specially fine harvest last year. Or of course,' she added, dropping her voice a little, 'I 'spect he could find you some French brandy if your tastes run to it…'

'Brandy,' declared Clifford, pushing aside his empty wine glass. 'Although I don't doubt it will be poor stuff.'

Selina glared at him for his bad manners, but before she could speak Lord Deveril jumped in.

'Nonsense,' he said cheerfully, 'I do not believe an establishment that can produce such an excellent repast could serve up an inferior brandy. Madam, pray tell the landlord we'd be honoured to try it!'

Selina did not miss the charming smile he gave the landlady, who blushed with pleasure and left the room with a jaunty spring in her step.

'Turning her up sweet, my lord?' she murmured, finishing her wine.

He grinned. 'By no means, I meant every word. Will you join us in a glass of brandy, ma'am, or would you prefer something else—more wine, perhaps. Or they might have sherry.'

Selina hesitated. Dinner had gone better than she

had expected and she was tempted to stay, but knew it would not do.

'Thank you, my lord, but no,' she said, rising. 'I shall bid you both good night and leave you to your brandy.'

The gentlemen stood, but it was Lord Deveril who stepped across to the door and opened it for her.

'Good night, Miss Wynter.' He looked towards the window. 'It has stopped snowing. Let us hope we shall be able to return you to Reigney Abbey in the morning.'

'Yes, I hope so.'

She glanced up to find him smiling down at her and it threw her off balance, as if she had missed her footing. Her heart began to thud, she felt dazed, shaken. She quickly looked away and gave him no more than a little nod as she left the room. Heavens, she had never known a man who could unsettle her so.

Selina did not sleep well, despite the best efforts of her hosts. Mrs Jennock provided her with a plain but clean nightdress and sent Mildy up with the warming pan and a hot brick to put between the sheets. She could not complain that the bed was uncomfortable, and Mildy, sleeping on the truckle bed in the corner, did not snore. However, when Selina finally blew out her candle sleep eluded her. She tossed and turned, wondering what was happening at Reigney. Had her father discovered she was not at Fremington

Court; had Clifford's man even passed on her message? Whatever the case, poor Papa must be very worried by now.

Eventually, she told herself that there was nothing she could do about that for the moment, and very sensibly tried to put such thoughts aside. When at last she did drift off to sleep, her rest was disturbed by dreams of Lord Deveril and his ability to turn her rage to laughter with no more than a look.

Selina awoke feeling little refreshed and opened her eyes to find the grey dawn was peeping in through a gap in the bed curtains. When she sat up and pulled them back, she discovered she was alone. Mildy had already left the room, but not before she had rekindled the fire.

Selina slipped out of bed and crossed to the window, her heart sinking as she stared out. The snow was even deeper than last night. It continued to fall silently, swirling around and covering everything in a white blanket. It had been blown against walls and hedges, forming thick drifts. Everywhere she looked the snow was smooth and untouched, no sign that anyone or anything had yet ventured out of doors.

She sighed, her breath misting the glass.

'It must have snowed all night.'

There was a knock at the door and the maid came in, carefully carrying a large jug.

'We 'eard the creak of floorboards, ma'am, so I

knew you was up,' she said cheerfully. 'Mrs Jennock would've come up herself but she's finding the stairs too much for her this morning so she sent me up with the 'ot water and bids you to come downstairs for breakfast as soon as you're ready. Oh, and I'm to ask if you needs 'elp with your stays?'

'That is very kind, yes,' replied Selina, hiding her despondent thoughts behind a smile. 'It would be easier if you can lace me up. But I shall not keep you longer than necessary,' she said, going over to the washstand. 'I am sure you must have a thousand things to do.'

'Aye, ma'am, but Master Jennock says I'm not to feed the hens yet, as missus'll be needin' one for the pot and it'd be a waste.'

Selina had no reply to this artless speech. She quickly washed and dressed. It would seem that her worst fears were realised, and they were stuck here for another night. Or more.

Chapter Thirteen

Deveril was in the parlour, contemplating the snowy scene outside the window, when he heard the door open.

'Good morning, my lord.'

He turned to see Selina had come in. She looked neat as a pin with her thick glossy curls tamed and swept up into a topknot. Her Prussian blue jacket hung open to display the matching walking dress, the skirts of which had been brushed, and she had replaced yesterday's torn muslin with a piece of snowy white linen.

Aware of his scrutiny, she put a hand up to her breast, saying with just a hint of defiance, 'I begged this from Mrs Jennock, my fichu being too badly mauled to wear again.'

'It looks very well, ma'am,' he said politely. 'I see nothing wanting.'

She relaxed a little.

'She found me a comb, too, and some more pins for my hair.' She walked over to join him at the window.

'I am not hopeful of being able to leave here today, are you?'

'No. I spoke with Jennock earlier, and he agrees there is nothing to be done until the snow stops. I only hope they have sufficient supplies to feed us.'

'I am reliably informed one of the hens is, er, destined for the pot.'

His brows went up. 'Drastic measures, then.'

'Indeed.'

She met his eyes, her own twinkling with shy amusement, but before he could say anything more the landlady came in carrying a tray of cutlery and glasses which she put down on the table. Deveril thought the woman looked a little pale and he watched as she stood for a moment, one hand gripping the top of a chair, the other pressing on the small of her back.

'Let me do that for you, Mrs Jennock,' said Selina, hurrying over. 'I am quite capable of setting the breakfast table.'

'Bless you, ma'am, but that wouldn't be right.'

But Selina was already laying out the knives and forks.

'Nonsense,' she said. 'I know exactly what needs to be done. You may safely leave it with me.'

'Well, if it's all right with you then, Miss Wynter, and thank 'ee. I'll go back and prepare the tray for Mr Fremington, who says he will take breakfast in his room.'

'That he shall not,' declared Selina. 'With your condition, and only Master Jennock and Mildy to help, I will not countenance him making extra work for you.' She looked across at Deveril. 'My lord, I pray you will go up and inform Mr Fremington that he will break his fast here, or not at all!'

Shocked by this robust declaration, the landlady protested, but Deveril put up his hand, saying, 'I think we must allow Miss Wynter her way on this, Mrs Jennock. She knows just how much work is entailed in running an inn, is that not so, ma'am?'

He was rewarded with a furious look from Selina, which he met with a bland smile before going off to give Fremington the news.

'Oh dear, oh Lord,' muttered Mrs Jennock, once his lordship had departed.

Selina patted her arm. 'Pray do not fret. You are looking after us splendidly, but we must not impose too much upon you.'

'I thank 'ee for that, ma'am. I can't deny it, I ain't feeling that good today, but don't you worry, I will have breakfast on the table for you in a trice!'

With that the landlady waddled off to the kitchen and Selina went back to setting the table, a slight frown creasing her brow.

Breakfast was finished, the table cleared and all three stranded travellers were sitting before the fire in the parlour when Jennock came in with more logs. In response to a question from Clifford, he confirmed what Selina had feared. There could be no travel that day.

'The lane's blocked in both directions and the snow in the fields has blown into great drifts in places, too deep to push through. We's cut off good and proper, at least for a few days,' he told them, shaking his head.

'Damn and blast, I won't have it!' fumed Clifford. 'It's stopped snowing now, surely you can get together a few fellows to help dig out the road.'

'Impossible,' retorted Selina. 'Master Jennock has just said one cannot even get across the fields.'

Clifford glowered at her. 'Well, I don't believe that. I have a good mind to send Merton out to see for himself just how bad things are.'

The landlord scratched his head. 'You *could*, sir, but your driver discovered my barrel of strong beer last night and made free with it. Drank himself into a stupor, he did, and he was still sleeping soundly when I went to the hayloft this morning to check on 'im. I don't reckon you'll be seein' much of him for the rest of the day.'

'*What?* We'll soon see about that!' Clifford pushed himself out of the chair and almost ran out of the room, slamming the door behind him.

The landlord turned back to Selina and gave her a reassuring smile.

'If you be worrying about how we'll go on here, ma'am, there ain't no need. The missus keeps us well stocked with provisions, hams, cheeses and the like, plus all manner of pickles. And we've the milch cow in the barn. There's plenty of wood, too, for the fire,' he added, dropping the logs into the wood basket. 'You won't go cold nor hungry.'

'No, I am sure we won't, Master Jennock,' she said. 'Thank you.'

With a nod the landlord went out and Selina wandered over to the window to stare out at the white world. It had started to snow again, fat white flakes sticking to the glass and obscuring her view.

'If it has snowed this heavily around Torrisford no one will be travelling anywhere,' said Lord Deveril. 'Your father will not expect you to return for a few days.'

She shook her head.

'But he will not know what has happened to me,' she said, her voice not quite steady.

'Most likely he will think you are snowbound at Fremington Court.'

Selina swung round. 'Will he? I am not so sure.'

'I heard Fremington's man telling your driver you had been called away to visit a sick friend, presumably Lady Fremington. I thought it sounded a little suspicious at the time.'

'Oh. Then my sixpence was not quite in vain!'

She felt quite giddy with relief and sank back down on her chair. She saw his lordship looking puzzled and even managed a little laugh before she explained.

'I purchased some linen, which Clifford's man was

to take back to the driver with my message, and I gave him a sixpence for his trouble. Clifford had instructed the man to say nothing. He will be so cross when he knows of it.'

'The servant is not such a rogue as his master then.'

'No.' For a moment they shared a smile across the table, then she sighed. 'As long as Papa does not discover the deception, he will not fret.'

Deveril did not miss the note of concern in her voice. She continued frowning for a moment, then seemed to gather herself and she looked up, attempting another smile.

'Not that it will do any good for me to worry about that, so we must go on here as best we can.'

She fell silent again, staring down at her hands, clasped in her lap, and after a few moments he prompted her.

'Is there something you wish to say, Miss Wynter?'

'Last night.' A faint blush painted her cheeks. 'I am sorry you had to witness…that scene with Clifford Fremington.'

'I am glad I arrived in time to prevent matters going any further.'

'Yes, thank you. And thank you for not pressing me for an explanation.'

'Oh, I think I have a pretty fair idea of what happened.'

She was silent, biting her lip for a moment.

'I have known Clifford Fremington since we were

children,' she said at last. 'He has always been a bully, but I never thought he would stoop to such a trick as to, to abduct me.'

'You do not need to worry upon my account, Miss Wynter. You can rely upon my discretion.'

She raised her head and fixed her eyes upon him. 'Can I, though?'

Deveril knew they were no longer speaking of Fremington or his attack upon her virtue. He waited. She looked uncomfortable, but her clear blue eyes met his gaze steadily.

'About that night,' she said at last. 'At the White Horse.'

'What of it?'

'My father knows nothing of what I do there. It would grieve him very much to learn of it.'

'I have told no one. Nor do I intend to do so.'

'Then why did you threaten me with it, at the assembly?'

'Did I do so?'

She bristled at that. 'You know very well you did, and you have done it again, since! Why, only this morning you referred to my knowing how to run an inn!'

'I admit to teasing you, Miss Wynter, nothing more sinister than that.'

'Really? When I was standing with Mrs Frith, at the assembly, you said we had not formally been introduced, but you said it in such a way that implied if I declined your invitation to dance, you would disclose to her just how we had met.'

'Ah, I see. It was never meant as anything more than a jest, madam. A moment of shared amusement. But it was very wrong of me, and I beg your pardon.'

He hoped his frank apology would disarm her and was relieved when she inclined her head a little. He went on.

'I should like to know why you were at the posting inn, though. Was that some sort of wager?'

'Of course not! *I* do not indulge in such foolishness!' She gave him a speaking look. 'It was necessary to keep the White Horse running as a posting inn while we were without our new innkeeper. I took two of my people from the Abbey to help me but unfortunately there was a...a disagreement that the servants could not resolve.'

'So you took it upon yourself to do so.' His lips twitched. 'With a broom.'

'Yes. It was not the wisest thing to do, perhaps, but I am not ashamed of it.' She flashed him a defiant glance. 'And I will not allow you to turn it to your advantage.'

'I have no wish to take advantage of you. Although I am very glad you agreed to dance with me. I enjoyed it.'

He thought he detected a gleam in her eyes. Amusement, perhaps? He hoped so, although her response was cool enough.

'I decided one dance with you could do no harm.'

'You are wrong, Miss Wynter. One dance can turn a life upside down.'

She blushed at that, but frowned, too. 'Are you trying to flirt with me? I pray you will not, my lord.'

He said lightly, 'Having witnessed your temper on more than one occasion, ma'am, I wouldn't dare.'

Deveril saw her trying not to laugh at that, and was satisfied. He went over to the hearth to add another log to the fire.

'One thing I should like to know,' he remarked, straightening. 'Why you were in Torrisford without a chaperone?'

'At five-and-twenty I do not need one.'

'No? Fremington would not have been able to carry you off so easily if you had been accompanied.'

'He would not have been able to do so if he had not lied to me!'

'True.'

'I should have known better than to believe him when he told me Lady Fremington was ill.'

'But you have already told me you did not think him capable of such ignoble actions. Don't be too hard on yourself, madam.'

The awkwardness between them had gone, but when he suggested they sit down by the fire she shook her head.

'It will not do for me to be alone with you for too

long, my lord. But, thank you. I feel we have cleared up the misunderstanding between us.'

'I am glad of it,' he said, walking to the door and opening it for her.

'Tell me, Lord Deveril,' she said, pausing in front of him, 'Why did you change your mind about going to London? What made you return to Graddon Hall?'

'I wanted to solve a puzzle.'

'And have you solved it?'

'In part.'

Deveril hesitated. Had she guessed the truth, that she was the puzzle? He did not think she had done so and he was tempted to tell her now. It would be amusing to see her reaction.

But at that moment, a woman's piercing cry rang out.

Chapter Fourteen

Hearing Mrs Jennock's scream, Selina picked up her skirts and ran along the passage. Deveril dashed after her, following her into the kitchen.

They found the landlady clutching the edge of the large table in the middle of the room. It was still covered with a jumble of bowls and cooking utensils plus a liberal dusting of flour and Mrs Jennock was bent low over it, drawing in long, painful breaths while Mildy looked on anxiously, hopping from foot to foot and wringing her hands.

'Mrs Jennock!' Selina hurried over to her. 'Is it the baby?'

'Aye, 'tis coming,' cried the maid. 'I knows it. My mother was just the same!'

Mrs Jennock straightened slowly.

'Now, now, Mildy, there's no need to worry the lady,' she said, struggling to sound calm. 'You go back to plucking that chicken, my girl, or we'll have nothing for dinner tonight. Go on.' She shooed the girl back out to the scullery, then she rested her floury hands on her distended stomach. 'I'm that sorry we disturbed you, ma'am, my lord. 'Tis just a warning. I was told to expect things like this, but it fair took me by surprise. I pray you will go back to the parlour, for I'm very well now.'

Selina did not move.

'Perhaps you should go and lie down,' she suggested.

'No, no, I shall know when the time comes—oh!' Mrs Jennock gasped as another spasm came on, but this time she merely pressed on her stomach and looked at Selina. 'They's getting stronger, but not too bad yet. Besides, I have the bread to make. Mildy can't do it, I need her to finish plucking the bird.'

'Then I will stay and help you,' said Selina, shrugging off her jacket and hanging it on a hook behind the door.

'Is there anything I can do?' asked Deveril, as she slipped an apron over her gown.

The outer door slammed, and Fremington could be heard, shouting for the landlord. Selina looked at Deveril.

'Yes there is, my lord. I pray you will keep Clifford out of the way!'

He nodded. 'I'll head him off and take him to the parlour.'

He went out, and as he closed the door, Selina turned to Mrs Jennock, saying cheerfully, 'Now, ma'am, I am a little out of practice with bread making. Remind me what we have to do here!'

Dusk was falling when Selina finally returned to the parlour, where she found the gentlemen at the table, playing cards.

'About time, madam,' grumbled Clifford, laying down his hand. 'It is nearly time for dinner. Where the devil have you been?'

She gave him a haughty stare. 'Ensuring that you will not go hungry.'

'How is Mrs Jennock?' Lord Deveril enquired, escorting her to a chair by the fire.

'Tired, but coping. She is adamant that my help is not required with the final preparations for our meal.'

Clifford scoffed. 'Of course it's not. What use could you be in a kitchen? You should leave these things to those who understand them.'

She bridled at his jeering tone, but Deveril caught and held her eyes, his own filled with laughter. She felt her anger evaporating and was obliged to look away before a giggle escaped her.

'I managed very well, under Mrs Jennock's instruction,' she said mildly. 'I trust you two gentlemen have been able to amuse yourselves?'

It was Deveril who replied. 'We have. As you see, Jennock found us a pack of cards.'

'Dog-eared and creased.'

He ignored Fremington's mutterings and raised his tankard.

'And he has also tapped a fresh cask of ale for us. Can I fetch you some refreshment, Miss Wynter? Madeira wine, perhaps, or lemonade? No need to disturb the servants,' he added, when she hesitated. 'Jennock has shown me where everything is stored and will keep a tally of what we use. He will not be out of pocket.'

'Thank you, that is kind, but I need nothing for the moment.' She turned to Clifford, 'Speaking of drink, how is Merton? Did you send him out to inspect the lanes?'

He threw her a withering look. 'Damned fellow spent the whole morning snoring in the hay so I was obliged to go myself, with Blackbourne here, once the snow had stopped. Drifts in the lane are too deep for the horses. Up to their withers.'

'I climbed one of the banks,' said Deveril, adding another log to the fire. 'The lane's blocked most of its length in both directions. Nothing moving. Didn't see another soul.'

'But it has not snowed since noon, has it?' put in Selina. 'And the wind has dropped.'

'True.' Deveril wanted to reassure her, but was anxious not to raise false hopes. He said, 'It is possible we shall see a rapid thaw tomorrow.'

'Let us hope so.'

She smiled, meeting his eyes quite naturally. There was no restraint in her manner and Deveril was sure she was about to invite him to sit with her by the fire. The danger now was that he very much wanted to do just that. To sit and talk with her like good friends. He waited, not sure if it would be wise to accept. He found the woman too damned alluring…

The decision was made for him by Fremington, who rapped sharply on the table.

'Come along, Blackbourne—it's your turn to play. We can't leave this game unfinished.'

'What? Oh, yes, of course. If you will excuse me, madam?' Selina could almost believe there was disappointment in Lord Deveril's eyes as he gave her a little bow before going back to the table. Something like a sigh escaped her as she settled herself more comfortably into the chair and she stared into the fire.

In another place, another time, they might have been friends.

Selina had instructed Jennock and Mildy not to hesitate to call her if help was needed, but despite her fears, dinner arrived on time, and was perfectly cooked, even if there were considerably fewer dishes on the table than the previous night.

'An excellent meal, in the circumstances,' declared Lord Deveril, when the covers had been removed.

Selina nodded. 'I admit I was concerned, with Master Jennock and Mildy having to do everything between them.'

'In small inns such as this it is not unusual to find a

landlord turning his hand to everything when things are quiet.'

Clifford sneered. 'Ha! I doubt you have visited many such places, my lord!'

'I have some experience of inns where there are not enough servants. In fact, I visited one such place quite recently.'

Selina sat up, suddenly on her guard, and regarded Deveril suspiciously. This must be a reference to the White Horse! Those brown eyes were full of mischief, but she saw something else in their dark depths. A gleam of understanding. The tension drained from her. He had no intention of disclosing that encounter to anyone else, but he was inviting her to share his amusement. And she *did* share it.

The revelation was like a lightning bolt. It stunned her and she stared down at her plate. It made no sense. This man was virtually a stranger and with a fearsome reputation as a notorious rake, but she trusted him so much more than Clifford Fremington, whom she had known all her life.

Clifford drained his glass and scowled. 'Where's that rascally landlord with the brandy?'

Unnerved by her thoughts, Selina jumped up from her chair.

'I will go and find out.'

Selina returned with a tray some ten minutes later, and Deveril immediately came across to take it from her.

'Has our landlady retired to her bed?' he asked her.

'Not quite, but she must do so, and soon,' she told him. 'I walked in to find the poor woman collapsed in a chair and her husband administering brandy and water. Mrs Jennock had insisted on remaining in the kitchen until dinner was finished, but now her pains are so frequent she can scarce draw breath.'

Deveril put the tray on the table and held a chair for her, but she shook her head.

'Thank you, but I cannot stay. I only came to bring you the brandy. I must go back and sit with Mrs Jennock while Mildy runs the warming pan over the sheets. I have already sent Jennock upstairs to light the fire. It will be cold as ice up there.'

'I hope he don't forget our rooms need warming, too,' muttered Fremington, reaching for the decanter.

Deveril's lip curled. The fellow had been drinking steadily all evening and was showing a complete unconcern for anyone but himself.

He also read the contempt in Selina's expression, but she replied with honeyed sweetness.

'I told Master Jennock he is not to worry about us tonight. You must tend your own fire, Clifford.'

Fremington's face darkened. 'I'm damned if I will! Merton must do it. But who is going to look after you, eh, Selina?' He picked up his glass and sauntered over to her. 'When you find ice in your water jug tonight, perhaps you will change your mind and beg to join me in my warm bed.'

Deveril tensed, ready to intervene, but Selina wasn't

listening to the fellow, in fact, she waved him away as if he was of no more consequence than a bothersome fly.

'Merton, of course!' she declared. 'Now why did I not think of that? He can look after the fires for all of us, and in exchange I will arrange a bed for him here, in the house! I must find Jennock and tell him to set Merton working immediately. Thank you, Clifford!'

She gave the bewildered Fremington a dazzling smile before hurrying away and Deveril was obliged to turn away to hide his amusement at this masterly treatment of a bully.

'Confound it, that is not what I meant at all!' exclaimed Fremington. 'Merton is *my* servant. I should have the ordering of him!'

'Oh, stop your whining, man!' Deveril hesitated, then said, 'But Miss Wynter thought it was an excellent idea, did she not? She even thanked you for it.'

'She did, didn't she?' said Fremington, much struck. 'Well, well, perhaps she is warming to me.'

'I shouldn't be at all surprised if that's the case,' Deveril agreed. 'Strange creatures, females. No understanding them at all.'

Grinning, he poured himself some brandy and carried it over to the fire, adding another log to the flames before sitting down in one of the armchairs.

It was not long before Selina reappeared and Deveril enquired after the landlady.

'Aye, is the child born yet?' asked Fremington, jumping up and offering her his chair beside the fire.

'It could be some hours yet,' she said, sitting down. 'It might even be the morning before the baby comes. Mrs Jennock is presently pacing the floor. Her husband and maid are with her, so she is well looked after. I have told them to fetch me if I am needed.'

'There is no need for you to put yourself out, Selina,' Fremington told her. 'These are country folk and will manage very well without you.'

'If we could fetch a doctor or midwife I would agree, but snowed in as we are, I am more than ready to help, if I can.'

He waved an airy hand. 'Pho, what use could you be?'

'More use than you,' she retorted. 'I have delivered more than one litter of puppies, and helped a cow to calve, which cannot be all that different, can it?'

She turned her head to look at Deveril, who quickly raised his hands. 'Pray acquit me, ma'am, I have no experience at all in that quarter.'

'No, of course not, but one must do something. Mildy is not yet sixteen, and although she is a sensible girl and a hard worker, she is little more than a child herself. There is no other female here, so I shall do what I can to help.'

'If you will take my advice, you will stay well out of it,' said Clifford. 'It's bad enough we are stuck in this place with so few servants, there is no need for you to play midwife as well! For heaven's sake, let be, Selina. The Jennocks will manage very well on their own.'

She made no response to that, but Deveril knew enough of the lady by now to guess that when the time came, she would be ready to assist in whatever way she could.

Clifford, however, took her silence for agreement and smiled.

'Now, Selina, allow me to pour you a glass of brandy.'

'What I should really like,' she said, 'is Madeira.'

Deveril saw Fremington glance towards the single decanter on the table as Selina went on.

'I noticed a carboy of Madeira wine in the cellar when I was exploring earlier,' she said. 'You will find clean decanters there, too.'

'Oh. Ah. Yes…well, I will go and fetch some.'

Fremington lounged away and, as the door closed behind him, Selina turned to Deveril, her face alight with puzzled amusement.

'Goodness, that is a surprise! What on earth has come over Clifford?'

'He is, er, trying to win your favour.'

'Dear me, is he?' She laughed. 'It will take more than a glass of Madeira to do that! Why on earth should he think it?'

'Because he told you that his coachman could make himself useful and you considered it a splendid notion.'

She looked blank for a moment, then she shook her head.

'But he only wanted Merton to wait upon *him*!' She drew in a breath and exclaimed wrathfully, 'First he runs off with me in the most outrageous manner and then thinks a few small gestures will make everything right. What a silly gudgeon!'

'Yes, he is, isn't he?' Deveril agreed affably.

'I have very little experience of the matter,' she went on, frowning, 'but I cannot believe abduction is the best way to go about seducing anyone. I should think one would be obliged to exert a great deal more charm, is that not so?'

She was looking at him quite innocently and Deveril waited for the moment when she realised just what she was implying. It did not take long. A fiery blush stained her cheeks and she put her hands to her mouth.

'Oh dear, I beg your pardon,' she said, between mortification and mirth. 'This is not a conversation we should be having is it, my lord?'

He grinned. 'I am very happy with it.'

She choked back a laugh, shaking her head, and Deveril waited, eager to know what she would say next.

He was to be disappointed. There was a hasty knock on the door and the maid came in.

'Beggin your pardon, Miss Wynter, but Master Jennock says please can you come to the bedchamber? The mistress is fretting fit to burst!'

'Oh dear!' Selina jumped to her feet. 'Yes, of course I will come with you, Mildy.'

She hesitated, glancing uncertainly at Deveril, who nodded.

'Go on now. And if there is anything I can do you must tell me. I will help you if I can.'

She had reached the door but stopped and looked back at him, an arrested look in her eyes.

'Thank you,' she said slowly, 'I believe you would.'

Deveril listened to the footsteps receding along the passage. Whatever else one might think of Selina Wynter, she was not a lady to sit by when anyone was in need. She had come very close to flirting with him tonight, but the maid's obvious distress had put to flight all such ideas.

He pushed himself to his feet and went over to refill his brandy glass. Perhaps that was for the best. He enjoyed a dalliance with those ladies in Society who knew the rules, but Selina Wynter was not of their number. For all her independence and her infuriating self-assurance, she was an innocent when it came to the art of coquetry, and he did not want to be the one to break her heart.

Deveril had only just resumed his seat when Fremington returned in triumph with a decanter half full of Madeira in his hand. His good humour vanished when Deveril informed him that Selina had gone off to tend to Mrs Jennock and he slumped down at the table to drown his sorrows in brandy. It was not long before he was asleep, his head on his arms and snoring gently.

A quiet settled over the parlour. Deveril knew the Jennocks' bedchamber was at the other end of the house and the creaks he could hear were nothing more than the old house settling. An hour went by. Deveril tended the fire and trimmed the lamps. At one point he went off to the cellar to refill the brandy decanter. When he returned, he found Fremington was awake and looking owlishly around the room.

'What time is it?'

Deveril glanced at the clock on the mantelshelf. 'Just past midnight.'

'Is that all? Damme, if feels later!' He pushed himself to his feet. 'It's been a devilish long day. I'm going to my room. What about you, Blackbourne? You waiting for Selina to return? Thinking you might try your luck with her, is that it?'

He scowled suspiciously at Deveril, who waved him away.

'Oh, go to bed, man! Miss Wynter has more important things on her mind than either of us tonight.'

He stood aside and watched the other man shamble unsteadily out of the parlour, then he resumed his place by the fire and settled down to keep a solitary vigil.

It was some time later when he heard a step in the

passage and Jennock came in, his usually merry face creased with worry.

'How goes it?' asked Deveril.

'Terrible bad, my lord.' The man shook his head. 'Poor old besom. I never seen her like this before. She's thrown me out of the bedchamber! Says she can't abide the sight of me and a lot more besides. I ain't to go back 'til I'm summoned.'

The man was shifting miserably from foot to foot and Deveril waved him to the empty chair.

'Come and sit down. What you need is brandy,' he said, going over to the table.

'Ah, no, sir, wouldn't be proper. I just came in to ask if you needed anything.'

'I do. Company!' He filled a glass and held it out. 'Come, man, sit by the fire and drink with me.'

With a sigh the landlord took the glass and sat down.

'It wouldn't be such a worry, my lord, if the wife's mother could have been here to help her through this. Or even the farmer's wife. But what with the snow...'

'A worrying time for you,' murmured Deveril.

'Aye. It's our first, you see.' He gave a gusty sigh. 'I shouldn't have married her, some'd say. Her being a good ten years younger than me. But she's the love of my life, my lord. There's never been anyone else. I knew it the moment I first clapped eyes on 'er.'

'You were fortunate to meet such a woman.'

'Aye, my lord, that I was. Don't you be thinking I

don't know how lucky I was to find her. She keeps house exceeding well. She is a good cook, too, and has a good head on her shoulders. She could run the Rising Sun as well as I, if she needed to. But this.' He looked up towards the ceiling. 'I knows 'tis a dangerous time, giving birth, and I don't want to lose her.'

Deveril merely nodded. There was nothing he could say or do to reassure the man and they sat with only the crackling of the logs to break the silence. Another hour passed and the landlord pushed himself out of his chair.

'I can't stand this waiting. What is happening up there?'

'Be assured if anything had gone wrong they would have come down to tell us,' said Deveril, trying to sound confident.

The landlord heaved another gusty sigh and returned to his seat. Deveril reached across and gripped his knee.

'Patience, man, I believe these things do take a long time.'

'Aye, so I've heard,' muttered Jennock. He looked up and said simply, 'She's everything to me, my lord. She is my world.'

It was at that moment that the door opened and both men jumped to their feet. Selina came in with what looked like a small bundle of shawls in her arms.

'All is well, Master Jennock,' she said, giving the landlord a dazzling smile. 'Your wife is sleeping now and Mildy is sitting with her while I bring your daughter down to meet you.'

Deveril watched the landlord slowly cross the room and look at the tiny figure she was holding. The candlelight shone on the little group, and his gaze moved to Selina.

She had removed her fichu and her lace cuffs, and some of her curls had escaped the pins to hang in glossy dark ringlets against the creamy skin of her neck as she smiled down at the baby in her arms.

A band of iron tightened around his chest, making it difficult to breathe. How beautiful she looked. Positively radiant. She held the baby as if it was the most precious thing in the world. She was soft, gentle. Not a harridan at all. An angel.

At that moment she looked across at him, meeting his eyes with a warm look that sent his thoughts spinning wildly towards a future he had never considered before. A life with children, and a wife. A soulmate.

He was so shaken by the unfamiliar feelings that he couldn't even smile. He needed action, to be doing something. To hide his confusion, he busied himself with the fire.

Selina cradled the baby girl in her arms while Jennock stared at his daughter. The man was clearly overwhelmed, murmuring 'my little maid' over and over in a tone of reverential wonder.

But not so Lord Deveril, she thought, her happiness dimming a little. She had seen how quickly he turned away.

What else had she expected? Bachelors had no interest in the birth of a baby. In Deveril's world children were little more than property, the girls married off to the family's advantage, boys raised to carry on the family name.

Was she being unfair, she wondered, watching as he stabbed at the logs smouldering in the hearth. Perhaps he did care. Mayhap he was thinking of what might have been, if his beloved fiancée had lived. He must have loved her very much indeed, to still feel it so deeply.

'Thank 'ee, ma'am, for bringing the little mite down for me to see,' muttered the landlord, wiping his eyes with a large handkerchief. 'I shall rest easier for that.'

Selina nodded. 'I shall take her back to her mother now.'

Deveril, she noticed was still tending the fire and did not look up. She turned and carried the baby back upstairs, aware of a heaviness in her step. A tiredness she had not noticed before.

Chapter Fifteen

Deveril rose early the next morning, but the ice on the window pane dashed any hopes of a thaw. Clearing a small patch, he could see that more snow had fallen during the night. Not much, but sufficient to prevent them leaving the inn that day.

He dressed quickly and went downstairs. Hearing voices in the kitchen he went in to find Selina and the maid working by the range. Selina turned as he came in, but he thought her smile a little strained.

'Good morning, my lord. What may we serve you?'

'If there is any coffee in that pot beside you, I should be glad to take a cup, if I may?'

'But of course. Pray sit down and Mildy will pour it for you. I hope you do not mind breaking your fast here in the kitchen, but there is no fire in the parlour yet. Merton has promised to see to it later, but he and Master Jennock are at present sawing up more wood ready for splitting.'

'Then I am more than happy to stay here and eat in comfort.'

She relaxed a little at his easy response and went on in a more friendly tone.

'As you see, we have plenty of ham and I am about to prepare some eggs. We have bread rolls warming in the oven and there is also a game pie, plus butter and preserves. There is also some pound cake left, if you would like that.'

He was impressed and said so. 'Have you both been up all night?'

'Not quite. We have been taking it in turns to sit with Mrs Jennock and the baby, and thankfully Mildy is adept at making bread, else you would have had to make do with the remains of yesterday's loaf.'

'Then I am very grateful to you, Mildy.'

He smiled at the maid, who blushed hotly before hurrying out of the room, muttering that she needed to collect more eggs. He sipped his coffee and watched Selina as she carried the various dishes to the table.

'You appear to have had a busy night,' he remarked. 'Did you get any sleep at all?'

'Sufficient,' she replied, removing the rolls from the oven.

'But without a chaperone in your room.'

She was carefully placing the hot rolls into a basket, which she carried to the table before replying.

She said, 'I took the precaution of moving the washstand across the door before I lay down to sleep. It would not keep out an intruder, but it would have woken me if anyone tried to enter. I shall do the same tonight, if necessary.'

He said lightly, 'I shall consider myself warned off.'

Her blue eyes rested on him for a moment and he knew from the way she looked at him that he was not the object of her concern.

'Yes do,' she returned cheerfully. 'Although I do not believe Mrs Jennock will require anyone keeping watch tonight. She and the baby are doing very well.'

'I am very glad to hear that.' He glanced up as he helped himself to a bread roll and saw she was regarding him, a tiny crease in her brow. 'What, are you surprised I should be concerned for our landlady and her child?'

'No, no of course not.' She turned away to busy herself at the range again. 'If you would like ham then pray help yourself. You will find a carving knife on the table.'

Selina pottered around the kitchen and tried not to think of the man sitting at the table behind her. It was all too easy to respond to his teasing and joke with him. She had to keep reminding herself that he had made her the object of a wicked wager and yet she could not dislike him. On the contrary, she knew she was in danger of liking him too much!

She had just refilled the coffee pot when Clifford walked in, bleary-eyed after his excessive libations of the previous evening. When Selina explained why he must eat his breakfast in the kitchen his face darkened.

'Mrs Jennock and her baby must have a fire day and night, and with so many other rooms to keep warm we have used a great many logs,' she informed him as she added a dish of eggs to the table. 'What we save by not lighting the parlour fire in the mornings means there will be wood for your bedroom fire this evening.'

'So we must all live like peasants,' Clifford muttered as he filled his plate. 'Damme but things have come to a pretty pass!'

She put her hands on her hips and glared at him.

'Jennock and your coachman are even now sawing up more logs, but they will be too thick for burning until they have been split. Perhaps instead of complaining, Clifford, you should consider how you might assist them.'

'It ain't my place to chop logs!'

'La, I quite forgot, sir. You are *gentleman*,' she scoffed at him. 'You would never sully your hands with such a menial task, even for your own comfort!'

The maid came back in at that moment, hesitating in the doorway at the sound of the angry voices. Selina took a calming breath and picked up one of the trays resting on the far end of the table.

'Mildy, my dear, if you can bring the second tray and follow me, I have prepared a breakfast for Mrs Jennock. Mr Fremington can help himself to coffee if he wants it.' She gave him a scathing look. 'I shall leave you to carve yourself some ham, too. I trust you will know how to do that!'

Deveril listened to this interchange, thankful he was not on the receiving end of the lady's tongue-lashing. Not that Fremington didn't deserve it, damn him. The man was a boor and a bully, selfish to a fault. He would dearly like to pick an argument with the fellow and thrash him soundly, but in their present circumstances that would only make life more uncomfortable for everyone, especially Selina.

Deveril waited until she and the maid had gone, then he looked up from his plate.

'You know, Fremington, that's not a bad notion. We should go and help.'

'You are being quite ridiculous!'

'Dear me.' Deveril raised his brows. 'Am I to understand you cannot wield an axe?'

'Well, of course I can! Damme, I ain't useless.' His lip curled a little and he added, 'I doubt that you, the son of the Marquess of Revesby, was ever required to split logs.'

'My father never expressed a wish that I should learn such a skill, but I have of course tried my hand at it,' drawled Deveril. He glanced at Fremington. 'Perhaps we should make a wager. See which of us is best at it.'

'Out of the question!'

'No, you are right. Miss Wynter would not approve

of that,' mused Deveril. He went on, slowly, 'However I believe she would approve of a full woodbin. Very much.'

He walked over to refill his coffee cup from the pot on the hotplate, watching Fremington from the corner of his eye. The man was chewing on a mouthful of ham, and he could almost see him thinking the matter through.

'Aye, perhaps she would,' said Fremington slowly. 'After all, she's stepped into the landlady's shoes, and women like nothing better than to keep a good house, do they?'

'Very true,' Deveril agreed. 'And that includes keeping the fires burning.'

When Selina came downstairs some time later, she was surprised to find only the landlord in the kitchen, sitting with his feet stretched out towards the range and smoking his pipe. When he saw her he began to rise, but she quickly waved him back down.

'Have Lord Deveril and Mr Fremington retired to the parlour?' she asked him.

'Nay, ma'am, there ain't no fire in there yet.'

'To their rooms, then?'

'Not there neither.' He sucked on his pipe for a moment. 'They's gone out to the woodshed.'

'The woodshed?'

'That's right.' He nodded, his eyes twinkling merrily. 'Splitting logs.'

'What!'

He removed his pipe from his mouth and gently tapped it out into the fire.

'Got it into their 'eads to see who could chop the most logs,' he said, casting a grin in her direction. 'I reckon there's enough wood out there to keep 'em busy all day, if they wants it.'

'Truly?' Selina shook her head, then laughed. 'I must see this for myself!' she exclaimed, taking a shawl from the hook on the door and hurrying off.

The sun was shining, but it was still bitterly cold outside. There was a small garden at the back of the inn, but the path to the outbuildings had been cleared of snow and Selina followed it towards a large timber barn. As she drew nearer, she could hear the thud of an axe on wood and she hurried around the building. On the far side the big doors were propped open and inside, stripped to their shirts and breeches, were Lord Deveril and the Honourable Clifford Fremington.

Each was using one of the larger pieces of tree trunk as a makeshift chopping block upon which they were splitting the logs and tossing them into large woodbins beside them. They were both far too intent upon their work to notice her approach.

Merton, the coachman, was sitting on a barrel with a watch in his hand and she walked up to stand beside him.

'No, no, don't get up,' she murmured. 'What on earth has come over them?'

'The master bet his lordship that he could chop the most wood in an hour. They've been at it for almost that now and there's not much between 'em.'

They did indeed appear to be evenly matched. Each had filled two large wooden bins and now their split logs were spilling out onto the floor.

Hearing voices, both men glanced across, but although Deveril paused long enough to nod in her direction, Clifford kept going. Fascinated, Selina pulled her shawl about her and watched them.

It was difficult not to compare the two men. Clifford's face was red with exertion, his movements erratic and the axe often missed its mark. Lord Deveril, however, worked steadily, swinging the axe in one smooth, fluid movement and splitting the log cleanly every time. His raven-black hair had fallen forward over his brow, but despite this he looked the least flustered. He would surely be the winner today.

He was a sportsman, she thought, studying his broad chest and flat stomach before allowing her eyes to roam over the powerful thighs outlined by the buckskin breeches. With his sleeves rolled up above the elbow, she could see the hard muscle of his arms as he swung the axe again and again with a smooth, rhythmic movement that showed no signs of slowing.

Something stirred in Selina. His shirt was open at the neck and she could see the dark shadow of hair on his chest. She imagined resting her hand against it, sliding her palm across his skin and feeling those curling black hairs beneath her fingers. She had never done such a thing: would those curls be silky soft or crisp to the touch? Having gone thus far, she now imagined his lithe, athletic body naked and pressed against hers…

Selina's throat dried and she quickly stifled the thought, but not before her insides had liquified. Resolutely she dragged her mind back to the competition. With two full woodbins apiece, the winner would have to be decided by the extra logs each man had cut.

It was only when she looked at the logs on the floor that she noticed Deveril's heap was noticeably smaller than that of his opponent.

So much for your judgement, Selina Wynter!

'That's it, sirs, time is up, if you please!'

Merton's voice brought the proceedings to a halt and put an end to Selina's musings. The two men put down their axes and threw the last of the logs onto their respective piles.

Clifford wiped his sleeve across his brow and addressed his coachman.

'Well, Merton, you are to be the judge, but I believe I have won the day.'

'It certainly looks that way, sir.'

'I knew it!' He turned to Deveril, saying gleefully, 'That's a pony you owe me, my lord!'

'I do indeed, Fremington,' agreed his lordship, raking his hair back off his face. 'You are undoubtedly the victor. I shall have to give you a note of hand until we get out of here, but there are enough witnesses here, you may be sure you will be paid.'

'I think 'tis me that's the winner today, sirs,' said Jennock, appearing in the doorway. 'You've saved me a deal of time and work. I thank 'ee for it and I've brought ye some cyder to slake yer thirst.'

He held out two full tankards which both men accepted gratefully. Clifford swaggered over to Selina.

'What do you think of my victory?' he asked her. 'Impressive, don't you think?'

She was not listening. Her eyes on Deveril, who was chatting with the landlord. As if aware of her glance he looked across and raised his tankard to her. Then he smiled and she felt suddenly weak, as if her very bones were turning to water.

'Well, madam—' Clifford stepped in front of her, blocking her view, determined to have her attention '—ain't you going to congratulate me? Selina!'

'What?' She looked at him blankly for a moment. 'Of course. Very well done, Clifford. Now if you will all excuse me, I had best get back and help Mildy in the kitchen. I am sure you will both need something to eat after all your exertions.'

There was plenty to keep Selina occupied for the next few hours. She helped Mildy prepare a light repast for the men, took a bowl of soup upstairs for Mrs Jennock and sat with her while she drank it before going back to the kitchens to discuss dinner arrangements with the maid. Then, learning that a fire was now burning in the parlour, she was glad of the excuse to sit down in there with the landlady's sewing box and do some mending.

Selina picked up a petticoat with a torn flounce. She felt much more at ease now, and able to look back on the morning's events with amusement. What a ninny she was, to behave like a giddy schoolgirl over Lord Deveril. Watching him swing the axe she had become entranced by his athletic figure and muscled body. She was a fool to daydream over such a man. He was handsome and charming, to be sure, but he could have no interest in a provincial miss like herself. As long as she remembered that he posed no danger to her, she decided.

He was, however, much better company than Clifford, so when Lord Deveril walked into the parlour a short while later, she was very pleased to see him. She looked up from the torn shirt she was mending and he stopped in the doorway.

'Miss Wynter. I beg your pardon, I did not know you were in here.'

'No, how could you?' she said pleasantly. 'Do come in, my lord. I would be glad of a little company while I work.'

'I should leave the door open. For propriety.'

'And let all the heat escape? I'd rather you did not.'

'You will risk damaging your reputation?' he asked, shutting the door.

She shrugged. 'I have no idea how my reputation will fare after this little adventure, but I think it will not be seriously compromised if you sit in the same room with me.' She glanced towards the sewing basket beside her on the window seat. 'I have sufficient needles, pins and scissors here to protect me from any amorous advances.'

'But no broom,' he murmured.

'No.' She met his eyes briefly. 'No broom.'

Deveril laughed and sat down beside the fire, from where he might watch her as she bent her head over her sewing.

'Do you never stop working?' he asked, after they had been silent for some time.

She chuckled. 'This is not really *work*. A little mending to help Mrs Jennock. I like to keep busy.'

He frowned. 'This is a damnable position for you.'

'It cannot be helped.' Her busy fingers stopped, the needle half in the material. She said, without looking up, 'I did not elope, if that is what you think.'

'That was never my opinion.'

She began plying her needle again. 'I have never thanked you for following Clifford's carriage out of Torrisford. That was what you were doing, was it not? I cannot think why you would otherwise have arrived at this place.'

'You are right. I had earlier seen him drive off at

speed, but not towards Fremington Court. I thought he might be up to mischief.'

'He was, and I am very glad you followed us. You were the last person I expected to see.'

She was keeping her head down but Deveril thought he could see a faint blush upon her cheek. He said, 'You believed I had some plan of my own regarding you.'

'Well, yes. Which is why I am at a loss over your behaviour today.'

'My behaviour?'

She finished her stitching and snipped the thread before fixing him with a steely look.

'I am not fooled by that tone of innocence, my lord. You lost to Clifford deliberately.'

'Whatever makes you think that?' he asked her, stretching his legs towards the hearth.

'I was watching you both.' She picked up another item for mending, this time a chemise with a broken seam. 'I believe you could have beaten him if you had wished to.'

'Such faith in me, Miss Wynter. I am honoured.'

Deveril expected her to respond in kind to his teasing, but she said nothing. She was concentrating on setting her stitches, a faint crease in her brow, and he waited. At length she gave a little tut of exasperation.

'You realise that Clifford will be quite unbearable now! Why on earth would you make a bet with him if you intended to lose?'

'For the pleasure of seeing him work for his supper. And your being there spurred him on, you know.' She looked at him blankly and he added, 'Fremington wants your good opinion.'

'Impossible! I shall never forgive him for abducting me. Just as I shall never forgive you, my lord, for your disgraceful wager!'

'It is merely five-and-twenty pounds, and in a good cause. We now have enough fuel for several days. What is the harm in that?'

'I do not mean this one!' she said, her cheeks very pink. 'I mean the bet you made with Lord Graddon and his friends. C-concerning myself.'

His brows snapped together. 'I made no wager with them.'

'No? I have it on very good authority that you have done so. In fact, I know you made a wager of five hundred pounds with *each one of them* that you would be the first man to, to seduce me!'

Deveril sat up very straight. He said, slowly, 'You are mistaken, madam. There is no such wager.'

It was then that he remembered the evening they had returned from Tawton and taken shelter from the rain in an inn. The Fremingtons had come in and there had been some drunken banter, some teasing about his youthful follies. Surely no one present that night would repeat any of that to a lady?

'Where did you learn about this?'

She shook her head. 'I cannot tell you. It was relayed to me in confidence.'

'And do you really think I would serve you such a trick?' he demanded.

'Yes, I do!' she went on, her voice dripping with scorn. 'I understand it is not the first time you have made such a wager concerning a lady!'

'I admit I did it once, and not recently. It was very wrong of me.' He shook his head. 'Believe me, madam, there is a great deal in my past life that I am not proud of, but nothing concerning you.'

'And you expect me to believe that?'

'Yes, I do.'

Deveril stopped. His first thought was that Clifford Fremington was guilty of spreading the lie, but now he recalled Lord Fremington's overloud remarks to him in the hall of Reigney Abbey. Remarks that Selina was sure to have overheard. Was the man as big a scoundrel as his son?

He said steadily, 'Whatever you have heard is a fabrication. Dreamed up by someone for their own advantage.'

'Hah! What advantage could there be...'

Her words trailed away and Deveril saw her countenance change, her eyes widening with a mixture of shock, anger and disbelief. He nodded.

'Aye, madam. My fellow guests at Graddon Hall talked quite freely before Lord Fremington and his son when we were all sheltering from the rain one night.

They did speak of an old wager, something that happened years ago, but nothing more than that.'

'You deny my name was mentioned?'

He hesitated. 'No, I cannot deny it. Your name came up in conversation, but Clifford Fremington gave everyone to understand that you and he were betrothed.'

Her eyes flashed at that. 'How dare he! And you believed him?'

'Why not?' He shrugged. 'I admit, once I knew you better, I found it difficult to believe you could be happy with such a dolt. And now I know he is not only a dolt but a liar, too.'

She acknowledged that with a little nod and silently went back to her stitching. The colour had drained from her cheeks and Deveril wondered what grim thoughts were eating away at her.

'What is it—will you not tell me?' he asked, when he could bear it no longer.

Her busy fingers stilled. She said, 'I believe the whole family are complicit in this. Lord Fremington carried the story to Sir Alfred Kenton, who is the local magistrate, knowing full well that he would not intervene in any private wager. The Kentons are close friends of my father, and of me. His lordship must have known it was likely—nay, almost certain—that they would immediately put me on my guard against you.'

'Thus ensuring I did not get in the way of young Fremington's courtship.'

'Clifford put an end to that himself with his attempt to abduct me.' She gave a small huff of exasperation. 'I do not doubt his lordship was behind that, too, since it was he who obtained the special licence. Clifford planned to keep me locked away in some remote lodge until I agreed to marry him.'

'Damme but the fellow deserves to be called to account!'

'A duel, you mean?' She gave him a look of disdain. 'Men think that is the only way to settle their differences! No.' She shook her head. 'I abhor violence and have no wish to be the cause of it.'

'Even though Fremington served you such a trick?'

'He did not succeed, thanks to you.' Her look softened. 'You have proved to be a good friend, Lord Deveril.'

A friend! That was all she wanted of him, while he—

Deveril pushed away the ideas taking root in his mind. He was loath to admit anything, other than that he was no longer sure what he wanted.

'Reigney Abbey marches with Fremington's land,' she went on. 'His lordship is eager to add it to his estates, but I cannot understand why he thinks Clifford and I would ever marry. You see, I can remember, when I was still in the schoolroom, Lady Fremington called upon Mama and suggested a match between us. Later, I overheard Mama laughing with Papa at the idea of it. She was quite certain, even then, that our temperaments were so different that we should never be happy. I can quite clearly remember her saying that, unless she was sure it was a love match, upon no account would she countenance such a union.'

'Yet many neighbours do welcome such a match between their children. Mine included.'

'And I understand that in many cases the marriage is very successful,' she replied, smiling slightly.

Selina returned to her sewing, bending her head again over the linen, and after a moment she decided to risk asking a question that had been in her mind for some time.

'What was she like, your fiancée?' She glanced up and said hastily, 'I beg your pardon, I should not have— That is, it is not my business. If it is too painful, then please, let us talk of something else!'

To her relief he did not look offended.

'Belinda Roding was quite beautiful,' he told her. 'Guinea gold hair and soft grey eyes. She had all the accomplishments required of a lady, too. She excelled at painting and dancing, she also sang and played the pianoforte. Such a sweet obedient creature, everyone loved her. She had any number of admirers but never gave her parents a moment's unease.'

He fell silent, a brooding look upon his face, and Selina looked down at her dry, rough hands, imagining the beautiful Miss Roding. She had been everything Selina was not. A quiet, ladylike creature who shone in the salon, not one who spent her days bargaining with merchants or traders and who had ruined her skin riding out in all weathers and working in kitchens.

At length Deveril stirred, shaking off whatever unpleasant memories had besieged him, and went on.

'We had known each other forever. It was always understood we would marry, when the time came. Sadly, she died just months before the wedding.'

'I am very sorry.'

He acknowledged that with a slight nod. 'Would I have made her a good husband? I doubt it. My father swore I was born to be hanged, so perhaps it is best that we never married.' The brooding look disappeared and he said lightly, 'It is clear to me that I was born to be a bachelor.'

She flinched inwardly. He could not have been plainer that he had no interest in her.

'No more do I intend to marry anyone,' she told him. 'Papa's health is not good. He cannot manage the business of the estate and I have taken charge of everything. Reigney is my life now. It provides me with an occupation, which suits me very well.'

'But that might change. You might meet someone.'

'Any suitor would have to agree to live at the Abbey, since I cannot leave Papa there alone.'

'I am sure there are many men who would be prepared to marry you on those terms.'

'But would I be prepared to marry *them*? I do not think so.' She went on, a little defiantly, 'I am past the age of falling in love and it is my belief that a true, lasting love is exceedingly rare. I can think of only two couples of my acquaintance where there is what Shakespeare describes as a marriage of true minds.'

'Your own parents, perhaps?'

'Yes. They were devoted to each other and I had a very happy childhood, despite Papa never enjoying good health. Mama ran the estate until she died, and then, thankfully, I was of an age then to take over. I am content to spend my life looking after Papa and the Abbey. That will be enough for me. I have seen enough unhappy wives to convince me I shall do better alone.'

Deveril shrugged. 'I cannot blame you for that. My own parents' marriage is very far from the ideal. They can never be in the same room for more than an hour before they are arguing. It is why I so rarely visit Revesby. It was never a home for me, merely a place I was obliged to live, and where I did my best to keep out of everyone's way.'

'Poor boy!'

Selina's utterance took him by surprise. He felt a flush of discomfiture mounting his cheeks.

He said coldly, 'I was not looking for sympathy, madam.'

'You have it anyway,' she said cheerfully. 'I have an abundance of sympathy for those who have never known the felicity of a loving family. I was very fortunate, I think.'

'You were. Extremely so.'

His tone was uncharacteristically bitter and Selina immediately wanted to cheer him.

'But there is no reason why you should not find happiness, my lord. You might yet have a family of your own.'

'I have already told you that will never happen!'

'You do not know that.' She took breath. 'Forgive me, it is not my place to say so, but just because you suffered a—a tragedy when you were younger does not mean you cannot fall in love again.'

She paused, waiting for an angry response, a demand that she should not meddle in what did concern her. When he did not speak, she was emboldened to continue.

'You are not confined, as I am, to a small town like Torrisford. You have the whole of Society in which to look for a bride who can make you happy. The ladies cannot all be fortune-hunting harpies!'

To her relief he laughed at that.

'You said yourself, ma'am, happiness in marriage is rare. Being a younger son and with a fortune of my own, I have no need to wed. I intend to remain a bachelor.'

'What, when ladies are tripping over themselves to win your regard?' she teased him.

He acknowledged this sally with a grin, but shook his head. 'My wealth means women only want to marry me for my fortune. They never see the man.'

Which was a great pity, Selina decided. Beneath his

insouciance there was a kind, thoughtful individual, and the more time she spent with Lord Deveril the more she liked him.

Which was a very unsettling thought.

'I had best put this away,' she said, gathering up her mending and the sewing basket. 'Mildy will soon be requiring my help to prepare dinner.'

Chapter Sixteen

'Good morning, Miss Wynter.'

Selina was surprised to find Deveril alone in the kitchen when she went downstairs the next morning.

'Good morning, my lord.' He had removed his coat, rolled up the billowing sleeves of his shirt and was standing in front of the range. She regarded him with a quizzical frown. 'What are you doing?'

When he turned, she saw that he had donned an apron to protect his waistcoat and breeches from the spitting fat in the pan that rested on the fire.

'Cooking my breakfast. Yours too, if you will join me.'

'Where is everyone else?' she asked him.

'Fremington—of course!—has not yet arisen, but Jennock and the maid have broken their fast. Jennock is gone out with Merton to try if they can reach the next farm and Mildy has taken a dish of porridge up to her mistress. She had already baked the bread and I thought she would enjoy a little time helping with the baby.' He grinned. 'She was reluctant to go, but I assured her I was quite capable of preparing my own breakfast. Now, what do you say, would you like to join me? There is more porridge here, or I could add something extra to the pan for you?'

The cooked bacon smelled delicious and she did not hesitate.

'I will have some of the bacon and an egg, if I may. Is there anything I can do to help?'

'You do more than enough,' he told her. 'Such as arranging for our shirts to be laundered and persuading Fremington to let me have one of his in the meantime.'

'That was reward for your efforts in providing so much firewood,' she told him. 'And besides, there was washing to be done for Mrs Jennock, too! Now what can I do to help?'

'You may pour yourself some coffee and fill up my cup, if you would.'

Selina collected a cup and moved across to collect the coffee pot from the warming plate beside the fire. Deveril was finishing the eggs and, aware of the dangers of working near fire and hot pans, she put one hand on his back before she reached past him.

She had put out her hand without thinking, but the feel of that hard, solid back beneath the fine linen was like an electric shock. She froze, suddenly aware of how intimate it was to be standing there. So close she could slide her arms around his broad chest and hug him.

She forced the thought from her mind, but could not drag her eyes from his bare, muscled forearm with the shadow of fine dark hairs and the strong fingers gripping the pan. Her heart was pounding so fast she felt dizzy, unsteady, and was obliged to breathe deep and gather her wits before she could pick up the coffee pot and back away.

Making sure her hands did not shake, Selina filled both coffee cups and returned the pot to the warming plate. This time she kept to one side, well away from Deveril's large masculine figure. Glancing up at his face, she did not know whether she was most relieved or disappointed that he was still busy cooking the food, unaware of the earth-shattering moment she had just endured.

Selina continued to potter about the kitchen, slicing and buttering the bread, clearing space at the table and fetching cutlery and plates. Once her pulse had returned to normal and she had regained her composure she began to enjoy herself. It felt very companionable to be working together like this.

But these were exceptional times and this friendly companionship could not last. Once the snow was gone they would return to their own worlds.

Do not be foolish enough to think he could ever think you truly attractive, said that annoying voice of reason in her head. Glancing down at her red and work-roughened hands, Selina had to agree. She would be no more appealing to such a man than a scullery maid.

***

Deveril shared the bacon and eggs between the plates and sat down opposite Selina. He was relieved he had not spoiled the food. It had been the devil of a job to concentrate on what he was doing knowing she was in the room. And when she had touched his back, it had taken all his self-control not to drop that pan and drag her into his arms.

They said very little during their meal, but finally Selina pushed her plate away and smiled at him across the table.

'That was excellent, my lord. I am impressed.'

Relieved, he grinned at her. 'You are not the only one who spent time in the kitchen as a child, madam.'

'Clearly not.' She put her elbows on the table and rested her chin on her hands, regarding him from eyes shining like sapphires in the morning light. 'Tell me how it comes about that the son of a marquess can cook as well as wield an axe.'

'My parents never spent much time at Revesby. Nor did my brother, who is several years my senior. When I was not at school or visiting friends I returned to the stately pile, supposedly to live under the guidance of our old nurse, who by that time had developed more of a fondness for wine than looking after a boy too old for the nursery. I was therefore left very much to my own devices and spent a deal of time out of doors with the gamekeepers and the woodcutter.'

'That explains why you are so proficient at splitting logs, my lord, but what of the cooking?'

'I often sought warmth and company in the kitchen.'

'And your cook did not object? From my experience they are tyrants in their own domain.'

'I charmed her into allowing me to stay.'

She laughed at that. 'Of course you did!'

'I used to watch her and even, occasionally, I was allowed to help.' He grinned. 'It does no harm to know how to feed oneself.'

He was surprised to see her suddenly look serious.

'Perhaps, sir, but they are hardly skills that would equip a younger son to make his way in the world.'

He shrugged. 'What little education I received at school was considered sufficient for one of noble birth. I could read and write, add a column of figures. What more is required of a nobleman?'

'A great deal,' she retorted.

His lip curled in a sneer of self-deprecation. 'My parents knew I would inherit my godfather's fortune, why would I need to know anything more than how to spend it?'

It was clear the lady was not amused. She pressed her lips together, as if to prevent a further angry outburst, and he laughed.

'Your indignation on my behalf is unnecessary, ma'am,' he said, his bitterness melting away. 'I may not have had a formal education, but I am not quite a savage. Fortunately I enjoy reading, a trait I inherited from my grandfather. He left the library very well stocked and I devoured all manner of books on mathematics, medicine, astronomy and natural philosophy, plus works by Tobias Smollett and Mr Fielding; adventurous tales that were designed to appeal to a young man. Once I came to London there were debating clubs, philosophical societies and of course the Royal Society lectures all available to me. I believe I can now acquit myself well enough in any company, Miss Wynter.'

She flushed. 'Yes, of course. I did not mean to imply...'

He cut her off. 'You think me a wastrel, do you not, Miss Wynter? A rakehell whose sole intent is his own pleasure.'

'And are you not?' she fired back at him. 'Oh, you can be very charming, but everything I have heard indicates you are not a man to be trusted.'

'Ha!—"*at every word a reputation dies*"—is that it?'

She sat up, an arrested expression on her face.

'That is Pope, is it not? *The Rape of the Lock*.' Mischief twinkled in her eyes as she said, 'I will acknowledge you are well-read, my lord, but does that make you any more trustworthy?'

Deveril realised that her anger had quite vanished and she was positively enjoying this exchange. As was he!

He grinned at her. 'Not in the least, but I am far more entertaining than Fremington.'

She laughed, that joyous, throaty sound that made his spirits rise. '*That* I cannot deny.'

Her voice was full of merriment, just as it had been at that very first meeting when she had held him off with the broom. The air crackled, something hot and fierce rushed through Deveril and he felt his world tilt.

At that moment the door opened. He looked up to see Fremington glaring at him from the doorway, his hair tousled and looking as if he had dressed in a rush.

'Good morning, Clifford.'

Fremington ignored Selina's cheerful greeting and snarled at Deveril.

'Trying to steal a march on me, are you, Blackbourne?' he demanded. 'How dare you sneak down before me. You should not be alone with her!'

'Oh, do pray be sensible, Clifford,' snapped Selina. 'Did you think to find him making love to me here, in the kitchen?'

The very thought of that sent a wave of desire crashing through Deveril. He remembered the touch of her hand on his back. What if he had turned then and dragged her into his arms? He might have kissed her, backed her to the edge of this very table and lifted her up...

He glanced up to find Selina staring at him, her eyes dark as a moonlit sky. He had the sudden conviction that she knew exactly what he was thinking, but the look was gone in an instant, and it was only the faint heightened colour in her cheeks that told Deveril he had not dreamed the whole. The next moment she was informing Clifford in the most matter-of-fact way that he had missed breakfast.

'The devil I have!' exclaimed Clifford, glaring down at their empty plates.

'It is your own fault for not coming downstairs in good time,' she replied.

'What the devil am I supposed to do now?'

'There is plenty more bacon, and eggs, too,' said Deveril, 'but you will have to cook them yourself.'

He thought for a moment Fremington was going to explode. His face darkened, but before he could say anything more the maid came into the room. She was carrying a tray laden with dishes and bobbed a very slight curtsy towards the gentlemen before addressing herself to Selina.

'The mistress and baby are resting now, ma'am, and she sent me downstairs to get on with my work.'

'And in good time,' barked Fremington. 'I need something to eat!'

Selina took the tray from the girl and gave her a reassuring smile.

'Perhaps your first job should be to prepare breakfast for Mr Fremington, Mildy,' she suggested.

'Very well, ma'am, but what about lighting the fire in the parlour?'

'I can do that,' offered Deveril, getting up.

He was rewarded with a quick smile from Selina before she turned away. The warmth he had seen in her eyes set his heart pounding again. He desperately wanted to go over and drag her into his arms, there and then, and devil take the consequences. Instead, he left the room, shutting the door carefully behind him and standing for a moment, his eyes closed.

He could not recall ever feeling like this about any woman. Just a look, a smile was enough to set him on fire. He wanted to take her to his bed, to make her eyes darken with desire, but it was so much more than that. He wanted to carry her off and keep her safe, shower her with every luxury. To make her happy.

To make her his wife.

The admission shocked Deveril to the core. He knew there was no such thing as happy ever after. That existed only in fairy tales, or for heroes. In his world, love only ended in pain and disillusion. The match his father had arranged for him might have had a chance of success if Belinda had not died before they could be married, although now he wondered if theirs had been a truly deep and lasting affection. They had been very young, with no knowledge of the world.

Since then he had lived recklessly. He had taken mistresses, fought duels, lost and won fortunes at the gaming table. He had done nothing to be proud of. Nothing to make him worthy of a woman like Selina Wynter. Thankfully, she had turned her face against marriage. All he had to do was avoid compromising her.

* * *

Selina busied herself in the kitchen, gathering up the used dishes from the table, and did not see Deveril leave the room, but she was very much aware of him doing so. She listened to his firm tread as he walked away, heard the door close behind him and immediately wished he would come back.

What on earth was wrong with her? She had laughed at Clifford's insinuation that Deveril might want to seduce her and yet the very idea of his doing so, of his kissing her there and then, had made her heart jump and race. Why was it that a mere look from those deep brown eyes could turn her insides to water and at the same time make her burn for him?

But it was more than just a look. It was his voice, his very presence. His scent, that mix of sandalwood and musk and something indefinably male that made her body ache to move closer. She had never experienced such a strong attraction to any man: it made her feel something very close to panic.

'What are you doing?' Clifford's petulant voice dragged her thoughts to safer matters. Unwelcome, but safer.

'Clearing space for you to eat.'

'Surely you don't need to do that.' He sat down at the table. 'Leave it for the maid.'

She replied with icy calm. 'It may have escaped your notice, Clifford, but there is only Mildy to do everything here this morning and she is currently preparing your breakfast.'

'Where's the landlord, why can't he come in, or Merton?'

'They have gone off across the fields. They are hoping to reach the next farm and bring back some fresh meat.' She poured the last of the coffee into a cup and put it on the table in front of him. She went on, knowing it would upset him, 'They may not succeed, of course. In which case, Clifford, if you want to eat this evening it will be up to you to find a hen and wring its neck!'

Selina heaved a long and heavy sigh. She had avoided the parlour all day, fearing that one or both of the gentlemen would be using that room, and she had thrown herself into a flurry of housework. Keeping busy had lightened her mood, but it had done nothing to improve her hands.

It was just before the dinner hour and she was in her bedchamber, preparing to join the gentlemen in the parlour. Staring at her palms in the candlelight, she was dismayed to see how the skin was beginning to crack in places, leaving them red and sore. These were definitely not the hands of a lady.

'More like those of a washerwoman,' she muttered crossly, before good sense reasserted itself. 'But at least they are clean. As is my fichu.' She turned her attention back to the mirror and gave the linen around her shoulders a final tweak. 'When I get back to the Abbey, I shall ask Mrs Babbage to order some chicken skin gloves for me. If one is to believe the advertisements in the newspaper, they are supposed to work miracles.'

For now, however, there was nothing to be done, and with a final nod at her reflection she turned away. Then, head held high, she sailed off down the narrow stairs.

Both gentlemen were waiting for her in the parlour and they rose as she entered. A fire blazed cheerfully in the hearth and the room glowed with candlelight. She glanced towards the table and gave a little nod of approval. It had been set in readiness for dinner. Not, perhaps, in the first style of elegance, but good enough to equal the standards maintained at the White Horse, which was quite a feat for such a small country inn.

'You have been busy today,' remarked Lord Deveril, following her glance.

'Oh, this is not my doing. Mildy did it, and she has remembered everything I told her. She has hopes of moving up rapidly from maid of all work and I believe she will do so. She is quick to learn and eager to please.'

'But despite all that we have scarce seen you today,' grumbled Clifford Fremington.

'Do you expect me to sit in here doing nothing when there is work to be done?'

'It ain't a lady's place to do it! Every feeling must be offended.'

'Oh?' she said, brows raised. She turned to Deveril and said sweetly, 'Then pray, my lord, when we sit down to dinner, do not pass Mr Fremington that stew of beef rump. Nor the ragout of roots. It will only offend him. In fact, Clifford, you should not eat *anything*, since I was responsible for it all, in some part of the preparation.'

'Enough, enough,' snapped Clifford. 'Pray forget I said anything!'

Scowling, he threw himself back into his chair beside the fire.

'Here, ma'am, I have poured this for you.' Lord Deveril handed Selina a glass of Madeira.

His eyes were warm with understanding and she felt an answering smile bubbling up. Quickly she turned away, angry with herself for wanting to respond. Blast the man, why would he not leave her alone?

Dinner was served. Selina took her usual place between the two gentlemen, and tried to swallow her irritation against Deveril. It was ill-founded and petty. He had a natural charm, and what else would one expect of a rake? *Forewarned is forearmed*, she told herself. It should be quite possible to enjoy his company without endangering her good name. Or her heart.

They were left alone to serve themselves, and for a while there was silence, save for the occasional request to pass a dish. At length it was Lord Deveril who made some attempt at conversation.

'It would appear Jennock's attempt to reach the farm was successful,' he remarked, helping himself to more of the beef.

'It was,' replied Selina. 'They found the roads still blocked with snow, too deep for wagons to move, but they managed to trudge across the fields and only had to do a little digging through the drifts to reach their neighbour. They were able to procure the beef and a generous supply of provisions, and the farmer has promised to send over a leg of mutton tomorrow, if the weather does not improve.'

'I hope to God it does, then!' muttered Clifford.

'I am thankful for the clean linen, too,' said Deveril, ignoring him. 'It is good to wear my own shirt again. Although I am indebted to you, Fremington, for the loan of one of yours.'

'You must both take credit, too, for all the firewood,' she said, supporting Deveril's attempts to charm Clifford out of the sulks. 'Without your efforts, we would not have enough to heat the water for the laundry. But it was Mildy who took on that task, not I.'

Deveril lifted his glass to salute her. 'None of this would have happened if you had not arranged it.'

Selina blushed. A lady should accept the compliment with decorum, a word of thanks, perhaps, but then she should change the subject. Selina knew that, but she made the mistake of looking at Deveril, and after that she forgot about decorum. The smile in his dark eyes encouraged her to respond, and in a most unladylike way.

She returned his salute, saying, 'I am a very managing female, my lord. As you know.'

Deveril watched as she put the glass to her lips, looking at him over the rim, and he almost choked on his wine. By heaven, she was *flirting* with him!

No, not flirting, he corrected himself. Those sapphire eyes looking steadily into his were innocent of any trick to enslave. She was inviting him to share a memory, a moment of companionship. And yet the way his body was reacting, she could have been offering herself to him!

She lowered the glass and his eyes fixed on her mouth, stained now with wine. How sweet it would be to kiss those full lips again, to explore her mouth with his tongue, while that luscious body pressed against his. He wanted to awake in her the passion he was sure she possessed. He had glimpsed it, felt it simmering, just below the surface.

If—when—she gave herself to a man, it would be… shattering.

'Damn you, Blackbourne, pass me the onion tart, will you—I have asked twice!'

Deveril started at the sharp voice. He handed over the dish to Fremington who took it, glaring at him.

'I know your sort, Blackbourne,' he snarled. 'A damned rakehell, turning all the ladies' heads with your compliments and then off you will go, back to your London mistresses and leaving a string of broken hearts behind you. But don't you worry, those of us who remain will step in to mend them.'

Deveril did not respond but glanced at Selina. She gave him a small smile, as if they were conspirators. Fremington, meanwhile, having piled his plate with food, was now devouring it greedily. How could the fellow be so complacent? Selina would never marry him.

Would she?

There was sure to be some speculation, when she eventually returned to Torrisford. Would her friends stand by her, or would the gossip that was bound to arise in such a small town destroy her?

Deveril pushed the food around his plate, his appetite gone. She did not deserve such a fate.

'Listen!' Selina's voice interrupted his dark thoughts. He watched her hurry across to the bay window and pull aside one of the heavy curtains.

She turned back, smiling. 'It is raining.'

Chapter Seventeen

The long-awaited thaw continued through the night, greatly reducing the covering of snow although it had less effect on the frozen drifts filling the lanes, as Master Jennock informed Selina when she came down to the kitchen soon after dawn.

The return of the stable lad earlier that morning meant there were extra hands to tend the fires while Mildy prepared breakfast, and Selina was informed, politely but firmly, that her help in the kitchen was not required.

'Nay, ma'am, tedn't proper for you to be working in here,' the landlord told her, when she protested. 'Howsomever, I'd consider it a kindness if you'd look in on Mrs Jennock. She's mortal tired, and frettin' that she should be up and doing something.'

Selina readily agreed. It suited her very well to spend time with the landlady. It gave her an excuse not to break her fast in the parlour. More specifically, to delay a meeting with Lord Deveril. She was becoming far too comfortable in the man's company.

She was not a fool; he might flirt with her but Selina knew nothing could come of it. He was the son of a marquess and she was nothing more than a country miss. She glanced down at her hands. He must think her more of a hoyden than a lady. An amusing diversion, to be forgotten once he returned to his own world.

It was gone noon by the time Selina finally went into the parlour. She found both gentlemen there and was greeted by Clifford, demanding to know why she was not at breakfast.

'I have been with Mrs Jennock. Keeping her company.'

Clifford grunted. 'You have been elevated from skivvy to the role of companion. That is something I suppose!'

'Did Jennock tell you he and Merton went out to the lane this morning?' she asked, ignoring this.

It was Deveril who replied.

'Yes, he did. He also said his stable boy has returned, although he only managed to do so by scrambling over the walls and coming cross country.'

'We should make a push to have the lane cleared today,' declared Clifford. 'With Merton, Jennock and the stable boy to work at it, a few hours should do the trick.'

'You think so, Clifford?' Selina reached for a bread roll. 'You would be willing to leave at dusk, not knowing what difficulties you might encounter on the way back to Torrisford?'

'I will take that chance rather than spend a moment longer than I must in this damned place!'

Deveril was watching Selina, noting the slight crease in her brow.

'What say you, Miss Wynter?' he asked.

'You may both go, with my blessing,' she replied, buttering the roll. 'But I have no intention of leaving.'

'By heaven, madam, have you lost your wits?' exclaimed Clifford. 'I suppose it is because you do not wish to ride in the travelling chariot with me.'

'There is that, but it is not my reason. Mrs Jennock and the baby appear to be doing well, but I am loath to quit the inn until the midwife has visited her.'

'Phsaw! You would stay here and nurse the landlady? A woman who is nothing to you. By heaven but you have some very strange ideas, madam.'

'I hope I will always do my duty to a woman in need,' retorted Selina.

'I see what it is,' he snapped. 'You want me to leave, so you can throw yourself at Blackbourne. I have seen the way you look at each other—you will be in his bed in the blink of an eye, once I am gone. He is known as Devil Blackbourne for a reason, madam. But don't think he'd ever marry you. He'll take his pleasure and cast you aside like all his other conquests!'

'Enough!' Deveril's voice cut like a sword across Clifford's furious tirade. 'There is no question of my remaining here if you leave, Fremington. And unlike you,' he added, 'I have no intention of seducing Miss Wynter.'

Selina's spirits sank. Despite knowing he had broken countless hearts, deep down she had thought she was different, that he felt something for her. Such bluntly spoken words showed her how wrong she was. He had no interest in her at all. Well then, the sooner he was out of her life the better!

Deveril went on, 'It is to the lady's credit that she wishes to remain and look after Mrs Jennock. I have a suggestion.'

She pushed down her own unhappiness and said politely, 'Pray go on, my lord.'

'The thaw *is* continuing, but I would suggest we wait until the morning before attempting to leave. The drifts between here and Torrisford should all be gone by then, or at least diminished. Fremington and I will carry word to Reigney Abbey and explain the situation. Mr Wynter can then send his own carriage for you, ma'am, together with your maid. That would allow you to remain here in perfect propriety and return to Reigney Abbey at your own convenience.'

Clifford scoffed. 'Ho, and what will the gossip mongers make of that?'

'Nothing, Fremington. As long as we both maintain Miss Wynter's reputation was never compromised.'

Deveril had fixed Clifford with a steely glare and uttered the words in an equally hard tone, one that promised dire consequences if he should dare to say anything different. Selina knew he was acting in her best interests. He was trying to protect her good name, making it quite unnecessary for either man to offer her marriage.

She should be grateful, but instead she felt despondent. Although she was determined no one would ever know.

'That would suit me very well, my lord,' she said. 'And I doubt I should be here for long. It is very likely the midwife will be able to call here tomorrow.'

'Very well, but if a doctor is required, tell Jennock not to hesitate. I will pay for him to attend her.'

'That is very kind of you, my lord. Thank you.'

Clifford's chair scraped back.

'It ain't kindness at all, Selina. He's trying to buy your approval,' he snarled, throwing his napkin down on the table. 'Have a care, madam, or it will be you needing the services of a midwife!'

Barely had the words left his mouth before Deveril leapt up from the table and was upon him, delivering a crashing blow to the jaw that sent Fremington sprawling on the ground.

'You have insulted the lady once too often,' he snarled, standing over Fremington with his fists clenched. 'I swear you will meet—'

'Enough!' Selina was gripping his arm. 'I will not allow you to fight a duel over me!'

Deveril's lip curled as he glared at the man climbing slowly to his feet.

'Then we'll settle this now,' he growled. 'Outside!'

'And just how is that supposed to protect my good name?' she demanded, her voice scathing. 'Perhaps your mistresses appreciate these grand gestures, my Lord Deveril, but I assure you, I do not! And as for you, Clifford Fremington, your actions have been beyond the pale. If you or any of your family importune me in future then I shall have no hesitation in making this whole sorry business public and making a formal complaint to the magistrate. As you know, Sir Alfred is a very good friend and he will not treat lightly any accusations I make.'

The red mist that had enveloped Deveril began to clear and he made an effort to compose himself while Selina continued to ring a peal over Fremington. By the time she had finished and dismissed the fellow, he was looking so dejected that Deveril could almost feel sorry for him.

As the door closed behind Fremington, he looked across at Selina. She was very pale, although her eyes were sparking with anger. His heart went out to her; he wanted to take her in his arms and kiss away her rage, but he knew she would repulse him. For once, when dealing with a woman, he felt at a loss.

'Damn the fellow,' he said lightly. 'He has insulted

you several times over now. I wish you would let me call him out.'

She blinked at him, as if gathering her thoughts, then shook her head.

'I pray you will not,' she said, trying to match his flippant tone. 'You might kill him, and only think of the trouble that would cause!'

'I have never yet killed a man. Although it is probably the only sin I have *not* committed!' he added, bitterly.

She shook her head. 'To be serious, my lord, we should do nothing that could give rise to more gossip.'

'I know, but it is a shame. I should dearly like to punish him for how he has treated you.'

'I do not need you to defend me, my lord.'

She went back to the table and began to gather up the dishes, piling them onto a tray to carry off to the kitchen.

'Here, let me.' He reached for the tray but she evaded him.

'Thank you, but no, I would rather do it. I need to talk with Mildy.'

With that she hurried out of the room.

Selina spent the rest of her day between the kitchen and Mrs Jennock's chamber. She tried to tell herself it was necessary for her to sit with the landlady while she rested, but she knew in her heart she was avoiding Deveril.

She could no longer ignore the fact that she liked the

man, and far more than she should. He had the power to disconcert her, to turn her anger into laughter in a moment and to set her pulse racing within nothing more than a smile.

She sighed, thinking of the way he had jumped to her defence earlier. She had told him she did not need his help, but a tiny part of her acknowledged that sometimes it would be a comfort to have someone to lean on. Not to fight duels for her, heaven forbid, but to have someone to confide in. Someone who could share her problems, to take from her shoulders some of the weight of looking after her father as well as Reigney.

But she knew that person could never be Devil Blackbourne. He was rarely serious and lived for his pleasures. She could not think of a more unlikely partner.

The light was fading when Jennock came into the kitchen and announced that he expected the road to Torrisford to be passable by the morning. Selina wanted to feel nothing but relief, but much as she would be glad to see Clifford leave the inn, she knew she would miss Deveril's cheerful presence and the way his smile could lift her spirits.

The depressing thought followed her when she went upstairs to tidy herself before dinner and she was obliged to scold herself.

'You had better get used to it,' she told her reflection, as she sat before the looking glass in her bedchamber. 'After being snowbound for almost a week your reputation must already be hanging by a thread. Any hint of familiarity between you and Devil Blackbourne would sever it completely.'

A soft noise made her turn. A folded paper had been pushed under her door. Selina picked it up and carried it across to the lamp to read the short message it contained.

Five minutes later she entered the parlour to find Lord Deveril pacing back and forth.

'You wished to talk to me, my lord?'

He stopped.

'Yes. Thank you.' He did not invite her to sit down but stood, hands behind his back, regarding her with a dark, brooding look. 'I have been thinking. About your reception when you return to Torrisford.'

'So too have I. There will be gossip. I am prepared for it.'

'Are you? Fremington could make it very uncomfortable for you, despite my attempts to warn him off.'

'He may try. My true friends will not believe it.' She raised her chin and said, with a hint of defiance, 'I shall manage without the good opinion of the rest.'

'It would be easier if you took a husband.'

'I will not marry Clifford under any circumstances.'

'I am not talking about Fremington.' He came closer. 'I think you should marry me, Selina.'

She reached out for the support of the nearest chair back.

'Y-you?'

Her eyes searched his face, but it was unreadable; the dark eyes, usually so expressive, were shuttered.

Deveril turned away, unable to bear the mix of dismay and surprise in her countenance. It was clear this was the last thing she expected of him. He began to pace back and forth, staring at the floor.

'When my Belinda died, I vowed never to marry, but I am in part responsible for your situation and I must do my duty. As your husband I would be able to shield you from snubs, and the worst of the gossip.' He stopped pacing and fixed his eyes on her. 'Miss Wynter, I would be honoured if you would accept my offer.'

There, the words were out. She was staring at him, the colour in her cheeks changing rapidly from blush-red to alabaster. He scowled down at the worn carpet at his feet. Hell and damnation, he was making a mull of this!

'I know it is not ideal,' he said. 'You have told me you cannot leave your father and I would not ask it of you. It is true I have houses and estates that require attention, but it would not be necessary for you always to accompany me. You could remain for most of the year at Reigney Abbey, if that is what you wish. The point is that once we are married you would have the full protection of my name, even when I am not here.'

He looked up to see she was now as pale as her fichu and gazing down at her hands, which were tightly clasped in front of her.

'Thank you, my lord, but I cannot accept.'

He said gently, 'Could you really not bear to be my wife?'

A tremor ran though her. 'Really, it is not necessary.'

'Necessary?' He came closer. 'Perhaps not, but I think we might rub along very well together.'

He took her hands, turning them palms up. His heart contracted at the sight of the cuts and scratches on the red, chapped skin.

'My poor Selina,' he murmured, bending to press a kiss into one palm.

She snatched her hands away, cradling them together against her breast.

'On the contrary. I do not think we would do well at all. In fact, it would be…a punishment to be married to you!'

'As bad as that?' Her answer startled him. 'Selina—'

'No, I pray you, say no more,' she begged. 'I am—I am honoured by your offer, my lord, but I cannot accept. I am content as I am. I do not wish to marry *anyone*.' She turned and walked over to the window, staring out at the melting snow. 'You will be leaving here in the morning and…and I should be obliged if we could forget this conversation ever happened. Lord Graddon rarely stays in Torrisford beyond March, which means you will only be in Devonshire a few more weeks, but if—' she took a breath '—*if* we should meet, I should like to be on friendly terms. If that is possible.'

'But of course.'

'Thank you.'

Selina blinked rapidly, fighting back tears. She would not give in to such weakness. She would *not*. Taking a deep breath she turned to face him, head up, her voice cool and composed, at variance with the tumult inside that threatened to rip her apart.

'We still have some time before the dinner hour. If you will excuse me, it will be best if I go now and return once Mr Fremington has come downstairs. I would rather he did not know anything of this.'

'He will not learn of it from me, madam.'

Selina gave a stiff little nod and left the room. She managed to hold back a sob until she was halfway up the stairs, then she ran the rest of the way to her room and threw herself on the bed, where the tears came thick and fast. He felt sorry for her. That was why he had made his offer.

If there had been any hope that their feelings could grow into something stronger, Selina might have considered a marriage of convenience, but Deveril had told her quite clearly that he had set his face against marriage when his fiancée died. He was even willing for her to remain at the Abbey with Papa, leaving him free to continue with his life as if he was still a bachelor.

No! A thousand times no! That would be the worst

of all possible worlds. She hated to be regarded as an object of pity.

Then stop snivelling and get up off this bed!

The voice, her stronger self, almost made Selina smile. She sat up and dried her eyes. She should be flattered that the son of a marquess should propose to her. When she was an old lady, it was something she might boast about, but for now, having refused this very advantageous offer, she must act with propriety, put it behind her and get on with what she needed to do.

Which, at that moment, was to wash all traces of distress from her face, tidy her hair and go down to dinner.

'So, Selina, you are determined, you will not come with us,' said Clifford Fremington, pausing beside his carriage.

Deveril was talking with the stable lad who was holding his horse, and had watched Selina step out of the inn to see them off.

'I am,' she said. 'You have my letter to give to my father.'

'And if he asks me how such a misadventure came about,' said Fremington, peevishly. 'What am I to tell him?'

'What we agreed. Your driver mistook the way in the snow. Papa will think it foolish, but at least he will not think you a rogue.'

He scowled, but without another word jumped into his travelling chariot. Deveril waited until the chaise had moved off before walking over to Selina.

'It seems a little harsh that Merton should be the one to bear the blame for your misadventure,' he remarked.

'I know, but I hope it will be enough to avoid a scandal. I really do not want it known that Clifford abducted me. But I will disclose the fact,' she added, with a fierce look, 'if he does not keep to our agreement. Papa must be extremely anxious by this time, I do not want anything or anyone to add to his distress.'

'Don't worry, I shall follow him to Reigney Abbey and make sure he delivers your letter. He knows he will have me to deal with if he says anything to disparage you.'

'Thank you.'

She held out her hand to him and he took her fingers and bowed over them, even though what he really wanted to do was to pull her into his arms and kiss her.

'I am at your service, ma'am. Anything at all. You have only to ask.'

He looked up, willing her to ask him to repeat his offer. But she merely smiled and bade him a safe journey as she gently pulled her hand free.

Chapter Eighteen

Three days later Selina travelled back to Reigney Abbey in her father's carriage. The thaw had been rapid and the lanes were now free of snow, although there was still some on the surrounding hills.

She was accompanied by Nancy, her maid, who was uncharacteristically quiet. Selina had no proof, but she suspected her faithful servant had heard enough from Mildy and the landlord to guess her mistress had been tricked into going off with Clifford Fremington. Not that it mattered: Nancy was far too loyal to spread malicious gossip.

As soon as the carriage came to a halt at the Abbey door, Selina jumped down and ran inside. Pausing only to remove her cloak, she hurried to the drawing room, where she found her father and Mr Chewton sitting before the fire.

Both men rose when she entered, her father coming across the room to meet her.

'Selina, my love, you are back, at last!'

'I am, Papa,' she said, hugging him. 'But do sit down, my dear sir.'

She kissed his cheek and gently eased him back down into his chair before turning to greet his guest. Horace Chewton was about the same age as her father, but his lean figure was very upright compared to Papa, whose spare frame was stooped by constant bouts of ill health. Mr Chewton looked very hale and hearty, an energetic man with thick white whiskers and a cheerful twinkle in his blue eyes.

She held out her hand to him. 'I cannot tell you how sorry I am that I was not at the White Horse to meet you, sir. I hope my driver told you what had occurred.'

He nodded. 'Yes, I had already arrived when the servant came and delivered your message, that you were off on an errand of mercy.' His merry eyes twinkled. 'But it would seem matters did not turn out quite as anticipated.'

'No. I was grieved beyond measure not to be able to get back to you both.'

Her father tutted loudly. 'I was quite distraught when young Fremington arrived here without you!'

Mr Chewton patted his shoulder, saying cheerfully, 'Now, now, William. We said, did we not, that with it snowing so heavily, it might have happened to anyone.' He turned to smile at Selina. 'You appear to have had quite an adventure, Miss Selina, but all's well that ends well, and you are safe back with us now.'

'I am, sir, but I must apologise for not being here to play hostess.'

'Pray do not fret yourself, my dear. It could not be helped, and your housekeeper has provided for us very well, has she not, William?'

'Yes, Mrs Leighton made sure we never wanted for anything,' remarked her father. 'Leighton, too, has been most attentive.'

'I am very glad of it, Papa.' She sat down on a stool beside him, relieved to see him looking so cheerful. 'I am sure the Leightons are as happy as we are to have a guest at the Abbey. We have lived very quietly these last few years, haven't we? And I am glad you did not fret over me.'

'When the snow showed no sign of stopping, I did not expect you to return immediately, and was quite content to think you safe at Fremington Court. Of course, when I read your letter, I was shocked to learn you had been stranded at a wayside inn all that time. And for Fremington's driver to lose his way like that, well, he should be turned off! It was badly done, Selina. Very badly done.'

His hands began to twitch nervously, a sign that he was growing agitated and she reached out to take them, holding them firmly in a warm clasp.

'But I was never in any danger, Papa,' she assured him, stifling her conscience. 'Naturally, I was most put out about it, but once we reached the inn there was nothing to be done. We were obliged to stay.

'And the landlady, you see, was very near her time. It was a blessing that I was there, because she was brought to bed much earlier than expected and there was no one else to help her with the baby.' She squeezed his hands. 'I hope my letter explained enough to stop you worrying, Papa. You would not have had me act any differently.'

'You believed you were needed, my love, and knowing your kind heart, I quite understand that.'

'I could not leave until I was sure the new mother and her baby were going on well. When the midwife arrived yesterday, I was very reassured to find her such a sensible, knowledgeable woman and I know she will take care of everything.' She smiled, 'Believe me, Papa, it pained me excessively to delay my return. My only comfort was knowing that Mr Chewton was with you.'

'Well, well, it was not so bad you know,' said her father. 'In fact, we have had a most enjoyable few days, have we not, Horace? We have been playing cards, chess and backgammon, reading together and of course talking, you know. It has been like old times!'

He broke off as the chiming clock on the mantelshelf announced the hour.

'Is that the time? We should be making our way to the dining room, Horace. Mrs Leighton has taken to preparing a small nuncheon for us,' he explained, observing Selina's look of surprise. 'Perhaps, my dear, you would like to join us, once you have changed out of your travel clothes?'

'Thank you, Papa, I should like to join you, very much, if you can wait for me!'

Selina hurried away to her bedchamber, her mind spinning. She had expected to find Papa in a frenzy of anxiety over her absence and she was relieved that it was not so. In fact, she thought him far more animated than she had seen him for a long time. She could not remember the last time Papa had eaten anything at midday.

One thing was clear: Mr Chewton's visit had put new life into him, and Selina was very glad of that. It was very selfish of her to be disappointed that he had not missed her more.

As the weather improved, local Society began to stir again. When an invitation arrived from Lady Kenton for all three of them to dine at Torrisford Manor that Friday, Selina was pleased, if a little surprised, when her father accepted without demur.

'The squire said he was eager to renew his acquaintance with Horace,' he reminded her, as they set off in the carriage on Friday evening. 'We shall have a very pleasant evening, I am sure.'

They were welcomed at the door by the squire himself.

'You must be very glad to have your daughter back at Reigney, safe and sound, Mr Wynter,' he said. 'So unfortunate, to be snowed up for a week, but there, one has to expect snow at this time of the year. Now, come in, all of you and warm yourselves. We are only a small party at dinner,' he explained, as he ushered them into the drawing room. 'Just Helena and her husband, Harvey Frith: you met them on your last visit I believe, Mr Chewton? And I have invited a few friends to join us after, so I hope you will be well entertained, sir. There is a very lively group of gentlemen staying at Graddon Hall presently, here for the hunting, you know. And of course, you are acquainted with the Fremingtons.'

'Lady Fremington is up and about already?' exclaimed Mr Wynter. 'Oh dear, is that wise?'

'What?' His host looked towards his wife, perplexed.

'Her illness could not have been as serious as was first thought, my dear,' replied Lady Kenton, glancing at Selina.

'With all this snow the news has been a little slow to spread, has it not?' The squire gave a hearty laugh. 'Well, well, that will soon be remedied, I am sure,' he declared jovially. 'Once you ladies begin to circulate again!'

The Kentons went off with Mr Wynter and his friend, leaving Selina free to join the Friths on the far side of the room. After exchanging pleasantries, Harvey moved off and Helena immediately put her hand on Selina's arm.

'Oh, my dear, tell me truthfully now, how are you?'

Selina was immediately on the alert. 'What have you heard?'

Helena hesitated, then drew her a little further towards the window, where they would not be overheard.

'I was in Torrisford with Mama yesterday. Some unkind people were saying the driver mistaking his way was all a hum and that Lady Fremington's illness was only a story concocted to explain your absence.' She took a breath and went on, her eyes wide and slightly questioning, 'They say you were eloping with Clifford Fremington!'

'That is completely untrue!'

'Of course it is,' said Helena, looking relieved. 'Anyone who knows you would never believe it.'

'But who was spreading such lies?' Selina demanded.

'We heard it from Mrs Hexham, whom everyone knows is addicted to servants' talk. Mama quickly refuted the story, but you know how gossip can grow.'

Selina could not shake off the suspicion that Clifford was responsible for spreading the story, but there was little she could do. And Helena was right: there was always going to be some talk and speculation.

'I spent most of my time at the Rising Sun attending the landlady and her baby,' she explained. 'I suppose everyone will think that was beneath me, too!'

'Some will, of course, Selina. Ill-natured people love to think the worst!'

Selina put up her chin. 'Let them. My true friends will stand by me, I am sure.' She saw Lady Kenton making her way over to them and turned to her. 'Helena was telling me of the ridiculous rumour going around the town, that I eloped with Clifford Fremington.'

She was comforted by her hostess's cheerful response.

'Yes, such nonsense! My dear, when Mrs Hexham mentioned it to me, I vow I almost laughed in her face, did I not, Helena? We were in the haberdashers at the time and I made sure everyone heard me when I corrected her. After all, why on earth would you distress your friends and family by eloping when there is not the least obstacle to your marrying young Fremington, if you so wished? Now, my dears, I am just waiting for our last guest and we can go in to dinner. I invited Julia Allen to join us, to make an equal number of ladies and gentlemen—ah, here she is now!'

Lady Kenton went off to greet the widow, who entered in a flurry of silk skirts, her golden curls glinting in the candlelight. Selina heard Helena give a little sigh.

'I know she is Papa's cousin, but I cannot like Julia Allen. She is so very *forward* with the gentlemen. She even tried to flirt with Harvey, you know, at the last assembly. He says she is tiresome, but I think he was flattered, all the same.'

'Helena, surely you don't think—'

'No, no, dear Harvey is far too loyal to respond to her advances. Besides, he is too much of a dull dog for Julia!' She giggled. 'Mama has put her between your father and Mr Chewton at dinner, so I hope they will enjoy having a pretty woman beside them!'

Selina hoped so, too. The widow appeared to be quite satisfied with her lot and exerted herself to engage both gentlemen in conversation during the dinner. By the end of the meal everyone appeared to be in the best of spirits as they returned to the drawing room to await the arrival of the evening guests.

The coaches from Graddon Hall were the last to arrive at Torrisford Manor. The gentlemen piled out and were shown into the drawing room, which was already noisy with chatter.

Deveril spotted Selina at once. She was wearing a robe of striped green silk, with her glorious hair pinned up in curls about her head and shining like polished mahogany in the candlelight. Much as he wanted to speak with her, after what had occurred it would not do for him to single her out. He took his time, moving about the room, conversing with several acquaintances and then making his way across to the small group gathered about Lady Fremington. It included Mr and Mrs Keith, as well as another couple he recognised as living in Torrisford.

They all greeted him civilly, and after a few pleasantries he turned to address Lady Fremington.

'I am pleased to see you out and about, ma'am. Your son told me how worried he had been about you. I trust you are quite well now?'

Her blush was visible even beneath the thick white powder on her cheek. She stammered an incoherent response and looked relieved when her husband and son came up to join her. Undaunted, Deveril included them all in his smile before he turned back to the lady.

'You must be pleased to have your son home again, ma'am, and none the worse for his adventure.'

'We are all thankful the snow has gone,' replied Lord Fremington, his eyes snapping angrily. 'But it seems an odd coincidence, my lord, that you should find yourself stranded at the self-same inn.'

'Yes, wasn't it?' Deveril knew his cheerful response would infuriate his lordship even more. He went on, his fingers playing with the ribbon of his quizzing glass, 'Providential, though. We could both attest to Miss Wynter's good name being upheld during our time at the Rising Sun. Ain't that so, sir?'

'What?' Clifford Fremington started. 'Oh, yes. Yes.' A deep flush mounted his cheeks as Deveril continued to look at him, waiting for more. 'Nothing untoward happened. There was never any danger to the lady's reputation. None at all.'

Deveril nodded approvingly, but he was not done with the family yet. He paused, just long enough for the man to think he had finished, then:

'That reminds me, Fremington, I have not yet settled with you for our wager.'

Mr and Mrs Keith did not react, but the Fremingtons looked decidedly uneasy at his words. Smiling, Deveril pulled a small purse out of his pocket and handed it to Clifford, who quickly stuffed it into his pocket.

'There, the matter is settled.' He glanced at Lady Fremington. 'You look concerned, ma'am,' he said. 'Pray let me assure you it was mere funning. A little contest, to see who could chop the most firewood. Your son was easily the best, ma'am, proved himself to be quite adept with an axe!'

'Oh. Oh yes, I see,' murmured the lady, fanning herself vigorously while her husband stood in silence, his countenance red with anger.

'Ah.' Deveril assumed a look of chagrin. 'I see I have erred. His lordship is quite put out with me for mentioning such a matter, and before a lady, too. I beg your pardon, madam, I hope you can forgive me. I have no idea when I shall see Mr Fremington next, you see, and one should always settle matters of honour as quickly as possible.

'Yes, yes, I see I have erred badly,' he went on, shaking his head. 'It is one thing to discuss a wager in private, after a good dinner, perhaps, but the matter should never be aired elsewhere. Ain't that so, my lord?'

Lord Fremington's countenance darkened further. Deveril did not wait for a reply. He made his bow and wandered off.

He delayed a little longer before speaking with Selina, pausing for a word with her father and then, avoiding Mrs Allen's attempts to catch his eye, he went over to exchange a little light-hearted banter with Viscount Graddon. That brought him neatly to the side of the room where Selina was standing beside their hostess.

'Lord Deveril,' Lady Kenton greeted him cheerfully when he came up. 'I was just talking to Selina about your recent ordeal at that wayside inn.'

Selina was taken aback by her friend referring so directly to what had occurred, but Deveril took it in his stride.

'Not at all, ma'am, merely a little inconvenience,' he said. 'More so for Miss Wynter, who was obliged to make do with the services of a kitchen maid and the landlady. All perfectly respectable, ma'am. As Fremington will confirm.'

'Yes, I have heard him say as much and I confess I am very glad of it.' Lady Kenton's eyes remained fixed upon him as she went on, 'Sir Alfred and I would take it very ill if any slur were to be cast upon dear Selina's good name.'

'I am pleased to hear you say so, my lady,' murmured Deveril, with a little bow. 'We all have Miss Wynter's best interests at heart.'

Her ladyship's duties as hostess would not allow her to remain in any one place for long, and when she had moved off, Deveril glanced at Selina.

'It *was* an ordeal for you,' he said quietly. 'You must be relieved it is over.'

'I am, of course.'

He frowned a little. 'You do not sound too sure of that, Selina.'

'Despite what Lady Kenton says, I am aware the gossips are already at work,' she said bitterly. 'It is said I went off willingly with Clifford.'

'You know as well as I that ill-natured people will always think the worst,' he reminded her. 'As long as we all maintain your reputation was never compromised, we shall get through this. And if Fremington should stray from that,' he added lightly, 'then I shall call him out.'

'Now you are being ridiculous!' She laughed, but to Deveril's ears it sounded strained.

'What is it, Selina? What is worrying you?' He glanced across the room. 'Is it your father, was he very upset by your absence?'

'No, not unduly. Not as much I expected.' She stopped, waving one hand to dismiss whatever it was she had been about to say. 'Oh, please, take no notice—I know very well that I am being foolish about this.'

'Tell me.'

She hesitated for a moment. Then, 'Papa accepted quite readily that I had gone to the Fremingtons and did not fret over it, possibly helped by the fact that Mr Chewton was with him. And because of the snow he knew nothing of the true state of affairs until Clifford delivered my letter and even then he was quite sanguine.' She bit her lip. 'In fact, he hardly appears to have missed me at all!'

Deveril's lips twitched. 'You have clearly trained your household too well, madam. You should be relieved they know how to go on without you.'

'You are right, of course. I should be glad of it. I *am* glad of it.' She sighed. 'The thing is, you see, I have only been away from home once before. When I was eighteen. My aunt invited me to London for the Season but I had to cut short my visit when Papa was taken ill. I have been with him ever since.'

'Then I can quite understand you were concerned that he would miss you,' said Deveril. 'And I have even more admiration for your fortitude when you learned you might be obliged to remain at the Rising Sun for some days. In fact, I am surprised you did not fall into hysterics!'

That brought the twinkle back into her eyes.

'You know I am not that sort of female. Besides, we would have been in an even worse fix if I had taken to my bed! No, I should be thankful Papa had Mr Chewton to keep him company, and that my absence caused them both so little inconvenience. And I am, truly. Only…'

'You think Chewton has usurped your place in your father's affections.'

'I do not think Papa's affection for me was ever that strong,' she said candidly. 'Oh, he loves me, but never as much as he loved Mama. Which is as it should be. He worshipped her, you see. He was crippled with grief when she died and I was desperate to cheer him. I realised that I could be useful by taking over the running of the house and the estate, so that is what I did. It had always been Mama's province, because Papa's health had never been good.'

'How old were you then?'

'Sixteen. Pray do not look so surprised, my lord. It is not such an arduous task. I enjoy it, truly. Ashworth, our steward, handles the day to day running of the estate and I deal with the accounts and look after any correspondence. The squire, too, is very happy to advise me if I need assistance.'

'And your father takes no part in the running of it all?'

She shook her head. 'Papa likes to be informed, and I never make any major decision without discussing it with him beforehand. But he has always been a scholarly man. He prefers to lose himself in his books than wrestle with practical matters.'

'Leaving you to take up that burden.'

'I do not see it as a burden. I am my own mistress and have far more freedom than most single ladies of my acquaintance, and far more to occupy me, too.' She shook her head. 'You must not feel sorry for me, Lord Deveril, I will not allow it.'

'I would not dare!'

His reply made her smile, but before she could reply Helena Frith came up.

'I hope you will excuse me, Lord Deveril,' she said, taking her friend's arm. 'I have come to take Selina away. Mama has asked that we play a duet together.'

'Of course, Mrs Frith.'

Deveril bowed and watched the two young ladies walk off. He had made a laughing retort to Selina, but in truth his heart went out to her. She had devoted her young life to her father and Reigney Abbey, years when she should have been out exploring the world. At the very least she should be going to the theatre, attending soirées and ridottos.

Dancing until dawn and falling in love.

Selina joined her friend at the pianoforte to play one of the pieces they had practised together many times. She tried to concentrate, but could not help wondering what Deveril was doing. Was he talking with his friends, or flirting with the ladies?

Not that it was her concern. She had made her position perfectly clear before they left the Rising Sun.

Her only interest in him was as a friend. They had spoken very easily tonight; they were comfortable together and she valued that.

Raising her eyes from the keys she saw him talking with Julia Allen, his partner for those last two dances at the assembly. The widow was touching his arm and smiling up at him in the friendliest way and Selina's insides roiled. Her fingers stumbled over the keys and she had to work hard to find her place again.

She had no right to be jealous. He had offered her his hand and she had refused him. He was free now to flirt with anyone he wished.

Chapter Nineteen

Springtime was always busy at Reigney Abbey estate and Selina had plenty to do each day. Horace Chewton's presence in the house meant her father had a constant companion and she was no longer obliged to keep such a watchful eye on him. That was a relief, and if she sometimes felt a little excluded from their conversation during dinner that was a small price to pay when Papa was so much happier. She threw herself into looking after the house and the estate, but something had changed since her enforced sojourn at the Rising Sun. She no longer felt the same satisfaction at the end of each day.

Selina was forced to acknowledge that she missed Deveril. At the inn they had seen each other every day. They had talked together, teased one another. He had challenged her, made her feel alive. It was as if they had known one another for years. As if they were friends.

But it was one thing to be friends within the confined world of the Rising Sun, quite impossible outside it. They could meet only in company and exchange nothing more than a little polite conversation. She thought it would be better when Deveril left Graddon Hall. Then she would be able to forget him.

It was a week after the Kentons' party that Selina ventured into Torrisford to do a little shopping. It was a fine March day and the town was busy, so she was not surprised to find a number of customers already in the haberdashers. As she entered the shop their lively chatter stopped momentarily, picking up again once Mrs Babbage had hurried over to serve her.

While she waited for her purchases to be wrapped, Selina wandered over to inspect a display of coloured ribbons near the window. She looked up as Mrs Hexham and her daughters came into the shop and gave them a friendly smile but received only a cold nod as they hurried past her.

Selina thought little of it and might have forgotten the matter, if she had not received a similar reaction from several acquaintances she met on the street. These were people she had known since childhood, but now, although they returned her greeting, they seemed uneasy in her company, most looking away and not meeting her eyes.

The change was so marked that Selina decided to call upon Lady Kenton on the way back to the Abbey. When she reached Torrisford Manor she was shown into her ladyship's sitting room and was relieved that her old friend's greeting was as warm as ever.

'Selina, my dear, this is a pleasant surprise,' said her ladyship, kissing her cheek. 'I had not thought to see you today.'

Selina gave a perfunctory smile and asked her bluntly if she had heard any fresh gossip.

'It is as if I had suddenly grown two heads,' she said, pacing back and forth. 'People I have always thought of as friends keeping their distance.' She forced a laugh. 'I think one even gave me the cut direct!'

'I think I know the cause of this, my dear, and I am very sorry for it,' said Lady Kenton, taking her arm and guiding her to a sofa.

'Then I pray you will tell me, ma'am,' cried Selina. 'I thought those early rumours had been nipped in the bud.'

'I thought so, too. This latest, however, is…different.'

Selina was alarmed by her friend's anxious tone and begged her again to tell her anything she knew.

Lady Kenton did not answer immediately but clasped her hands in her lap and stared down at them.

'When I was at church on Sunday, I heard some of the ladies talking. Your carriage had already departed, Selina, or I do not think they would have been speaking so freely.'

She began to rearrange the lace at her wrists until Selina put her hand over hers.

'What were they saying?'

'That you *did* elope with Clifford Fremington, but changed your mind about marrying him once Lord Deveril turned up at the inn.'

Selina stared at her in horror. 'They think I rejected Clifford Fremington in favour of Deveril? That is despicable!' She put her hands to her heated cheeks. 'And completely untrue!'

'So I told them,' said Lady Kenton. 'But…is it, my dear? His lordship is very attractive. It would be no wonder if you were to feel a partiality for him.' She hesitated. 'I dare say you have not noticed, but there are times when you forget to use his title.'

Under her friend's keen gaze Selina knew she could not lie.

'I do like him, Lady Kenton. He is charming, and witty and very kind, but I think of him only as a friend. I am not foolish enough to believe it could ever be more than that.'

'Because he is a rake?'

'Yes. Although I have seen very little evidence of that in his behaviour towards me.'

'Oh, my dear, I fear you are too innocent to understand such men!'

'I do not deny that, ma'am.' Selina hesitated, then she said slowly, 'His lordship may well be a libertine, and a complete rogue, but I promise you he was the model of propriety during our sojourn at the Rising Sun. Far more so than Clifford Fremington, I assure you!'

Lady Kenton was looking alarmed and Selina decided she should explain. In fact, it would be a relief to tell someone.

'Clifford did abduct me, ma'am, but his plans were thwarted by the snow and we had to put up at the Rising Sun. Lord Deveril arrived shortly after and came into the parlour just as Clifford was trying to, to ravish me. It was only his presence at the inn that kept me safe, I think.' She plucked at her skirts. 'He even asked me to marry him, to save my reputation.'

'Good heavens! And you refused him?'

'Of course. Why on earth would I not? He cannot love me on such short acquaintance. Nor I him.' She sat up a little straighter before going on. 'It could never work. He is the son of a marquess and…and I could never leave Reigney. My life will always be here, with Papa.'

She met Lady Kenton's eyes steadily, knowing all the time that she was nowhere near as confident about this as she sounded. After what seemed like an age, her ladyship sighed and nodded.

'You have always been one to know your own mind, Selina, but…well, it does not matter now. What's done is done.'

'Quite, ma'am.' Selina rose and shook out her skirts. 'I am only sorry I spent so long talking with him Friday evening. I shall make sure I do not give anyone further food for gossip.'

'It will be easier once he has left Devonshire,' said Lady Kenton, accompanying her to the door. 'I understand the Viscount plans to travel to London in a se'ennight.'

'They are leaving so soon?'

'Why yes. Sir Alfred had it from Lord Graddon himself on Friday.'

Having taken her leave of Lady Kenton, Selina climbed into her coach for the short drive back to Reigney Abbey, her concerns about the gossip quite eclipsed by the news that Deveril would soon be gone. He had become so much a part of her world that she felt quite bereft at the idea of his going away.

The depression on her spirits had not lifted by the time she reached Reigney Abbey, where she was met with the news that her father and Mr Chewton were playing chess in the library.

'Very well, Leighton, I will not disturb them,' she said, removing her cloak and bonnet. 'I have work to do in the study. Pray have a glass of ratafia brought in to me.'

'Of course, Miss Selina.' The butler gave her a fatherly smile. 'And perhaps a slice of cake, or some bread and butter?'

The weight pressing on Selina had quite destroyed her appetite and she shook her head.

'No, nothing, thank you.'

* * *

Entering the figures and tallying up columns occupied Selina for a couple of hours and did much to restore her equilibrium, but there was still an element of relief mixed with her surprise when she learned from her father that he and Mr Chewton were dining at the George that evening.

'I am very sorry to be leaving you to dine alone, my dear,' he said, when she joined the gentlemen in the hall to see them off. 'The squire sent over the invitation this morning, while you were out. It needed an immediate reply, you see, and since Horace was eager to go…'

'There is no need to apologise, Papa, I am delighted that you feel well enough to attend.' She kissed his cheek. 'I am sure you will have a very pleasant evening.'

'I do hope so. Sir Alfred has arranged the dinner for the gentlemen from Graddon Hall, you see, and he thought Horace and I might like to come along.'

Horace Chewton laughed. 'I think what he really wants is a couple more old heads amongst what will be a room full of young bucks, eh, William?'

'Just so, Horace.' Her father chuckled. 'As Shakespeare put it, "a man loves the meat in his youth that he cannot endure in his age". We shall be able to enjoy a good dinner, lively company, but we will also leaven the proceedings with more serious conversation.'

Selina's heart swelled to hear her father sounding

so cheerful and she was genuinely happy to give him and his guest her blessing.

'Then you must go and enjoy yourselves,' she told him. 'I shall not wait up for you, so you may both be as late and as riotous as you please!'

With that she escorted both men to the door and waved the carriage away before going upstairs to change into an evening gown in readiness for a solitary dinner.

Papa was quite right, of course, about age and youth. It was quite understandable that the older gentlemen should seek out each other's company. For herself, tonight she was happy to be alone and consider what might be done about the gossip swirling around in Torrisford.

The answer, of course, was nothing. She would go on as before, ignore the gossip and eventually it would die down. When Deveril Blackbourne returned to London the gossip mongers might conclude that she had tried and failed to attract him, but she would weather that storm, too. Her true friends knew the truth and that was all that mattered.

Chapter Twenty

Deveril was in no mood for company. At least, for the company of anyone other than Selina Wynter. He could not get her out of his mind. In all his thirty years he had never felt this strongly about a woman before. Not even his long-deceased fiancée.

Belinda had been his first love. They had been childhood friends and his parents were very happy to promote an alliance that was so advantageous to both families. When she had died of a fever, Deveril had been distraught.

He had mourned for a full year, and when he did return to Society, his handsome face and charming manners soon made him a favourite with the ladies, but not one of them roused in him more than a passing fancy. It had always been understood, by himself and his friends, that Belinda's demise was the reason he was determined to remain a bachelor. Until now.

Selina filled his dreams as well as his waking hours. He could not forget her joyous laughter or those blue eyes that twinkled with merriment, or darkened to deepest sapphire when she was angry. Her presence lit up a room, her smile brightened the darkest day. He had never wanted anyone as much as he wanted Selina.

Deveril knew she could not love him after such a short acquaintance, but he did think she might at least have considered his proposal. Her refusal had been brutal, and since returning to Graddon Hall all he wanted to do was to be alone with his thoughts, wondering what, if anything, he could do to change her mind.

Tonight, however, the squire's invitation could not be refused. His friends would want to know the reason if he was the only one to remain behind. He therefore dressed with his usual care, offsetting the starkness of his black evening coat and breeches by the addition of an embroidered waistcoat, and accompanied them to the George.

Their host was waiting for them in the dining parlour, and Deveril was surprised to discover that Mr Wynter and Horace Chewton would be coming.

'Years of illness and a retiring nature has made William Wynter old before his time,' Sir Alfred explained in his bluff, good-natured way. 'Horace Chewton's visit has done wonders for his spirits and I thought there could be no objection to their joining us.'

'We shall be delighted to see them,' returned the Viscount cheerfully. 'The more the merrier!'

'I am glad to hear that, my lord.' The squire looked relieved, and became expansive: 'Wynter is one of my oldest friends and I vow I haven't seen him this animated since the death of his wife. That was almost ten years ago, and the poor fellow took it very bad. He was never a practical man, you see, and his wife had taken care of him and the estate. He is fortunate to have his daughter to look after Reigney.'

'And has she always done so?' enquired Lord Graddon.

Most of the others were busy filling their glasses, but Deveril hovered near, eager to hear more of Selina. His host did not disappoint him.

'Aye, she quit the schoolroom when her mother died and took over the running of the household and the estate. William insisted she should have her come out, two years later. He sent her to his sister in London to be presented, but within a month or so he was seriously ill. Selina returned home to nurse him and has been at Reigney ever since.' Sir Alfred sighed. 'Fine gel. I would have liked to see her settled in her own establishment, but that seems unlikely now. She is devoted to her father.'

'No hint of marriage, then,' remarked Sir Henry Jesmond, who had wandered over. He cast a laughing glance at Deveril. 'Surprising, with all the talk going around…'

'Mere tittle-tattle,' drawled the Viscount, putting

a warning hand on Deveril's arm. 'You know how people love to gossip.'

'Indeed, they do, my lord,' Sir Alfred agreed.

With a nod he moved away, taking Sir Henry with him, and Deveril let out his breath.

'Thank you, Richard. A timely intervention.'

The Viscount grinned. 'Couldn't have you drawing Jesmond's cork, my friend. That would certainly not help the situation. Word would have been all around Torrisford by the morning that you have an interest in the lady.' He glanced around to ensure they were not overheard. 'And pray do not insult me by denying it.'

'I merely wish to protect her good name.'

'Is that all? I have known you too long to believe that.'

Deveril felt his cheeks flushing under his friend's knowing glance, but he shrugged.

'It is of no consequence, Richard, since she won't have me.'

'You have made her an offer?' The Viscount was visibly startled.

'Yes. She refused me.' Deveril turned as the door opened again. 'Ah, here's her father now, with Chewton.' He watched as the squire greeted his final guests then added, 'I have to agree with our host, Mr Wynter's health seems to be vastly improved since Chewton arrived. He looks years younger.'

Lord Graddon nodded. 'Aye he does, despite his recent anxiety over his daughter.'

Deveril suddenly found he had no wish to talk more of Selina, even with his best friend. It was unexpectedly painful. He made his excuses and went off to refill his wine glass.

He continued to brood while the dinner progressed, drinking more slowly than some of his companions, notably Charles Penkridge and Henry Jesmond who were sitting opposite. When at length the covers were removed and the wine bottles had been replaced with brandy, conversation turned to the recent heavy snow and his attention was caught when Penkridge remarked that the Wynters had been the most inconvenienced.

'That must have been a very anxious time for you, sir,' he went on, 'not knowing where your daughter might be.'

'I was not overly anxious,' replied Mr Wynter in his mild way. 'I believed her to be with Lady Fremington.'

'It would have been different if we had known the truth,' remarked Mr Chewton. 'However, Miss Wynter is returned to us safe and sound. As I said at the time, all's well that ends well.'

But Penkridge wasn't finished.

'Aye, 'tis a pity about all these rumours flying around now,' he said, draining his glass and reaching for the decanter. 'Gossip is never good for a lady's reputation.'

'Then it is best not repeated,' Sir Alfred interjected. 'The matter should not be talked of.'

But his frowning look went unregarded.

'There's Fremington insisting his driver lost his way in the snow and swearing it wasn't an elopement, but that sounds like a hum to me! Trouble is, no one really knows what went on at that inn.' He gave a crack of laughter. 'Apart from Blackbourne, of course!'

'My daughter would not do anything to damage her reputation,' declared Mr Wynter, with a quiet dignity that momentarily sobered the party.

The old man was looking very pale, and Deveril desperately wanted to speak up, but most of those around the table were now in a rollicking humour. Anything he said in Selina's defence would only make things worse, and might result in ribald jests.

Realising he had blundered, Penkridge now tried to make amends.

'No, no, sir, I meant no offence. I'm sure there's no truth at all in the gossip. Although it's common knowledge that young Fremington wants to marry Miss Wynter, and it's no wonder, the lady being such a beauty. Not that I believe she would ever consent to an elopement, of course! Or that she changed her mind when she saw a bigger prize.'

Deveril banged his glass down on the table. 'Enough, Charles, damn you! There is no truth in any of this.' He glared around the table. 'If I find anyone here repeating these lies, I will call them out. *Is that understood?*'

'Aye, 'tis all nonsense, Blackbourne, I have always

said so,' exclaimed Sir Henry Jesmond, waving his glass in the air. 'And as for setting her cap at you, my lord, I don't believe a word of it! And what would be the point? Everyone knows you are never going to marry!' He cast a bleary eye around the table. 'Y' know what everyone says—Blackbourne buried his heart with his childhood sweetheart.'

'Stow it, Jesmond,' growled the Viscount, who was sitting at the foot of the table.

Deveril could see the fellow was too drunk to take note of anything save a punch on the jaw. He shrugged inwardly. It was better the fellow chattered about the past than the lady whose father was sitting nearby and looking decidedly uncomfortable. Someone tried to turn the conversation but Henry Jesmond was fixed on his subject, and his loud, drunken voice commanded attention.

'Never met Miss Roding myself, of course, but she must have been a beauty for poor Blackbourne to be so besotted.'

Deveril saw Richard start to rise and shook his head at him. Let the fellow talk. He could bear it, as long as it kept everyone's attention away from Selina.

'Saddest thing I ever heard,' Jesmond continued. 'Betrothed, they were, and a putrid fever carried her off shortly before the wedding.'

'When was that, Blackbourne?' asked Charles Penkridge. 'Six, seven years ago?'

'Nine.' Deveril picked up his glass. 'Nine years last December.'

That awful winter had marked the end of his youth but it struck him now that memory of it no longer filled him with black despair.

'I am very sorry to hear of your loss, my lord.'

Deveril looked across the table to find William Wynter's eyes resting on him, full of sympathy that he was not sure he deserved.

He said, 'Thank you, sir. It was a long time ago.'

'But one never recovers from such grief,' said Wynter, unutterable sadness in his voice. 'The squire here will tell you, I speak from experience.'

'And so it is with Blackbourne,' said Jesmond, swaying a little in his chair. 'He has vowed he will never marry. Ain't that so, my lord?'

Deveril hesitated, but he was not thinking of his dead fiancée. Selina's words were ringing, crystal clear, in his head, every syllable was like a blade in his heart.

It would be a punishment to be married to you.

He sat up straighter. Only now, when it was too late, did he realise how much she meant to him. But not by the flicker of an eyelid would he let anyone know that.

'It is true, Henry.' He smiled around the table. 'Marriage would curtail my pleasures considerably. I have made it a rule to keep clear of all the single ladies in want of a husband!'

'Aye.' Lord Ancrum laughed. 'He pursues the married ones instead!'

'Only if they first pursue *me*,' retorted Deveril, grinning.

As he had intended, his light-hearted quip lifted the atmosphere. There was general laughter around the table and the Viscount quickly introduced another subject. Much to Deveril's relief.

Selina awoke early to a fine spring morning and the cloudless blue sky she could see from her window raised her spirits. She rang for Nancy, who brought hot chocolate and the information that Papa and Mr Chewton had not returned to the Abbey until well after midnight.

'Then I shall not wait to break my fast with them,' declared Selina, throwing back the covers. 'Pray, Nancy, bring me my olive walking dress—I shall be going out this morning.'

After her usual morning meeting with the housekeeper, Selina ordered her carriage and set off to call upon the Jennocks. The morning air was cold, but it was still a pleasure to drive out in the late March sunshine. The recent snows had quite gone and spring flowers starred the banks and peeped out beneath hedgerows that were white with blossom.

When Selina reached the Rising Sun, she was greeted at the door by Mildy, who informed her that Mrs Jennock was in the kitchen.

'If you'd be so good as to step into the parlour, ma'am, I'll fetch her for 'ee.'

But Selina would not allow this. She followed the maid back to the kitchen, where she found the landlady sitting in a chair at one side of the fire, the baby's cradle beside her.

'Miss Wynter! Whatever is Mildy thinking of, bringing you in here!'

'No, no, don't get up, Mrs Jennock,' said Selina, laughing, 'I do not stand on ceremony with you.' She put her basket on the table and turned to peer into the cradle. 'And how is the baby?'

'Oh, she's coming along very nicely, thank you, ma'am. The midwife came the day you left and stayed for a full week, until I was well enough to get up and get on with things.'

'I confess I am surprised to find you out of bed.'

'I couldn't leave Mildy and Jennock to cope with everything any longer than I had to, although his lordship did offer to pay for someone to come in.'

'You mean Lord Deveril?'

'Aye, that's right. That concerned, he was, tellin' Jennock to take on another girl, but as we told him, I ain't no fancy lady, wantin' to lie abed for weeks. Beggin' your pardon, miss.'

Selina laughed, not a whit offended, and at that moment the door opened. Mr Jennock came in, beaming when he saw their visitor. Selina suggested they should inspect the basket, and watched, smiling, as they pulled out the little gifts she had included.

'Miss Wynter you are spoiling us,' the landlady protested. 'A silver and coral teether for the baby, whatever next!'

'And look, Mrs Jennock, there's a bar of fine soap for you and tobacco for me pipe!' exclaimed the landlord.

'And pretty ribbons for Mildy.' Mrs Jennock waited until the girl had thanked Selina profusely before sending her off to put the ribbons away safely in her room. She shook her head as the maid danced out of the room. 'That girl will be gettin' above herself!'

'Nonsense, it is only a few ribbons.' Selina paused as the landlady gasped over a length of white lace she pulled from the bottom of the basket. 'And that is merely a scrap I came across in the linen store and thought you might be able to find a use for it.'

'Aye, miss, we'll keep it to wrap Baby for her baptism,' said Mrs Jennock, refolding the lace. The baby stirred and she began to rock the cradle, saying fondly, 'So fine as she'll be, lord love 'er.'

The landlord came over to stand by his wife, gazing down fondly at the little bundle in the cradle.

He said, 'Ah, 'twas a lucky day when you was all snowed in with us, Miss Wynter, and no mistake. We owes you a great debt, ma'am, and I don't know how we can repay it.'

'Apart from *not* gossipin' with strangers when they

comes asking,' declared Mrs Jennock, lifting the baby into her arms.

Selina frowned. 'Someone has been here, asking questions?'

'Only one of the carters from Torrisford,' Jennock told her. 'He'd heard some tale about elopements and suchlike. I gave him short shrift, told him we was a respectable house and sent him on his way. We neither saw nor heard nothing untoward, Miss Wynter. That's what I told him and what I'd say to anyone who comes asking about what's none o' their business.'

'Thank you, I am relieved to hear it.'

Selina took her leave soon after, disturbed to think the gossip had spread so far and so quickly. She hoped it would not come to Papa's ears. It would grieve him deeply to think she was the object of such salacious stories.

However, there was little she could do about it, she decided, as she travelled back to the Abbey. Just as there was nothing she could do about Deveril's leaving. She stared out of the window, oblivious to the sunshine or the burgeoning hedgerows. She had known it must happen, but hearing of his kindness to the Jennocks only served to remind her of what a good man he was.

And what she had lost by refusing him.

'But how could I accept?' she asked the empty carriage. 'He was being noble, offering me the protection of his name. And I do not want or need his protection!'

But the arguments rang hollow. Somehow Deveril Blackbourne had invaded her thoughts and her heart, leaving her restless and unsettled. So much so that she was no longer sure she wanted to spend the rest of her life at Reigney Abbey.

Not that there was anything to be done about that at present, because Papa needed her. He must be her first concern.

When the carriage drew up at the Abbey door Selina buried all these unwelcome thoughts. She summoned up a smile and walked into the hall, where she was informed that her father and his guest had gone out.

'Goodness, after their late night I thought I should find them both dozing before the fire!'

Leighton shook his head.

'No, Miss Selina. It being such a fine day they are gone out in the gig. Mr Chewton is driving them.' He added, smiling, 'It is good to see the master out and about again, isn't it? Quite like his old self.'

'Yes, yes it is.'

She went upstairs, thinking of the numerous times she had tried to persuade her father to drive out with her, but he generally refused, saying he was too tired, or too busy. Horace Chewton's presence in the house was acting like a tonic for her father, and she could not regret it. Before his old friend had arrived, Papa had few regular visitors. Even the vicar, Mr Gurney, could only come to play chess with him occasionally.

Selina devoted most of her spare time to Papa, reading to him, playing at cards or backgammon or trying to coax him to stroll out in the garden. It was a very good thing that Papa was not quite so dependent upon her now, but she could not deny it hurt, just a little, to think she was not quite so necessary for his comfort.

Having shed her cloak and bonnet and tidied her unruly curls, Selina made her way down to the morning room, where she wandered aimlessly around the room. She thought of the Jennocks, happy and content in the cosy warmth of their kitchen, and Papa and Horace Chewton, enjoying their outing. Going over to the window she stared out at the gardens. For once the view gave her little pleasure and she crossed her arms, as if to protect herself from the wave of loneliness that suddenly swept over her.

This was nothing more than a fit of the megrims, of course. Quite foolish. She had Papa and her friends in Torrisford, plus sufficient pin money to do very much as she pleased. So why on earth should she feel so sorry for herself?

Her thoughts were interrupted by a scratching on the door and the housekeeper came in.

'There's a delivery for you, miss.' She held out a package wrapped in brown paper.

'Thank you, Mrs Leighton.'

Selina took the package and placed it on the table.

Intrigued, she removed the outer wrapping and a layer of felted cloth beneath it to reveal a patterned bandbox bearing the name of a London perfumiers. Inside the box was a large jar of hand salve, nestled in straw. Spotting a folded paper tucked in one side, she pulled it out and scanned the contents.

Then she burst into tears.

Chapter Twenty-One

Selina did not weep for long and she was already wiping her eyes when she heard voices in the hall. It was Papa and Mr Chewton, returned from their drive!

Expecting them to come into the morning room, she quickly put away her handkerchief, but there was no time to remove the bandbox. All she could do was to school her face into a cheerful smile as the door opened.

'Ah, Selina, there you are. I hope you have not been anxious about us, my dear?'

'No, no, Papa. Leighton told me you had gone out,' she said, as he came over and kissed her cheek.

'We have had the most splendid time, Miss Selina,' declared Horace Chewton following his host into the room. 'We drove into Torrisford to take a look at some of its fine old buildings. Then we called upon Mr Gurney, who invited us to inspect the undercroft at the church. There are definite signs of a much older building beneath the existing structure, it was most interesting!'

'But what is this, Selina?' said her father, spotting the bandbox and its wrapping on the table. 'A delivery for you?'

'Why yes, Papa, it arrived shortly before you came in.' She waved one hand dismissively, in an attempt to make light of it. 'Shall we all sit by the fire? I should very much like to know about your outing.'

But her father was not to be distracted. He walked across to the table and stared down at the jar, still nestled in the bandbox, then he picked up the delivery note.

'Hand salve, Selina?' He gave her an enquiring look over the top of his spectacles.

'Very useful.' Mr Chewton nodded. 'The winter weather can be very cruel to the skin.'

She felt herself blushing, wanting to snatch the paper from Papa's hands but knowing that was impossible. She could only wait while he read it.

'Goodness me, it contains myrrh oil and jasmine. And from Jermyn Street, too! This must have cost a pretty penny—my dear, surely you did not send for this?'

'No, Papa, I—'

But he was already taking a closer look at the note. 'Ah, now I see: "prepared on the express instructions of Lord Deveril Blackbourne".'

'Lord Deveril?' repeated Horace Chewton. 'Why,

he is one of Viscount Graddon's party, isn't he? We saw him at last night's dinner.'

Mr Wynter had removed his spectacles and was staring at Selina.

'So, it is true,' he said slowly. 'What they are saying about you and his lordship.'

'There is a great deal being said, Papa,' Selina answered him cautiously. 'Perhaps you should tell me what it is you have heard.'

'Last night, at the George. Your name and Lord Deveril's were…were linked. It was said.' A spasm of disgust clouded his usually benign countenance. 'It was said that you *set your cap* at him while you were at the Rising Sun.'

'Perhaps I should go…'

Mr Chewton began edging towards the door but Selina put out her hand to stop him.

'No, please stay,' she said, her cheeks flushed with anger. 'I have done nothing to be ashamed of. I should like to know who has been spreading such vicious lies.'

It was Mr Chewton who answered.

'My dear, you must understand, this was a gentleman's dinner. Things are often said there that would never be spoken in mixed company. Wine and words were flowing freely. Some of the guests were in their cups.'

Selina frowned. 'You said Lord Deveril was there,

Mr Chewton. Did he not deny these malicious rumours?'

'Yes, and most forcefully.' He went on, trying to reassure her, 'His lordship was even willing to defend your honour. He threatened to call out anyone repeating the salacious gossip.'

'Did…did he?' asked Selina, a tiny flame of hope flickering into life.

Her father nodded. 'Yes, he did. I thought the better of him for that.'

'Aye, 'twas very chivalrous of him, when one considers his own tragic loss,' added Mr Chewton. 'After all, it is well-known that he has never shown a serious interest in any woman. What was it they said of him, William? Ah yes, he buried his heart with his fiancée. In fact, Lord Deveril said as much himself.'

'Oh,' The little flame flickered and died.

Her father nodded. 'I feel for the man, Selina, because it is very much the case with me. I have never recovered from your dear mother's death.'

'Although his lordship very bravely hides his anguish,' added Mr Chewton. 'He said in that joking way of his how much a wife would restrict his pleasures.'

Her father sighed. 'Poor fellow. One can never truly recover from the loss of one's first love, as I know only too well. I miss my dear Avril more with each passing day. However, it gives me some comfort to think she has been spared the grief of this present scandal.'

Distress was writ large on his countenance and Selina's heart ached for him, even as she raged inwardly against the gossip-mongers.

'There *is* no scandal, Papa! There is no truth in any of the rumours you may have heard.' She added bitterly, 'I suppose they also said I had eloped with Clifford Fremington?'

'It was mentioned. Naturally, I discounted it.'

'As you should, sir,' she replied angrily. 'I have no intention of marrying Clifford. Or anyone!'

He went on, as if he had not heard her, 'I did not believe any of the things that were said of you! But now, seeing this…' He waved towards the jar.

'Dearest Papa, believe me, Lord Deveril meant no harm by this gift. It was a kindly gesture, very much like the little presents he sent to the Rising Sun.

'You see, what with Mrs Jennock being so near her time and there being only Mildy, the young maid, to look after us all, I could not sit idly by. I set to work in the kitchen, helping to prepare the meals and all the other tasks that needed to be done.' She hurried across and took his hands. 'There, Papa, you can feel for yourself my hands are rougher than they should be.'

Her father pulled free and stepped back, staring at her. 'You worked as a—a *maid*?'

She blenched. If he thought that was outrageous, what would he do if he knew of her masquerading as a serving wench at the White Horse? She prayed he would not find out about that!

She said now, 'I could do nothing else, sir. We

would not have been half so comfortable if I had not taken charge. Then Mrs Jennock was brought to bed and I divided my time between looking after her and the kitchen. The circumstances were exceptional and, given the bad weather, I believed it was necessary for me to help. We had a bed made up in my chamber for Mildy and both gentlemen were very solicitous of my reputation, I promise you. Believe me, Papa, but there was no impropriety. You may go to the inn and talk to the Jennocks yourself, if you wish.'

Her father sighed and shook his head.

'*I* do not doubt you, my love. I am quite sure you would never act improperly. But it pains me deeply to think anyone would spread such lies about you.'

Mr Chewton sighed. 'Alas, William, it is the way of the world. Another scandal will occur in due course and this will all be forgotten.'

Mr Wynter nodded. 'You are right, of course, Horace. When Graddon Hall is shut up again and the visitors gone the Torrisford gossips will turn their attention elsewhere.' He released a weary sigh. 'Until then we must bear the scorn and disapprobation of our neighbours as best we can.'

'I am very sorry for it, Papa, but I did nothing wrong, save climbing into Clifford's carriage without my maid. But truly, I thought I would be safe enough. We were only supposed to be going to Fremington Court.'

'I believe you, Selina. Although perhaps now you

will see the wisdom of being accompanied when you go out. Your dear mama would never have thought of leaving the house without a servant in attendance.'

Selina's lively spirit rebelled at the idea, but Papa was already overset by the salacious talk, and she did not want to grieve him further with an argument.

The entrance of Leighton and a footman with trays of refreshments put an end to the conversation. Selina excused herself, leaving the two gentlemen to enjoy their cakes and wine while she carried the jar of salve carefully up to her room. She would treasure it. Not for its cost, but because it was such a thoughtful gesture. An act of kindness that had reduced her to tears, knowing who had sent it, and what might have been.

In her room she pulled a chair to the window and sat down, looking out at the familiar landscape. Mr Chewton had said Lord Deveril defended her. Was it possible that he still cared for her, just a little? Enough, perhaps, to repeat his offer of marriage? No, that was too much to hope for.

She fell into a pleasant daydream, thinking of Deveril, the way his mouth quirked up at the corners, always on the edge of a smile. The twinkling gleam in his dark eyes that sent tiny shivers of excitement running through her. He might never love her as he had done his childhood sweetheart, but perhaps they might be able to live comfortably together. He had already suggested he could go about his business while she remained at Reigney, looking after Papa.

She never doubted that he would spend some time with her in Devonshire, and she would be able to accompany him occasionally, to town or to visit one of his houses. There would surely be times when he would want her in his bed. The very thought of it made her light-headed with desire.

Perhaps she been too hasty in refusing him. She had always put her father first, but now she wondered if that was truly necessary. After all, the household had proved themselves quite capable of looking after him when she was stranded at the Rising Sun. Papa, too, had gone on perfectly well without her. She frowned, trying to be honest with herself. There had been other men in the past who had shown an interest in her, and looking after Papa had always been her reason for rejecting them. Perhaps it had become second nature to refuse them without actually consulting her own heart. She had only ever felt the mildest of regrets at turning them down. Until now.

She tried to distract herself with her embroidery, but the idea persisted. Finally, shortly before changing into her evening gown, she gave in to temptation and dashed off a note to Deveril, telling him that she would be riding out to Reigney Ridge before breakfast the following morning.

She was not so forward as to ask him to meet her there. She would leave that to him. But if he did turn up, well. She had left a door open, just a little.

* * *

Selina went down to dinner to find Papa still fretting over the rumours and she exerted herself to coax him into a happier frame of mind. In this she was ably assisted by Horace Chewton, who introduced subjects of a more scholarly nature to divert her father's thoughts.

Between them, they succeeded very well and Selina was pleased to see her father enjoy a hearty dinner. When the meal was over, Mr Chewton went off to finish some urgent correspondence, assuring his host that it should not take longer than an hour.

'Afterwards I shall come to the drawing room and you and I will have our customary brandy together, before we retire to our beds,' he declared.

Mr Chewton went out, and as the door closed behind him, Selina heard her father sigh.

She said quickly, 'It is a very fine evening, Papa. Shall we take advantage of the last of the light to stroll around the garden?'

She was pleased and somewhat relieved when he agreed without demur. She quickly fetched a wrap for herself, and a muffler for her father and accompanied him outside.

They walked slowly, Selina pointing out the autumn plantings that were already showing in the flowerbeds.

'Very good my dear,' he told her. 'You do not have your mother's flair for gardening, but I am sure they will provide a lovely display in the warmer weather.

Now, let us go through the arch. I am eager to see what changes have you wrought in here.'

They stepped into the walled garden, where fruit trees and bushes, flowers, vegetables and herbs flourished in its sheltered confines.

'I have changed very little here,' she confessed. 'Everything seems to grow so well I leave it to the gardeners to tend it as they will.'

She accompanied her father as he walked slowly along the path, using his stick to point at the various plants that caught his attention, until at last they came to a bench and he suggested they sit down for a moment.

'This was your mother's favourite spot,' he said, after studying the garden in silence. 'She loved to sit here on a summer's evening, when the air was heavy with scent. Those were halcyon days, Selina, when your mother was alive. We shall not see her like again.'

He sighed heavily and after a few moments spent in reflective silence, Selina suggested they should move on.

'The light is fading and I do not want you to catch a chill.' She helped him to rise, saying as she rearranged the muffler around his throat, 'Mr Chewton will soon be coming downstairs to join you in the drawing room.'

'Yes, he will,' said her father, brightening. 'It has been such a pleasure to see Horace again. I had forgotten how much I enjoy his company. My, but the lively conversations we have had since he has been here, they have quite lifted my spirits.'

'They have indeed, Papa, it is a long time since I saw you so animated.'

'But he will be returning to Oxford shortly. The Abbey will seem very empty without him.' He gave a long sigh, but then rallied, saying more cheerfully, 'At least I shall still have you with me, Selina. I confess, I am very relieved to know you have no thoughts of marriage—although with all the talk whirling about at present I do not think any respectable man would wish to…' He trailed off, then smiled and held out his arm to her. 'But enough of that. You are here, Selina, and I thank heaven for that. It is such a comfort, knowing I shall have you with me, always.'

Selina took his arm. 'Yes, Papa, you will always have me.'

She smiled, but inside if felt as if a door had finally been closed. And locked.

Chapter Twenty-Two

Selina woke early, but for once there was no eager anticipation for the day ahead. She had received no word from Graddon Hall; she had no idea if Deveril would ride out to meet her, or even if he had received her note. She wished now she had not written, but having done so she must keep her word. She would ride out, as planned.

It was a clear sunny morning and Orion was very lively when he was led out of his stall, but Selina declined her groom's suggestion that he should come with her, salving her conscience with the thought that she would be on Reigney land, and her father had not actually forbidden to her to ride out unaccompanied.

She was obliged to give her attention to Orion for the first ten minutes, but the big hunter soon calmed down, and Selina's nerves settled, too. If Deveril should appear she would thank him for the hand salve and his kindness towards the Jennocks and take her leave of him. There was no need to say anything else.

* * *

As she approached Reigney Ridge she spotted the grey gelding tethered to a bush, and Deveril standing nearby, his black cloak pushed back from his shoulders. Selina rode up, frowning. She had expected them to converse from horseback, safely and at a distance.

He said, by way of greeting, 'You have heard this latest nonsense that is being spread abroad.'

'That I ran off with Clifford and then rejected him for you?' Her lip curled. 'Contemptible rubbish. I suspect Clifford had a hand in starting these rumours, and I am furious with him. I am also angry that he thinks I would marry him just to save my reputation! But what angers me most is Papa's learning of it. He was very distressed.'

'And he heard of it from people who should have known better.' He took the reins from her and tethered Orion close to his own mount. 'You cannot know how very sorry I am for that.'

She dismissed his apology with a wave. 'I understand the wine had been flowing freely, my lord. It loosens tongues.'

'That was not why you wanted to see me?'

'No.'

He stepped closer. 'Shall we walk?'

Selina hesitated, then kicked her foot free of the stirrup and slid down. Deveril caught her, taking her weight and lowering her gently to the ground. For a moment they did not move. He was gazing down, his dark eyes devouring her face. Selina's heart missed a beat then began to pound, hard, against her ribs. Unable to resist, she lifted her chin, her lips parting, inviting his kiss. His arms tightened and he pulled her against him, lowering his head to capture her mouth.

A wave of shock crashed over her and she put her hands on his shoulders to steady herself while his lips worked over hers. She responded instinctively, her arms slipping around his neck clinging to him desperately while she gave him back kiss for kiss. When he raised his head, she pressed closer.

'Don't stop,' she whispered, her lips against his mouth. 'Don't stop now.'

He gave a ragged laugh. 'Sweetheart, I must, before it is too late.'

'No.' Desperately she took his face in her hands and kissed him. With a groan he lowered his head and began to trail kisses along her chin, each one sending a fiery dart arrowing deep into her body until she was burning with need.

She moaned softly as his teeth grazed her ear, then with a sigh he lifted his head, his arms tightening around her.

'This is madness, Selina.'

She closed her eyes, close to tears with frustration. She wanted him, with every fibre of her being. Inside, she was screaming at him to kiss her again, to prove to her just how much he wanted her. He was holding her close and she could feel the heavy thud of his heart against her cheek. After what seemed like an age his chest rose and he released a breath, like a long sigh of regret, then he gently held her away from him.

'We should walk.' He pulled her hand onto his arm. 'Come, Selina, I think we both need to take the air.'

Disappointment seared her, bitter as gall, but she fought it down as they began to walk towards the ridge. She had offered herself to him and he had rejected her. If anything was needed to prove he did not love her, this was it.

Deveril glanced down at the stiff figure on his arm. Her cheeks were flushed, and she was biting her lip, as if struggling with some strong emotion.

'Why exactly did you send me that message?' he asked, beating down the temptation to drag her back into his arms.

'I wanted to thank you. For your kindness in ordering the salve for me.'

'You could have put that in your note.'

'I wanted to tell you in person.'

'And that is why you kissed me, is it?' he said. 'To thank me.'

'Of course not.' Her head dropped and he saw the colour flood her cheeks. 'That was unfortunate. I could not help myself.'

He felt a little flicker of hope.

'Should I be flattered?' He kept his tone light, teasing. 'Have you, perhaps, changed your mind about marrying me?'

Selina's breath hitched. He must never know how much she wished that was possible, but she was committed to her father. Duty before self.

She managed a short laugh. 'Why on earth would I do that?'

'To confound the gossips.'

'That is not a good reason to marry. The gossip will pass, in time.'

Deveril stopped. 'Will you not reconsider my offer?' He took her hands. 'Marry me, Selina. Allow me to take care of you. To protect you.'

Still no words of love. He did not even utter the smooth insincerities of a rake intent upon seduction! For a long moment Selina could not speak, her heart breaking for him, as well as herself. How deeply he must have loved his fiancée to have forsworn marriage all these years. He was behaving like a gentleman, offering marriage to save her good name.

She wanted to accept, to put her trust in him, but how long would it last? She could never replace his beloved Belinda. Deveril was impulsive, restless. How long before he lost interest and regretted saddling himself with a wife?

It took all her strength to refuse him.

'Thank you, my lord, but no.' She gently disengaged herself and began to walk on. 'I cannot marry you.'

'Why not? I think we might be very happy together.'

'No, it would not work,' she said. 'Your offer was kindly meant—'

'Kind!'

'Yes.' She could not bring herself to mention Belinda and said instead, 'You suggested I might remain at Reigney, with Papa.'

'Yes, of course, if your father needs you.'

'I am his daughter. There is no one else.' The words sounded bleak, even to her own ears.

'I am not asking you to choose between us, Selina. I have already said you might spend a considerable part of the year here at Reigney, if you wish.'

A cold hand clutched around Selina's heart. If anything was needed to convince her it was this. It was not the speech of a man violently in love. She put up her chin.

'Thank you, but I am very content with my lot.'

'Content! I do not believe that. I have seen another side to you. A bolder, more adventurous side that wants—*deserves* more than this quiet existence. You are a courageous woman, Selina, made for a life of excitement and colour. Of new experiences. Adventure. I can give that to you.' He put his hand on her arm, obliging her to stop. 'Marry me, Selina, let me show you the world outside Torrisford!'

'Your world is one of intrigue and gambling, my lord.'

And mistresses, she reminded herself, to bolster her resolve.

'In London, perhaps!' He laughed. 'That is only a small part of it. There is so much more to be enjoyed, art, the theatre, good conversation. As my wife all doors would be open to you. We might travel abroad, too. I have been thinking for some time I should make the Grand Tour and there is no reason we should not do it together. Imagine it, Selina! France, Italy, Switzerland.'

She could imagine it all too clearly. A Grand Tour with Deveril at her side would be blissful, if he truly loved her.

'No,' she said, with more than a hint of defiance, 'I do not want to live anywhere but here. Reigney is where I have always been happiest.'

'You do not think I could make you happy?'

They had reached the edge of the escarpment and she stopped, silently looking out over the familiar landscape spread below. A tiny voice whispered that it was not necessary for her to remain at the Abbey. Mrs Leighton was perfectly capable of managing the house, while Ashworth and Papa's attorney could handle the business of the estate. But they were none of them related to Papa. They could not be company for him. They could not be a comfort.

And where would be your *comfort, if you marry a man who does not love you?*

He went on. 'You said once that marrying me would be a punishment, but surely it could not be as bad as that?' When she did not reply he sighed. 'Forgive me, this is all new to me. I am not accustomed to baring my soul in this way.' He raked a hand through his hair.

'I am offering you not just my hand, Selina. What I am trying to say is that... I love you.'

He buried his heart with his fiancée.

Selina shook her head. 'That is impossible, my lord. We have only known each other a matter of weeks.'

'It is nearly two months now. And I think I have loved you for almost all of that time.'

His smile almost broke her heart. She desperately wanted to believe him, but dared not do so. Fine words tripped easily from his tongue, but he couldn't mean them. How could she ever replace the fiancée to whom he had given his heart? He was known to be wild and reckless. While he might say he loved her now, it would not last. His passion would fade and he would look elsewhere for comfort. Then she would be a prisoner, locked into her worst nightmare.

'I am sorry, I cannot marry you,' she said at last. 'I do not love you.'

'But you want me, Selina, and that's a start—'

'It is true, I do want you. I want to lie with you here, now, but I will not marry you.'

She spoke the last words slowly, clear and deliberate, and they hung in the air between them.

'And that is your final word on the matter?' he demanded, his voice sharp. 'Answer me truthfully now, for I vow, Selina, I shall not ask a third time.'

'It is. My final word.'

She met his frowning gaze steadily, ignoring the tumultuous racing of her heart.

'Then you had best go home. I may be a rogue, but for all my rakish ways I do not tamper with innocents.'

She raised her chin. 'I am five-and-twenty. I know my own mind.'

'Not in this case, madam.' His lips quirked upwards, but his eyes remained dark, sombre. 'Trust me, I know far better than you what you are risking.'

He was looking impossibly handsome, his raven-black hair falling over his brow, and Selina wanted him so badly it took her breath away. If she could lie with him, just once, it would be a memory to comfort her through the coming years. She stepped closer.

'I am willing to take that risk. Please, Deveril, do you want me to beg?'

She reached up to smooth back the wayward lock but he caught her wrist.

'Oh no, Selina, I will not let you tempt me into such an indiscretion.'

Her face flamed.

'I thought you w-wanted me!' she cried, her voice catching on a sob.

'I do, but not like this. You refuse to marry *me*, but are young enough yet to meet someone you do wish to marry, a good honest man, no doubt, and then you would bitterly regret this encounter. I will not do that to you.'

The implacable note in his voice told Selina he would not be moved. She bit her lip, dragging together the remnants of her pride.

She raised her head and tried to smile as she quoted a line of poetry that had come into her head.

'Very well. "Since there's no help, come let us kiss and part".'

Deveril's eyes blazed and for a moment she hoped he might take her in his arms one last time, but he merely took her hand and pulled it onto his arm.

'I don't think that's a good idea, my sweet, do you?' he drawled. 'You should go home now.'

In silence they walked back to the horses. Selina kept her tears at bay by telling herself if it had to end, this was for the best. She should be thankful that for once Devil Blackbourne had acted so nobly.

One day, perhaps, she would be.

Selina allowed Deveril to throw her up in the saddle, and he gallantly held Orion's bridle while she made herself comfortable and secure on the saddle.

'Thank you.' She avoided his eyes. It was easier to keep her voice steady if she did not look at him. 'I wish you well, my lord.'

'And I you, madam.' He patted Orion's neck and stepped away. 'I had best get back to Graddon Hall. There is much to do before I leave for London later today.'

'Today!' Selina glanced up at the sky. 'But it will be past noon before you even get back to Graddon Hall.'

Deveril's mouth twisted. He needed to get away, to put some distance between them. Confound it, why could she not send him away? Every moment he remained in her company was torture!

He said, 'It is how I am. Impatient. I shall be away before dark and dine on the road. There is a clear sky and the moon is almost full. I shall travel through the night.'

'But surely, you would be better waiting until the morning.'

'No. There is nothing to keep me here any longer.' That sounded more bitter than he intended, but it was too late now. The words were out. 'The sooner I am gone, the sooner those damned rumours will fade.'

Deveril strode across to Colonel and untied him. It had taken all his willpower to refuse Selina and his body was still burning with frustration. Was he a fool, when the lady was so willing?

For years he had been feted by Society, courted and pursued by ladies all eager to marry him. He had taken some of them to his bed, but nowhere near as many as rumours suggested. Now, when he had finally found the woman he wanted to make his wife, she would have none of it. And the irony was that he loved her far too much to ruin her.

By the time he scrambled into the saddle he expected Selina to have ridden off, but she was still there, regarding him.

He said, 'If you have need of me, a letter to Revesby House, my brother's residence in London, will find me, wherever I am.'

He thought he caught a glimpse of regret in her face, a sheen of tears in those beautiful eyes, but it was gone in an instant. No matter, he would not torture himself thinking any more about the lady. He turned away, gave Colonel his head and they set off at a canter.

Selina watched Deveril ride away until tears blurred her eyes too much so see. It was done, she had sent him away and would never see him again. Dashing away the tears she turned towards home. She had made her choice and must live with it, even though a tiny voice in her head was telling her it was the wrong one.

Selina was thankful that Orion knew his way to the stables, because she paid scant attention on the ride back. It was as if a war was going on inside her. Sensible Selina insisted that her duty was to Papa. He needed her. But a more rebellious spirit had awoken. It had been mostly dormant and subdued since she had stepped into her mother's shoes and taken over the running of Reigney Abbey ten years ago, but it had been making itself heard more frequently of late. Now it whispered to her as she rode through the familiar lanes, heedless of the spring flowers and birdsong around her.

In truth you are not that necessary to Papa, whispered Rebellious Selina, with brutal honesty. *Since Mama's death you have always been there to look after him, to amuse him and keep him company. But since Horace Chewton arrived he has shown that he can manage very well without you. Better, in fact.*

Yes. Selina had to admit that since Mr Chewton had arrived Papa had been far more active, much less inclined to fall into melancholy.

You are not his wife, Selina. Deveril is right, there is a solution to all this.

'Stop, I pray you!' she exclaimed, silencing the birds and causing Orion to prick up his ears. 'It is too late. Deveril is going to London. He will have plenty to distract him there. He will soon forget me.' She glanced around the quiet, empty lane. 'And he will not ask a third time.'

The rebellious spirit did not reply, but it seemed to Selina that it was not quite banished. Rather it had retired to a corner of her mind, where it waited, arms crossed, observing her with disdain.

Chapter Twenty-Three

Arriving at the Abbey, Selina left Orion and the stables and slipped into the house through a back door. She made her way, unnoticed, to her bedchamber where she threw herself onto the bed and indulged in a hearty bout of tears.

When she finally stopped crying she felt so drained that she remained on her bed, thinking despondently that she had just proved beyond all doubt that she was not the courageous woman Deveril thought her. Why, she was nothing but a watering pot!

With a sigh she slipped off the bed and went over to the washstand to bathe her face. Nancy would be in soon to help her change for dinner and she must make an effort. She did not want Papa or Mr Chewton to think anything was amiss.

When Selina entered the drawing room she found her father alone and standing by the window, a partially filled wine glass in his hand. She was heartened by the sight; he had often stood thus when Mama was alive. Since her demise, he had taken to sitting down with a rug thrown over his knees, like an invalid.

He turned, saying, 'Ah, Selina, is that you? May I pour you a glass of Madeira?'

She was delighted to accept this change in their routine. It was normally she who poured wine for them both.

'I am glad to see you looking so well, Papa. What have you and Mr Chewton been doing today?'

'We have spent the morning talking, my love.' He beamed at her. 'I have news, my dear. News that I hope will please you as much as it does me.'

'Very well, Papa, you had best tell me.'

Still beaming, he walked away from the window and sat down opposite her.

'Horace is going to remain at the Abbey!'

'He has extended his visit?' She hoped her smile was convincing. 'That must please you exceedingly, Papa.'

'No, no. He is going to make his home here at Reigney. We have plenty of room, after all. Horace and I have decided the arrangement will suit us both very well.' He stopped. 'But, Selina, are you not pleased, my dear? Horace is such an easy-going fellow, I thought you would be delighted with the plan.'

'Why, yes, Papa. I think it is the very thing for you. It—it is just a shock to hear it is all decided.'

His brow cleared. 'I knew you would agree with

me. And I am sure it need make no difference to how we go on here. You will still have the running of the house and the estate.' He laughed. 'In fact, it will be even better. With Horace to keep me company I shall not be such a burden to you.'

'You could never be a burden, Papa!'

'Oh, but I am, Selina. After your mother died, I gave way to my grief with no thought for what you must be suffering, too. You were still in the schoolroom, too young to bear all that responsibility of the house and the estate.'

'But I wanted to do it. I know I could never replace Mama, but I wanted to make you happy.'

'And you did, my love. But you are right. Nothing could bring your dear mama back to me. The pain of it has never left me.'

She hesitated, then said slowly, 'Papa, if you had known how painful it would be to, to lose Mama, would you still have wanted to marry?'

He looked at her, uncomprehending.

'But of course, Selina. She was the love of my life.' He smiled. 'One never knows what the future may hold, my dear, but if I had been told I could only have a month—one day!—with my darling Avril I would still have jumped at the chance.' He paused as the door opened. 'Ah, there you are, Horace. I have told Selina about your staying on, and she is delighted with the idea.'

'It that really so?' Mr Chewton bent an earnest look

at Selina. 'I did suggest we should talk it over with you first, Miss Wynter, but William was adamant you would not have the slightest objection.'

He was looking keenly at Selina, who roused herself from her thoughts and smiled at him.

'No, Mr Chewton. No objection at all.'

'That relieves my mind of its only concern.' He gave a merry chuckle. 'I shall be in the nature of a companion for William, which will give you more time for your own interests, my dear.'

'Yes,' she replied, still distracted. 'Yes, indeed.'

Leighton came in to announce dinner just as the clock on the marble consul table chimed the hour. Five o'clock. Too late to send a note to Deveril. He would be on his way to London by now. If only this had been decided yesterday and she had known of it before she rode out to meet him. How different things might have been.

'Well, well,' declared Papa, as they sat down at the table. 'I was feeling quite dejected at the thought of your leaving us, Horace, but all that is changed now!'

Throughout dinner Selina listened to her father and Horace Chewton discussing their plans and she realised how little she featured in them. She had lost her place as Papa's companion, but she could not be unhappy about it. Mr Chewton was her father's equal at chess and they were able to converse on scholarly subjects that had never interested her. She had no doubt they would go on very happily together, here at the Abbey.

But what of her own future?

Horace Chewton picked up his glass. 'Well, well, it all looks to have worked out for the best, William,' he said, saluting his friend. 'But, Miss Selina, you are very quiet. I do hope you are not having any misgivings about this?'

She was so lost in thought that he was obliged to repeat his question. She looked at him blankly for a moment, then smiled.

'I was a little surprised when Papa first told me of it, Mr Chewton, but I can assure you I am very happy. In fact,' she said, raising her own wine glass, 'I think it is the very best thing, for all of us!'

The post-chaise swept into the yard of the White Horse and was immediately surrounded by ostlers ready to change the sweating horses.

'No hurry,' Deveril informed them, as he jumped down from the carriage. 'I am dining here.'

Throwing a coin to the postilions he followed the landlord inside and was shown directly to a private parlour. In his present mood he had no wish to sit in the public coffee room, even for ten minutes. Confound it, if he hadn't sent one of Richard's servants ahead to bespeak the room and a dinner, he would not have bothered to stop at all, for he had no appetite.

The sun had already set and a covering of low cloud

brought an early dusk. Candles burned around the room, reflecting on the polished wood panelling, and a cheerful fire blazed in the hearth, but none of these comforts improved his mood.

He shrugged off his coat and walked across to the window, which looked out onto the busy yard. A mail coach had just come in and the ostlers were racing to change the horses. The driver had climbed down to stretch his legs and was chatting and laughing with a servant who had brought him a tankard of ale.

He remembered how he had walked through the alley over there into the little service yard. That was where he had first seen Selina, flushed and bright-eyed, sending two drunkards about their business. He had thought her delightful, a strong, resourceful woman with a gleam of mischief in those beautiful eyes. But that was not the half of it! Only when they had been snowed up together had he realised how truly magnificent she was, taking charge of the inn, looking after the landlady and her baby.

Stealing his heart.

This was a mistake, there are too many memories here. You should have stayed in the coach while the horses were changed.

'Beggin' your pardon, my lord.' The landlord came in, interrupting his thoughts. 'I've brought your wine and some biscuits while Cook prepares dinner. It'll be a while yet, 'cos of—'

'I know, the mail coach.' Deveril interrupted him, nodding. 'I can wait.'

'That's mighty understanding of you, my lord,' exclaimed the landlord, looking relieved.

'Yes, yes. Off you go.'

Deveril waved him away and sat down at the table with his wine. He would drive through the night, only stopping to change horses, and he should still reach Revesby House by tomorrow evening. Possibly even in time for dinner. He would spend a few weeks in London to enjoy all it had to offer and then he would go on to Paris, with all its diversions. That would restore his spirits.

But would it? More importantly, would it restore his heart? He had never, truly, considered marriage until he met Selina. Belinda has been his childhood friend; he had been very fond of her but he knew now it had not been a true, lasting love. Nothing like the passion he felt for Selina. He had never felt like this before. The thought of her filled his very being. When she was with him everything was brighter, the air was sweeter. The birds sang louder.

Deveril rubbed his eyes. He had always considered a wife would shackle him, tie him down, but all that had changed. He wanted Selina, not just in his bed but by his side, forever. He wanted to show her the world and see it through her eyes.

Finishing the glass of wine, he poured himself another. He thought morosely that it might help, for once, if he drank himself into oblivion.

He glanced up as the door opened. A stranger was in the doorway, no more than a black shape in a riding frock and high-cocked hat, outlined against the lighted passage beyond.

'This room is taken!' The fellow did not move and Deveril growled in annoyance. 'Did you not hear me?'

'Yes, I heard you.'

He sat up quickly at the sound of that voice.

'Selina?'

He stared, wondering if he was dreaming. She walked in, closing the door behind her.

'I do not believe you can deny me access to my own property, my lord.'

'What are you doing here?'

Deveril pushed himself to his feet, still trying to gather his disordered wits.

'I came to find you,' she said, peeling off her gloves. 'You said you would be eating at the first change of horses, and I hoped it would be the White Horse.' Selina tried a smile but she was so nervous her lips felt too dry to stretch. Deveril was shaking his head and frowning. Her confidence deserted her.

'I am sorry. I should go—'

'No, no, stay! I…' He raked one hand through his hair. 'Do you often dress like that?'

She glanced down at her buckskin breeches and riding boots.

'When I need to ride like the wind, yes.'

'Did anyone recognise you?'

'I doubt it. It is too busy out there to take note of every traveller.' She put her hat and gloves beside his on a small sideboard, and when she turned back, he had pulled out a chair for her at the table.

'Thank you.'

She sat down and observed him as he resumed his seat. Had she made a mistake? His voice, when he spoke, was perfectly polite but he did not look in the least pleased to see her.

He said, 'Perhaps you will tell me why it was necessary for you to, er, ride like the wind.'

'I knew if I did not find you here, I might have to ride all the way to London.'

'You were prepared to do that?'

'Yes. I wanted—needed—to tell you that I had changed my mind. About your offer of marriage.'

'No!' She flinched as his hand crashed down on the table. 'Confound it, madam, did I not make myself plain the last time we met?' He jumped up and strode across the room to gaze out of the window. 'I swore I would not ask you again and I meant it!'

She fixed her eyes on his back. 'Perhaps you will let me explain.'

He did not move, his back ramrod straight and unyielding. Selina enduring the agonising silence for a few moments then took a deep breath.

'I was afraid, you see.'

'Afraid, you?' A bitter laugh escaped him. 'I find that hard to believe!'

'It is true. I did not want to risk marrying you and being unhappy.' She swallowed, her eyes fixed on her clasped hands. 'I saw what love had done to Papa. He never recovered from Mama's death. It destroyed his health, his happiness. I was afraid of marrying you, only to lose you.'

'Lose me?'

He turned, but with the light from the yard behind him the shadows were too deep for her to read his expression.

She flushed. 'You might grow tired of me and take a mistress. Or even worse, you might fall ill and, and...'

In two strides Deveril reached her, pulling her up and into his arms.

'I would never willingly do anything to hurt you, Selina. We can none of us see the future, but whatever it has in store for us, do you not think it worth the risk? Is it not better to have each other for a short while than not at all?'

'I think so, now,' she said shyly, looking up at him.

With something between a groan and a growl his head came down and he captured her mouth, kissing her with a savage intensity that set her pulse racing. Selina responded eagerly, inflamed with longing. She drove her fingers through his hair while he teased her lips apart and their tongues danced together, sending waves of desire pulsing through her body. Her very bones had turned to water and she gave a little mewl of dismay as he broke off their kiss and held her away from him.

'No more, madam! Have you not tortured me enough?' He released her and turned away. 'Go home, you she-devil,' he commanded. 'I have told you, I *will not* seduce you.'

'Then marry me.' She felt more confident now. After that kiss the blood was singing through her veins. It had shown her how much he wanted her and she would not give up just yet. He swung back to face her and she took a deep breath.

'My Lord Deveril, will you do me the very great honour of accepting my hand, and my heart, in marriage?'

He groaned and rubbed one hand over his eyes. 'Selina, stop it.'

'I am not a rich woman,' she went on, ignoring him. 'However, I stand to inherit a pretty little estate one day.'

She winced as he swore roundly.

'Pray, do not continue with this nonsense, madam,' he said roughly. 'I am a rogue, a libertine. I don't deserve you.'

She placed her hands on her hips and looked up at him. 'Who on earth told you that!'

'I told myself! Ever since I rode away from you this morning. The arguments are convincing. It is for the best, Selina. I am not a good man. Since Belinda died

I have lived wildly, gambling, taking mistresses, living up to my reputation as Devil Blackbourne! You deserve better. An honest, honourable fellow. Someone whose name is not touched by scandal.'

'He sounds terribly boring.' He did not laugh and she gave a sigh. 'So you will not marry me.'

'I will not.'

'And that is your final word?'

He scowled at her. 'Yes, madam, it is.'

Keeping her eyes on his she shrugged herself out of her coat and let it slide to the floor. Then she began to untie her neckcloth.

'What are you doing?'

'You need to see what else I can offer you.'

She pulled the neckcloth free and dropped it on top of her coat. When she began to unbutton her shirt, he raised his hand.

'Stop now, madam. I am not going to marry you!'

The shirt was undone now, revealing the top of her breasts and the lacing at the front of her stays. Quite shocking, but nothing worse than she had observed at the White Horse when the former landlord had been in residence. She tried to imagine how his saucy daughter would behave in this situation. The shirt remained securely tucked into her breeches and she put her hands on the waistband, smiling provocatively.

'But you are a rogue, Deveril. A libertine. You may take your pleasure without marrying me.'

She had unfastened the first two buttons of the fall flap before he reached out and caught her hands.

'No, madam! You will not persuade me to ruin you.'

'Why not, Deveril?' She could see he was gazing down at the exposed flesh above the edge of the stays. 'Tell me why you will not ruin me.'

Deveril's breath caught in his throat as she pulled back her shoulders, deliberately bringing the soft, creamy mounds of her breasts even closer to his waistcoat.

'I—I care too much to take advantage of you.'

'You care too much. What does that mean?'

She rested her palms on his chest and his heart began to thud even harder, as if trying to escape into her hands. He was burning with desire now. It was as much as he could do to keep still while she gazed up at him like that, her eyes dark and inviting.

She repeated, softly, 'What does that mean, Deveril?'

With a smothered oath he caught her hands and pushed them behind her back.

'I love you, you little witch!'

His savage tone appeared to make no impression on her, save to make her give a little crow of triumph.

'I knew it! So why will you not you marry me?'

'You know why, damn you! I have been foolish, irresponsible, all my life, never settling anywhere or with anyone for very long.' He looked over her head, forcing the words out. 'I am not good enough for you.'

'Oh, my darling, that is not true! You are prepared to sacrifice your own happiness to protect the woman you love. In my eyes that makes you the very best of men.' She pulled her hands free and reached up to cup his face. 'You love me too much to marry me, and I love you too much to let you go. What is to be done?'

She was smiling up at him, the message in her eyes causing his heart to lurch. He knew he was lost.

'Selina—'

The door burst open. 'Here we is at last with yer dinner, m'lord!'

The bustling entrance of the landlord and one of the servants broke the spell. Deveril froze, his body was shielding Selina from the men's view and he caught a glimpse of the ready laughter in her eyes before she turned away and sauntered off to the corner of the room where the shadows were deepest.

She had tied her hair back with a single ribbon, to hang in a queue down her back, and as long as she did not turn around, he was confident her identity and the true state of her undress would remain concealed. And as long as he did not move from this spot, they would not see the discarded jacket and neckcloth on the floor. Danger averted. For the moment.

Deveril took one deep, steadying breath and slowly swung about, raising his quizzing glass to observe the men who were busy setting out the dishes on the table.

'Yes, thank you.' His voice was admirably calm, considering his racing pulse. 'There looks more than enough food there, but perhaps you would lay another place for my friend, who has come to join me.'

'Aye, that I will, sir,' said the landlord, shooting an enquiring look towards the shadowy figure in the corner. 'An' I'll bring 'ee another bottle of wine, too, seeing as this one's half gone already.'

Selina remained with her back to the room, supposedly inspecting a small watercolour on the wall, until the landlord and waiter had retired. Only when she heard the door close did she peep over her shoulder.

'That was a close-run thing!' She came out of the shadows, chuckling.

'You are a minx, madam,' Deveril told her severely. 'You had best make yourself presentable before they come back.'

She stopped and looked up at him in surprise.

'What?' he demanded, his eyes narrowing.

'I thought you were going to tell me to leave.'

'Would it do any good?'

His mouth quirked, as if he was holding back a grin, and Selina was encouraged to smile at him. She was sure he had been within a breath of capitulating when they were interrupted and she had no intention of leaving now, when she was so close to success.

'No good at all,' she said cheerfully. 'We have not finished our conversation.'

'I thought we had gone far beyond talking.'

The look he gave her sent a delicious shiver down

her spine and her fingers trembled slightly as she refastened her breeches and buttoned her shirt.

Deveril bent to scoop up the neckcloth. 'Here, you had best let me tie this for you.'

'Thank you.'

She raised her chin obligingly as he set to work.

He scowled at her. 'After your tricks today, you deserve that I should throttle you with this rag!'

'I did not know how else to persuade you to marry me.' She paused. 'You are going to marry me, are you not?'

'That depends.' He put his finger under her chin to lift it a little higher. 'Now stop talking while I do my best to make you presentable!'

'On what does it depend?'

'Shush!' He finished tying the neckcloth then he stood back to inspect the result. 'Hmm. Not too bad. And just in time,' he muttered as the door opened again and the waiter came in to set the extra place.

Selina hung back, keeping in Deveril's shadow while he addressed the servant.

'Thank you. You may go now. I shall ring when I need you again. Until then we are not to be disturbed. Is that understood?'

'Yes, m'lord.'

Selina could almost imagine the waiter tugging his forelock and bowing himself out of the room.

When the door had shut and the servant's footsteps faded, she joined Deveril at the table. It was some time since she had dined and, while he poured them both a glass of wine, she took a small amount from each of the dishes on the table.

'Can I help you to some of this squab pie?' she asked him. 'It looks very good.'

'Yes, thank you.' He watched her cut a sliver of pie and slip it onto his plate. 'How very *housewifely*, Selina. Is this how you see our life together?'

She flushed a little at his mocking tone.

'Not at all. You promised me excitement, Deveril. You said you would show me the world.'

'And you wanted none of it.'

'Things were different then.' She hesitated, her fragile confidence ebbing a little. 'Perhaps we should finish eating before we discuss this.'

'A good notion. But will you not be missed, at the Abbey?'

'No. Papa thinks I have retired and will not look for me until the morning.'

And by that time I hope to be betrothed, she added silently.

Although, glancing at Deveril's inscrutable countenance, the outcome of this encounter was still in doubt.

Conversation was desultory during the meal, but Deveril was loath to end it. When they had finished eating he must send her away, and he was not looking forward to seeing her dismay when he did so. Confound it, could she not see that he was doing this for her sake? Far better to stop this madness now and send her back to her father with her virtue and, hopefully, her reputation intact. Damn the woman, how dare she put him through this, to twice rebuff him and then to follow him here!

Finally he could delay no longer. He pushed his plate aside and sat back in his chair, determined to get this over and done.

He said, roughly, 'Now, madam. You said things are different. What has changed?'

'You are not making this easy for me.'

'You have twice refused my offer.'

'And you want to punish me.'

Deveril saw the anxiety shadowing Selina's eyes and his anger melted away.

'No,' he said quietly. 'I want to understand.'

She sighed. 'I am not sure I understand it myself.'

'You told me you could not leave your father.'

'Yes, but it was more than that.' She picked up her wine glass, cradling it between her hands.

'My fear was that you might love me while we were together, but if I remained at Reigney, looking after Papa, you would be out in Society, a prey to all the temptations.' She glanced up at him. 'You are reckless, Deveril, wild and impulsive, as well as being far, far too attractive! I have seen how women look at you, how much they…they lust after you.'

'Most of them see only my title and my wealth,

Selina. They do not want the man, only what I can give them.'

She shrugged. 'Am I so very different?'

'Yes, you are. My rank and wealth mean nothing to you.'

'No, they were just another reason why I could not marry you.'

'Another reason?'

She stared at her wine glass. 'I did not think you loved me.'

'And now?' He paused. 'Now, Selina?'

She said, shyly, 'Now I think perhaps you do.'

He rose and came around the table to pull her up into his arms and kiss her.

'*Omnia vincit amor*,' murmured Deveril, when at last he lifted his head. She looked up, a question in her eyes, and he said, 'Virgil. It means *love conquers all*.'

She laughed at that. 'The odd Latin phrase must be very useful, for a noble seducer!'

'*You* are the seducer, madam!'

Her laughter died when she saw the look in his eyes. She slipped her hands around his neck and stretched up to touch his lips with her own.

'I am a woman in love,' she said softly. 'I was afraid the pain of losing you would outweigh any happiness we might have, but now I know I would rather be happy with you for a short time than not at all. I am ready to take the risk, if you will let me.' She gazed up at him meeting his eyes and praying he would read the message in them. She said, 'I love you so much, Deveril. I could not bear to wait for my letter to follow you to London. I needed to know if there was still a chance for us.'

'A chance? Oh, my darling girl, how can I begin to tell you how much I love you? You mean more to me than life itself!' His arms tightened. 'I want you for my wife, Selina. I want you by my side each day and in my bed every night.'

She shivered with delight.

'I want that, too. Forever. But I am prepared to take my happiness day by day. And if we find in the end that we are not suited, well.' She gave a little shrug. 'We will at least have the memories of our time together.'

'Oh, I think we are already very well-suited!'

He kissed again, a long lingering kiss that told her all she needed to know. When at last it ended she laid her head on his shoulder, feeling the thud of his heart against her cheek.

'I suppose you would not consider eloping with me, tonight?' Deveril asked her.

She replied with a warm, mischievous laugh that inflamed his blood and set his heart racing.

'Alas, no. I must go home.' She looked up, the love she felt for him shining in her eyes. 'But you can come with me. I shall find you a bed for the night.'

'Yours?'

'*Not* mine. The servants would know of it and be

scandalised. We must behave respectably. But we will see Papa in the morning, and tell him the good news.' She kissed him again, and then gave a little sigh. 'I hope you mean to marry me as soon as possible.'

'Yes. By special licence, and I intend our wedding to be the epitome of respectability. Therefore I agree that you must sleep alone at Reigney Abbey tonight.'

'Oh.'

The note of disappointment in that one syllable was not lost on Deveril.

'Yes.' He kissed her nose. 'It is, however, far too late for you to ride. I shall take you home myself, in my carriage. Your horse can be tethered behind.'

'An excellent idea,' she said, her eyes twinkling naughtily as she put on her coat. 'I thought you might want to seduce me in here, and there are only the hard wooden dining chairs in this parlour. I am sure your carriage will be more comfortable.'

'Undoubtedly it will, but I am not going to seduce you. The word comes from the Latin, meaning to lead someone astray, but I think you are already ahead of me there.' He picked up her hat and gloves and handed them to her. 'My chaise is designed for travelling, with a dormeuse boot. That means one can lie down and sleep. Or not.'

'And is there only room for one person to sleep?' she asked.

'I believe it will take two, although I have not yet tried it.'

'Then I think we should, do not you? Not that I have any intention of letting you sleep.'

He threw his head back and laughed at that.

'My future wife,' he murmured, kissing her again. 'Every inch a lady but the spirit of a tavern wench!'

'Do you disapprove?'

'Not in the least,' he assured her. 'I think it a perfect combination. Now come along, my darling girl. Our carriage awaits.'

She pulled his head down for one final kiss before they left the room. 'Our future awaits, my darling lord.'

* * * * *

If you enjoyed this story, be sure to read Sarah Mallory's previous historical romances

The Night She Met the Duke
Snowbound with the Brooding Lord
Wed in Haste to the Duke
The Earl's Marriage Dilemma
A Kiss to Stop a Wedding

MILLS & BOON®

Coming next month

ACCIDENTALLY WED TO THE PRINCE
Lucy Morris

What should I say? Magnus had made his decision in the library earlier, but now he was at a loss for words. The next sentence would seal his fate and that of his beloved Thrudheim forever.

He supposed he should just get it over with. 'Miss Mortimer, in light of our recent...accident. I think it only best that I ask for your hand in marriage.'

'What?' Miss Mortimer screamed the word so loudly that his ears rang and he winced.

She glanced up at the stagecoach, and he noticed that several people had gathered at the windows and doorway. Staring down at them expectantly like a nest of hungry chicks. Miss Mortimer scowled back at them and they hurried back into the shadows.

'Have you lost your wits?' She hissed, and then added, 'Your Serene Highness.' Belatedly and with a perplexed expression, as if she wasn't sure how she could remain polite and question his sanity at the same time.

'As we are going to be married, you may call me by my Christian name, Magnus, at least in informal settings such as this.'

She blinked with a slack expression as if she couldn't quite comprehend his words. After a moment of blankness, a strange iron-will seemed to take over her. She raised her chin and her spine stiffened, that odd conviction hardening within her eyes like granite. It was spectacular to watch, a goddess emerging from a fiery pit. 'I did not agree to your proposal!'

Continue reading

ACCIDENTALLY WED TO THE PRINCE
Lucy Morris

Available next month
millsandboon.co.uk

Copyright © 2026 Lucy Morris

COMING SOON!

We really hope you enjoyed reading this book. If you're looking for more romance be sure to head to the shops when new books are available on

Thursday 21st May

To see which titles are coming soon, please visit
millsandboon.co.uk/nextmonth

MILLS & BOON

FOUR BRAND NEW BOOKS FROM
MILLS & BOON MODERN

Indulge in desire, drama, and breathtaking romance – where passion knows no bounds!

OUT NOW

Eight Modern stories published every month, find them all at:
millsandboon.co.uk

LET'S TALK
Romance

For exclusive extracts, competitions and special offers, find us online:

- **f** MillsandBoon
- **X** @MillsandBoon
- **◉** @MillsandBoonUK
- **♪** @MillsandBoonUK

Get in touch on 01413 063 232

For all the latest titles coming soon, visit
millsandboon.co.uk/nextmonth